FALL OF HOUSTON SERIES BOOK FIVE

NO MAN'S LAND

T.L. PAYNE

NO MAN'S LAND
Fall of Houston Series, Book Five

Cover design by Deranged Doctor Design
Edited by Melanie Underwood
Proofread by Kay Grey

Don't forget to sign up for my spam-free newsletter at www.tlpayne.com to be among the first to know of new releases, giveaways, and special offers.

Check out other Books by T. L. Payne

The Days of Want Series
Turbulent
Hunted
Turmoil
Uprising
Upheaval
Mayhem
Defiance

Fall of Houston Series
No Way Out
No Other Choice
No Turning Back
No Surrender
No Man's Land

The Gateway to Chaos Series

Seeking Safety
Seeking Refuge
Seeking Justice
Seeking Hope

For Dockery

Contents

Prologue

Simone Perez held her badge up and batted her eyes at the guard as she approached the front of the historic red-brick mansion. The guard opened the gate and nodded for her to proceed to the next checkpoint. She could feel the soldier's eyes on her as she passed him, and she walked toward the portico covering the front entrance to the massive structure. She was accustomed to this type of attention. She knew how and when to use her charms to gain what she wanted, but there hadn't been much use for them lately. It seemed she had climbed as high up the career later as was possible— without replacing the general, and he wasn't going anywhere.

General Walter Dempsey never left the mansion that was now his headquarters and home. He rarely had visitors these days. He'd grown paranoid after repeated attempts upon his life. It seemed the citizens of his newly formed government didn't care much for his administration. Despite being fed and protected by the government,

1

they resented being forced into labor camps and separated from their families. It was all necessary of course, but they didn't see it that way. They had no idea what it was like out there in the rest of the country. Being assigned a job in the fields and factories, and working for their food, shelter, and protection, was such a small price to pay.

Perez thought they should have to see first hand what people outside the safe zone were having to do to survive. Despite the crackdowns on gatherings and organizing, groups had repeatedly attacked the capitol, and Homeland Security forces were on constant watch for plots against the governor's mansion. Springfield and especially the area around the mansion had been off-limits to anyone but the military guarding Dempsey.

Perez stopped outside the door and checked her uniform. She buttoned her blouse to cover her cleavage. She didn't need to use her charms on Dempsey. They'd known each other for years. He'd recruited her for the job at FEMA and encouraged her involvement with Gerald Aims, the director of Region Five's Response and Recovery Division. Now Dempsey had summoned her for another mission.

Perez knocked and Dempsey's aide opened the door. "Leave us," Dempsey barked.

His aide nodded and left the room. Dempsey pointed to the chairs in front of his desk and Perez took a seat. She leaned back, crossed her long, lean legs, and folded her hands in her lap. She waited for him to look up from the folder he was holding.

Dempsey leaned forward in his chair, placed his hands on the large mahogany desk, then leaned back and brought his hands together, interlacing his fingers.

"Simone, I have a mission for you. I want you to infiltrate Latham's government. I need intel. I've received word that they're putting together a unit to spy on me."

"I can do that," she said. She nearly choked on the words. It was the very last thing she wanted to do. She had worked very hard

2

to get the cushy job she now held. She had just finished decorating her new office, and her house on the edge of town was spacious and comfortable. Giving all that up to sleep on a cot in some filthy refugee shelter for weeks as she wedged her way into Latham's inner circle had not been in her career plan. She reached up and ran a hand down the length of her ponytail. She had pulled her long, jet-black hair into a ponytail for her visit to Dempsey. He was a stickler for his staff looking sharp and professional. Why it mattered now, she didn't understand. Who was there to impress? It wasn't like foreign dignitaries or anyone else important called on them.

"I want to know everything you can learn about this new president and what his intentions are when it comes to Region Five," Dempsey said.

"Do you really think they're a threat to us?" Perez asked.

She'd been in on all the briefings about Texas and the fight to repel the Chinese. Latham's success repelling the invasion had come as a shock to Dempsey. He had been misled by his communist handlers. They had oversold their capabilities—or they had underestimated the strength of the American military. Dempsey had never expected to have to defend his kingdom. Perez hadn't been so naive. She'd been concerned when she'd learned of Dempsey's alliance with the axis of evil that had attacked the country. She didn't buy into his excuse that it was the only way to save lives, and she wasn't convinced that the communist parties of China and Russia would leave them alone once they divided up their conquered territories. In fact, she was quite sure they would not, especially once they learned of the vast resources Dempsey had hoarded away.

"Threat?" Dempsey asked. He turned and looked out the expansive windows lining one wall of his office. "We are better armed and supplied. Our soldiers are capable of repelling any attack."

Perez noted a "but" in his tone.

"I want to head off any trouble before it reaches our doorstep. I will not allow anything to stop our progress. We are nearing completion of the repairs on the power station. Soon we will have electricity to power factories and be on our way to rebuilding our nation."

"Is the rumor true? Has Latham restored electricity to Texas?"

Dempsey huffed and leaned back in his chair. He glared at her.

"See, that is the sort of thing we need to stop. We can't have these rumors running rampant here. I have enough trouble with the folks in Peoria, Chicago and some of the other detention facilities. I don't need them getting misinformation like that and becoming upset with our progress."

"Who's going with me?"

"Watts and his team. You'll submit your reports to him and he'll get them to me."

Perez resisted protesting. She disliked Watts immensely. He had been a dirt bag before the EMP attack. Now he was an arrogant, misogynistic dirt bag. This assignment was going to suck so much. She wanted to hurry and get it over with.

"How long will I be down in Texas?"

"Until I find out everything I need to know about Latham and his plans."

Perez stiffened. She knew she couldn't refuse. She would just need to find a way to get the information quickly.

"What's my cover story?" she asked.

He smiled. "You'll come up with something. You're a clever and resourceful girl."

ONE

Will

Highway 10
Pulaski County, Arkansas
Event + Seven Months

The platoon had been marching since before dawn and it was past dinner time. Will Fontenot was more than ready to stop and make camp for the night. He was walking on point ahead of the group and as they approached Williams Junction, he noticed something odd at an abandoned convenience store at the intersection of Highway 9 and Highway 10.

Will knelt down and scrambled toward the ditch as he held a fist in the air to halt the platoon. Sergeant Talbot rushed forward and stopped beside him as everyone dropped low in the ditch closest to their side of the road

"What is it?" Talbot whispered.

"There—at the convenience store," Will said.

Talbot retrieved a pair of binoculars from his rucksack and scanned the store. "Looks deserted to me," he said.

"There's a cigarette smoking on the sidewalk by the door. I figure they heard us coming and pitched it before running inside."

"You're right, private. Good eye," Talbot said.

Talbot scanned the area again as the platoon leader, Lieutenant Brown, arrived and dropped down next to him.

"What do you have, Talbot?"

"Unknowns inside that store who probably saw us coming, sir." He handed the binos to Brown. "On the sidewalk outside the door."

"Shit fire," Brown said. He handed the binos back to Talbot.

"Sir, I'd like to send two men around back—I want eyes on any rear exit. I can send two teams to the west side and to the secure the side facing Highway 9."

"Get 'er done," Brown nodded.

Everyone stayed where they were as Talbot sent eight soldiers on their way. Once they were in place, Talbot told Will to cross the road and watch the side door. After he was in place, Talbot called out. "You inside the store, this is the United States Army. Come outside and with your hands in the air."

They waited for more than a minute, but no one exited the building. Talbot shouted the same instruction again and a second later a shot rang out on the opposite side of the store. Talbot watched as one team made entry into the store. Two minutes passed as Talbot waited for information from his soldiers.

"All clear!" one of the soldiers yelled as he walked out the front door of the store with his rifle pointed skyward.

Will, Talbot, and Brown approached and as they rounded the corner of the building, Private Ramirez was standing over a man in his early sixties. A few feet away, Private Rose picked up the man's shotgun. "It's empty," she said.

"Crap!" Ramirez said, dropping his head and turning away from the body. "Why didn't he just come out like he was told."

"We'll never know the answer to that question. You shot him before he could explain," Rose said.

"He had a freaking weapon, Rose. What was I supposed to do, let him shoot someone and then ask if it was loaded?"

Rose threw her hands in the air and stepped back. Ramirez huffed and knelt beside him.

The rest of the soldiers exited the store by the same door as the dead man. One by one as they filed by, each of them stared down at the frail looking man. His clothes were clean and, except for a patch on his left knee, they were in good condition. Will scrutinized the man's hands. His nails were clean and trimmed. Other than being thin, he didn't appear to be near death like most people they ran across these days.

"Roll him over," Lieutenant Brown said as he walked up to the old man's body, and gestured for Rose to hand over the dead man's shotgun.

As Rose handed Brown the weapon and knelt to roll the dead man onto his back, shots rang out from across the road. Everyone scattered, seeking cover, and began returning fire. Will dove to the ground and crawled around the corner of the building. Rounds dug chunks out of the side from the building peppering Will with tiny chunks of concrete. He rolled over, took up a good prone fighting position as he'd been taught, and began returning fire around the corner of the building.

Ramirez was pinned down; the dead man's body his only shield. A round struck his boot and he cried out.

"Medic! Medic! I'm shot! I'm hit!" Ramirez yelled.

"We got you, Ramirez. We'll get you out in a second," Brown shouted.

"Cease fire, cease fire!" Talbot hollered.

The shooting stopped abruptly, and Will scanned an outcropping of rock across the road where he believed the rounds had come from. He saw no movement, but to the right of the largest boulders, sunlight reflected off shiny new brass littering the ground.

Will pointed. "Sergeant Talbot—there to my twelve o'clock,

near the boulders." Talbot, who'd taken cover behind an ice machine, scanned the area through the scope of his rifle.

"Bryan, O'Neil, across the highway." He pointed. "Go check it out!"

Bryan and O'Neil took off across the road in front of the store as everyone else trained their rifles on the area where the boulders sat. They disappeared behind the boulders and a few minutes later, Bryan yelled, "All clear, Sergeant Talbot," and began walking back to the convenience store.

"They unloaded a magazine on us and then booked it," Bryan said as he approached Talbot. "Want us to pursue them?"

"Evans, Smith—go with Bryan and O'Neil and see if you can track them down," Talbot said. "Squad leaders, let's get these other buildings cleared around here so we don't get shot at any more."

Will and a few others began clearing the area north of the store. This was a rare encounter—they rarely ran into living people while out on patrol. They would see a few bodies in ditches or in homes they cleared near Robinson Maneuver Training Center in North Little Rock where Will and Isabella had been receiving their training. On the rare occasion they found survivors, they'd been instructed to escort them back to base for relocation to Texarkana. Most were eager to go. Some were not. Will assumed that the gentlemen lying dead on the ground and whoever had been doing the shooting were among the ones who didn't want to be "rescued."

Will and Corey approached a weathered old shed. Corey had been the only one from her family to make it to Texarkana after the Chinese overran their home south of Savanah's homestead. She'd been on her way to alert the Sugar Cove Road community when it happened. When she had arrived back home, she learned her entire family had been killed in a firefight. Corey had hooked up with other refugees and made it to the shelter in Texarkana a week after Will and the others. She and Isabella had grown close during their training at Little Rock.

"I volunteered for the horse brigade. I'd rather be out here than stationed in Houston or Dallas pulling security," Corey said as they consolidated ammo to ensure they both had equal amounts of ammo before they began clearing the building.

"Horse brigade? What type of missions could you do on horses?"

"I imagine what we're doing now," she said, as she approached the door of the wooden building. She gestured to the door that stood open, and Will tapped her on the shoulder. Moving quickly, she passed through the doorway and to the right, followed by Will who turned left. They each swept their side of the shed until the trajectory of their rifles crossed in the center on the far side of the shed.

"Clear," Will said.

"Where's this horse unit going to be stationed?" Will asked, surprising himself for considering it.

"In Little Rock."

"Have you spoken to Isabella about it?"

"Yeah. She's interested, but she didn't think you would be—not with Cayden being back in Texarkana."

The military wasn't allowing families to join soldiers on assignment outside of Houston, Dallas, and Austin. He and Isabella had discussed it. It seemed to be the only option for them to be with Cayden, Savanah, and the other civilian members of their group. Of course, Savanah wanted nothing to do with being relocated to any city. She was still talking about them finding an abandoned farm close to the shelter. Will hadn't told her yet, but the military wouldn't allow it. All civilians had to be within the safe zones.

Will wasn't looking forward to going back to Houston either. He'd need to talk to Isabella. They needed to find a way to have a group meeting so they could all discuss their futures and get on the same page. If Savanah remained adamantly against the city, maybe the horse brigade would be his and Isabella's best option. She'd love spending all that time with horses.

Will, Corey, and the other soldiers in their clearing party had cleared every structure on the right side of Highway 9 from Williams Junction to Thornburg and were heading back when a soldier ran up to meet them from the direction of the convenience store.

"Sergeant Talbot said to double-time it back. They found the shooters' compound."

"Compound?" Will asked.

"Yeah. There's a shit ton of people living there and they're all armed to the teeth."

Will, Corey, and the others took up a slow jog back to the store to meet up with the rest of the platoon.

"I have a feeling they aren't going to go willingly, sir," Sergeant Talbot said.

O'Neil handed Lieutenant Brown a piece of paper showing a drawing of the compound's layout.

"Maybe we should radio back for re-enforcements. We might need…"

"We've got this. It's our mission. We can handle it," Brown said, interrupting Talbot.

"What if they're as heavily armed as O'Neil says…" He nodded toward the squads who were squaring away their gear in preparation for battle. "They've not encountered anything like that yet."

They were nine weeks into their basic training and it was true, they weren't ready for a battle. They'd only come across one other person with a weapon. Most people had run out of ammunition months ago. Will was concerned—and damn glad Isabella wasn't with them. Who knew that a stomach bug could be a blessing.

The compound was huge. A pipe fence ran around it as far as Will could see, and armed guards walked the perimeter. He counted three main buildings, a large house, an even larger metal building about two feet from the house, and a rather new barn about one hundred yards from the metal building. Those were the only permanent structures and likely were original to the place. The rest reminded Will of the homestead back in Vincent with campers, tents, and shacks covering nearly all of the pasture.

Will looked through his rifle scope and panned to the right of the barn. "They have chickens."

"Chicken!" Corey smacked her lips. "I could really go for some southern fried chicken right now."

The suggestion made Will's stomach growl. The MRE he'd had for lunch was less than emotionally satisfying. It was full of the calories he needed, but lacking in flavor. He'd almost forgotten what fried chicken even tasted like after so long without it.

"It sure is a shame to disturb these people. They aren't hurting anyone and it seems like they're doing just fine on their own," Corey said.

Will nodded. The thought struck him, this could be them if they were to strike out on their own and form a community similar to this one. It seemed that an arbitrary rule was making it impossible for citizens to be self-sufficient and care for their own families. Surely there had to be an exception if the community didn't want assistance and could make it on their own.

A moment later, Will received his answer as the order to advance was given and the first shots were fired. Will joined his squad in moving toward the compound but didn't fire his weapon. It seemed wrong. They were the invaders in this situation.

"Medic!" someone cried out. "Corey's hit!"

Will turned and ran back to where she lay on the ground. She stared back at Will wide eyed. Blood spurted from a gash in her neck. "It's okay, Corey. Just be still. Doc, here, will get you patched up and we'll take you back to base," Will said, trying to calm her as his own pulse raced. The medic began applying pressure to her wound. Will ran around and dropped down on Corey's left side and took her hand. He looked up and the medic shook his head. Corey was dead. Shot by people just wanting to be left alone to survive. Will used his index finger to close her eyes and stood. He wiped the blood on his uniform pants and picked up his rifle. "This is just wrong," he said in a low voice.

"Orders are orders, Fontenot," Sergeant Talbot said as he approached Will.

"They're all just trying to survive."

"We all are," he replied.

TWO

Savanah

Texarkana Refugee Center
Texarkana, Texas
Event + Seven Months

A grouping of picnic tables had been placed on the outskirts of the camp, away from the shelters and children's play area. It was the only place for adults to gather and socialize inside the fence. Some of the camp residents had found a weakness in the perimeter fence and ventured outside to a shopping area nearby. They met at the picnic tables once a week to discuss conditions inside the refugee center. Savanah knew this because she had been invited to join them, but she hadn't attended until now. She was unsure of their motives for inviting her.

As she lowered herself onto the picnic bench, Savanah blocked the sun with an outstretched hand and looked skyward. It had rained for over a week straight, and after being cooped up with four bored children, she was relishing the warm sun and gentle breeze. The kids were all in school and she had just finished her shift at the dining facility. It was her first chance to be alone with her thoughts in weeks. With Jason, Will, Isabella, and most of the group she'd traveled with to Texarkana now gone on a mission with the military, much responsibility rested on her.

"Enjoying the sun?" Gabby said as she slid in across from Savanah.

"Yeah. I usually love spring, but..." She waved her hand gesturing toward row after row of tents and shelters that housed nearly one thousand people.

"You miss the farm."

Her cousin understood. Spring was one of the busiest times on a farm. There would be gardens to prepare and seeds to plant. Piglets, lambs, and kids would be born. Chicks would be hatched. The grass would be turning green and leaves beginning to bud. Here, all she saw was concrete and chain link fence—and people. Lots of people.

"Have you heard anything from Will and Isabella lately?" Gabby asked.

"Not in the last two weeks. Jason said they were on patrols. That makes me nervous."

"On horseback?" Gabby asked.

"Yes. It's part of their training." Savanah tossed her long braid over her shoulder and placed her hands on the table. She stared at them. She was only thirty years old, but you couldn't tell that by the way her hands looked. Day after day of harsh cleaning products were taking a toll on her skin. The guards had taken all her home-made lotions and herbal remedies when they had arrived. She'd protested of course, but they said it was for safety reasons. Safety? What did they think she'd do with goats' milk and honey lotion?

"How's Jason's foot?"

"He said he was getting around on it better. They're going to release him to light duty." Jason's horse had stepped on his foot and he'd been in a cast for six weeks. Savanah had hoped they would let her husband recuperate at the shelter with her, but they had required him to stay on base in Little Rock and do paperwork.

He ate with his unit and attended classroom instruction. He had been assigned work in the saddle shop and in the armory. Anything to keep him in training.

"Light duty means shoveling horse shit," Gabby said smiling.

"And grooming the horses," Savanah said.

Jason had been glad to be assigned to the Horse Detachment Unit. He enjoyed working with horses. Savanah had thought it was a good thing until she learned that the unit would be tasked with some of the more dangerous missions. They would be traveling without armored vehicles into rugged country. She had seen first hand how dangerous the backroads could be. Not everyone was happy to see the military.

At least he was with Will and Isabella. Pete and her cousins, Tank and Troy, had deployed with the 504th Military Intelligence Brigade to conduct intelligence, surveillance, and reconnaissance operations deep into the Midwest where some Army general had stolen government resources and forced citizens into labor camps. Savanah wasn't supposed to know about their mission, but Gabby was close to her brothers. Tank and Troy kept Gabby informed about where they were. How, Savanah didn't know. Gabby had refused to say.

"Have you thought any more about what Mac and Jeremy talked about?"

Savanah picked at a hangnail. She thought about the hours and hours she spent washing dishes each day. Had she thought about leaving the refugee center? Only a hundred times a day. But she wasn't sure about Mac or his son-in-law Jeremy. They, like her, weren't happy with all the rules and regulations they had to abide by living at a government-run facility, but they were being fed and protected there. Even though some of the rules seemed arbitrary and stupid to Savanah, her children never went hungry. That was the most important thing to her.

Mac Wilson and his son-in-law were the ringleaders of a band of disgruntled refugees at the facility. In the beginning, Mac had been quite vocal in his dislike for how things were run. When he had been threatened with expulsion, he had taken to complaining in secret where he found an audience of people with a distrust of the government.

Savanah met Gabby's gaze. "I've given it some thought."

"And?"

"As much as I hate being told I can't homeschool my children or have a say in what they're being taught, I'm not ready to leave the safety and security of the camp. Not with Mac and his bunch. When Jason and the others return, maybe we can set out and find someplace."

Gabby was quiet.

"Are you thinking about leaving?" Savanah said.

She nodded and looked away.

"Gabby?"

"They're planning on moving everyone to the cities as soon as they have power restored. The center will be closed."

Savanah gasped. "When? How much time do we have?"

"A month. Three months. No one knows right now, but they are preparing. They intend for us to work in factories making shit for the military. I'm not sticking around to spend ten to twelve hours a day sweltering in some factory in Houston making bullets and rockets."

Savanah didn't want that either. Was this just more of Mac's talk? It made some sense that they would need workers to manu-facture things in order to get the country running again. It wasn't like they could log onto their computers and order replacement parts from China. China was the enemy, and as far as she knew, China was also now in a big a mess after the United States had retaliated and dropped American bombs on them in response.

"What's the plan?" Savanah asked. When she'd last heard Mac speak on the subject, they really didn't have a plan for where to go or how to make sure everyone was fed.

"Mac and Jeremy are going to head north next week. They plan to find a deserted rural town that might be suitable as a home base, and near enough to a river to provide water and good river bottom crop land."

"Are they leaving their families here or taking them?"

"Leaving them for now—until they find a place."

Savanah pictured a little town like Vincent. She longed to return there and to her family's farm, but without knowing the condition of the place, everyone had been reluctant to leave the shelter. There had been reports of heavy fighting in the area. They could get there only to find the house and barn burned to the ground. If only Jason, Will, and the others hadn't joined the military. If the homestead had been destroyed, they might be able to rebuild by winter. Food would still be scarce though. That was always the major problem. Getting enough food to survive was the driving force in all their decisions now, something most people had taken for granted before the lights went out.

"So, when Mac returns for his family, you're heading out with them?"

"Me and the rest of the folks from Vincent."

She meant the band of folks that had called the casino home before war reached the town. Savanah had never learned what became of the people at the church. Father Johnson had done his best to care for the frail and elderly that sought sanctuary there. She prayed they had found their way to safety as well. Was anywhere safe outside Texarkana? If there were safe places, Savanah hadn't heard of them.

THREE

Stephens

Killen, Texas
Fort Hood Army Base
Event + Seven Months

Lieutenant Ryan Sharp stood at attention in front of the assembly of military and CIA attendees. CIA Analyst Rachel Stephens sat in the front row. Their eyes met. Stephens smiled and Sharp smiled back. Lieutenant General Robert Waltrip, post commander at Fort Hood, was the promoting official.

Brad "the Cad," standing behind Stephens, tapped her on the shoulder. "He won't be smiling when he's out there in no man's land without hot showers and hot meals."

Stephens ignored him. She wasn't looking forward to leaving the comfort of the base either, but she was ready to get to Little Rock and get their mission underway. It had taken some time to convince Waltrip to focus on General Dempsey and his emerging kingdom. Now that the fighting between the US and Chinese forces along the gulf coast had subsided, resources could be used to focus on General Dempsey's operation in the Midwest.

Promoting Sharp to lead 1st Cavalry's Horse Detachment Unit had been Colonel Williams' idea. She'd convinced Waltrip of the soundness of using the once ceremonial unit to conduct the recon mission. The mounted unit would be able to move in ways that motorized units could not—and they consumed zero fuel. It had taken a presidential order to promote Sharp from lieutenant to colonel, but with so few officers left to lead, President Latham hadn't required much convincing, though being promoted directly from lieutenant to colonel was a rarity, indeed. Sharp had the intelligence background as well as Ranger training. Waltrip had been reluctant, but Williams had convinced him Sharp was the right man for this mission. Stephens agreed. She trusted Sharp.

Following the ceremony, Sharp gave Stephens a tour of the stables and barracks for the forty soldiers, thirty horses, three mules, and two dogs that she'd be traveling with over the next several months. She had seen them exhibit their horseback marksmanship and saber skills. It was an impressive show. It reminded her of the shows at the rodeos she'd attended as a girl out in West Texas.

"You'll train with the unit starting tomorrow. Stop by in the morning and they'll get you a saddle and boots."

Stephens stared at Sharp for a long moment as she considered the long hours she would be spending in the saddle each day. It had been a lot of years since she'd ridden. Her butt hurt just thinking about it.

"Once we get to Little Rock, how long before we'll be set up for the Illinois mission?"

"It depends on how fast these guys can get our new recruits trained. We'll need to send out teams to round up more horses, break and train them—it could be a couple of months."

That wasn't what Stephens wanted to hear. With each passing day, more and more citizens were succumbing to starvation and disease. They desperately needed the supplies Dempsey was hoarding for himself. Despite President Latham's best efforts, with so few resources, recovery was moving at a snail's pace. And with the trouble on the west coast threatening to spill over in their direction, it wouldn't be long before everything was diverted to stop the enemy's advance across the Rockies into the heartland of America.

"I could use a smaller team. We could take a boat up the Mississippi."

"If I can spare anyone, you know I'll do my best, Stephens," Sharp said, turning to face her.

Her gaze fell to the silver eagles on his right and left shoulder boards. He had a monumental task ahead of him. Training civilians to become soldiers was one thing, but training them to become proficient mounted soldiers ready to go into battle on horseback was another. Dempsey had military vehicles and ample ammunition, or so they'd been told. The troopers of the Horse Cavalry Detachment Unit would need to be quick and agile as well as highly accurate with their weapons. They would need to pick their battles carefully. That was one of her jobs—to find out where Dempsey's army would be and how to exploit their weaknesses. She was more than ready to get started.

Stephens bobbed her head and smiled. "Let's get to Little Rock and get the show on the road."

Riding behind the convoy of horse trailers as they made their way north along Interstate 35 toward Texarkana, Stephens pored over the intel that had been gathered on Dempsey's operation thus far. She opened a folder labeled FEMA Region Five. Inside was the bio for the smiling African American director, Reginald Harding. Harding oversaw emergency management for Illinois, Indiana, Michigan, Minnesota, Ohio, and Wisconsin. He had been the source of much of the information they had on Dempsey's plot to set up his own government. After being targeted for assassination by Dempsey, Harding and his deputy director, Gerald Aims, had escaped and made their way to Missouri. They'd alerted military forces there and stopped them from joining Dempsey's forces. It had been said that one act might well have put a halt to Dempsey taking control of Missouri and Arkansas.

"We should go find him," said Brad "the Cad," who leaned over from behind her and poked an index finger at the photograph. "He knows Dempsey well. He also once had the respect of the men and women who worked for Region Five. He knows who on the inside might be willing to work with us."

She hated it, but he was right. Harding and Aims were valuable assets and a wealth of information. She made a note to have someone track them down. They'd last been seen at the shelter in Columbia, Missouri. She checked the date on the data sheet. "Shit!"

"What?" Brad asked.

"This says they left the shelter back in the fall. They could be anywhere now."

"Or dead."

Stephens looked up and glared at him.

"It's true. You've heard the same reports. Most of the country has died of starvation by now."

Stephens lowered her head and swallowed hard. She didn't need him to tell her that. She'd spent months trying to get this mission underway to try to save some of those lives. That it had taken this long broke her heart as much as it pissed her off. Of course, the military had been focused on fighting the Chinese and stopping them from overrunning the country, but in the meantime, those who resisted Dempsey were perishing while he grew stronger.

"Let's pray that Harding is still alive and willing to help us," Stephens said.

"We need to get to Missouri and find out."

Stephens raised her eyebrows. "We?"

Brad smiled, displaying his perfect shiny white teeth. "Missouri is on the way to Illinois."

Brad was scheduled to lead a team into the heart of Dempsey's territory. President Latham wanted numbers. He wanted to know how many prisoners they were holding and how many military forces they had guarding them. Waltrip believed freeing those prisoners in forced labor camps held the key to toppling Dempsey's kingdom. He might be right, but what kind of conditions would they find them in? Would they be malnourished and sick? Would they require more assistance than they gave? Stephens gave a sideways glance at Brad Smith. For all his faults—and there were many—he was still the right man for this job.

"You gonna miss me?" he asked.

She threw her head back and guffawed.

Brad's expression didn't change. He was so full of himself. His confidence was once one of the things that had attracted her to him, but his charms didn't work on her any longer. Not after learning he'd been cheating on her with multiple women. She'd heard that he'd given her engagement ring to his baby momma. *Whatever!*

FOUR

Savanah

Texarkana Refugee Center
Texarkana, Texas
Event + Nine Months

"Mom, Jason's home!" Karson yelled from the doorway of their shelter. Kylie jumped out of bed and Savanah had to lunge to catch her. "Back to bed, little lady. Doctor's orders, remember?" You're contagious."

"But, Mommy," the six-year-old whined.

"You don't want to give Jason your cold, do you?" Savanah said, placing her back into bed and tucking the covers in tight.

"But I don't feel sick anymore."

Savanah hurried to the door. It had been three months since she'd seen her husband, Jason. With him being away, training with the military at Little Rock, Arkansas, it had seemed like the longest months of her life.

"You can't come out of this room until the doctors say you can."

"That's not fair."

"I'll have Karson go see if Doc Sandman will drop by this afternoon. Maybe he'll give you a release since you're no longer running a fever."

"Can you send him now?"

Savanah nodded. "Stay put. I'll have Jason say hi from the doorway."

"Okay." Kylie smiled.

Savanah shut the door and turned the lock. She wasn't taking chances. She knew her daughter too well.

"Honey, I'm home," Jason shouted from just outside the shelter. He threw open the door and rushed inside. Savanah rushed into his arms, almost giddy to see him.

"I am so glad you're here." She'd almost said home, but this place wasn't their home. It was far from anything resembling a home. It wasn't that she was totally ungrateful for the life-sustaining food and protection that the FEMA shelter provided her and her family, but those things came with a price, and they'd had to give up a lot of their freedom to remain there.

They shared a long, passionate kiss, oblivious to the discomfort of Karson at witnessing the display of affection. Savanah heard the door shut. Karson had stepped outside.

"How long do you get to stay this time?" she asked.

"A week," Jason said, running a hand down her back and pulling her tighter. "Maybe we can get Gabby or someone to watch the kids and…"

"Gabby's on house arrest," Savanah said.

"House arrest? For what?"

"She tried to unionize the kitchen staff."

Jason chuckled. "I bet their supervisor didn't appreciate that much."

"No. No, he did not. He reported her as a subversive."

"Subversive?"

"It seems that disrupting order is a crime these days."

"How long is she stuck at home?" Jason asked, his smile fading.

"Until they find a place for her in Houston or Dallas. They don't want her anywhere near Austin or President Latham at the new capitol," Savanah said, leading Jason over to a grouping of lawn chairs in the corner of the space. It had taken two months for them to get enough chairs for everyone in her family to sit together. Lawn chairs were somehow a high-demand item in the refugee center.

"She's going to go crazy being locked up inside like that," Jason said.

"I'm afraid they will move her someplace just to get rid of her. She's not even allowed visitors, except for family. Troy and Tank are deployed so that means Gabby only has me."

"At least we'll have a babysitter."

Savanah shook her head. "Nope. They aren't allowing her to see the kids either."

"Why? That doesn't make any sense? Are they afraid she might lead the rebellion with children?"

"Something like that. Something about her poisonous ideas corrupting them at a critical time in their development."

Jason wrinkled his forehead. "Someone actually said that?"

"Don't get me started. They refused to allow me to appeal the decision and threatened to take the kids from me if I continued to push the issue. They hinted that I shouldn't even visit Gabby and implied that I was being watched too."

Jason tilted his head to one side and narrowed his gaze. "Watched? You haven't gone to any of those meetings again, have you?"

Savanah sighed heavily.

"Have you?"

"No! Mac and Jeremy left the shelter. The rest of them are meeting outside the fence. I wouldn't leave the kids alone like that."

"Good!" Jason leaned back in the chair and took her hand. "Listen, I know you're unhappy here. You never wanted to leave your homestead in the first place, and this place is far from perfect, but just give it a little more time. Will and I have been talking. We're planning to do some scouting next time we go out on patrol. We've seen a few areas we think might make a suitable place to set up a new homestead, once the military gets the area secured, that is."

"How long will that take? I thought they were using all their resources to get Houston, Dallas, and Austin secured?"

"We've been working on securing around Little Rock. There are a few spots near enough there that we might be able to move you all—and we might be allowed to come home more often if we move closer to base."

"That would be amazing." She leaned forward in her lawn chair and kissed him. Jason ran his hand down her arm and took her hand. They stood and were just about to retreat to their room when the door flew open.

"Jason!" Keegan squealed as he bounded inside. Jane's eyes grew wide and her lips parted. "Oh, I'm sorry. I didn't know you were home, Jason." Jane grinned. "I can take him to the park—if you need some time."

"I want you to take me to the park, Jason," Keegan said.

Jason sat him on the floor and took his hand. "Okay, let's go then."

Savanah smiled. She loved that her four-year-old son finally had a father that would take him to the park. She was so blessed to have someone who loved her children as his own. There were so many single mothers in the facility who were struggling to care for their children and keep up with the work demands required of them.

"You come too, Mommy," Keegan said.

"I can't, little man. I can't leave Kylie."

"Can't Jane stay with her," he whined.

"No. We wouldn't want Jane to get sick. It wouldn't be good for the baby."

Jane wasn't due to deliver her baby for another month. They were all hoping that Luca would be back from his assignment with the team working in Dallas in time for the delivery. Jane had put in a request to be allowed to be among the first refugees settled there so she could be close to her husband and have him there when their first child was born but hadn't heard anything on the request. Savanah wasn't sure where all the feedback and request cards went. They had them all over the facility, but as far as she knew, no one ever received a response back from anyone.

"They haven't released her from quarantine yet?" Jane asked.

"No. I'm still supposed to be wearing the hazmat suit when I go in to see her," Savanah said.

"Hazmat? Quarantine?" Jason asked.

"Kylie had a cold. The medical team freaked and said she couldn't leave her room. They dropped off a bunch of masks and gowns and said the rest of the kids couldn't go in there. That was a week ago. I've tried to get them to come out and examine her so she can be released from quarantine, but they haven't come yet."

"Poor baby," he said, heading toward her room.

"Don't!" Savanah shouted. "Don't go in there. You'll get into trouble. I don't want them to put us all under house arrest."

Jason stopped and turned back. "It's really that bad around here now?"

"That new director is an asshole," Jane said.

"New director?" Jason asked returning to Savanah's side. "What happened to Phillips?"

"He got promoted to some cushy job in Austin working with the president."

"And this new guy thinks the way to get himself promoted is to undo all the good things his predecessor put in place?" Jason asked.

Jane rubbed her expanding abdomen. "It seems so."

"So he's the one who cracked down on Gabby?" Jason asked.

"Her and anyone else who dares to question his orders," Savanah said, using air quotes around the words.

"Luca said they're preparing to close down the shelter, so his tenure here is likely going to be a short one."

"It could take months to completely close this place. They haven't trained enough police officers to secure the cities. There's a shortage of people, due to the needs of the military, for personnel taking priority over civilian jobs," Jason said.

"I'm not moving to Houston or Dallas. There's no way it's safe there. I don't care how much they screen people before sending them there," Savanah said.

"I don't think they would send everyone there and close the shelter if they couldn't provide security for the cities," Jane said.

"I'm not raising my kids in the city where they'd be reliant solely on the government for their survival. They need to be able to defend themselves, hunt for food, and find water."

"But they'll have all that provided for them," Jane said.

"Until they don't. What if this new government fails? What if the Chinese invade again?"

Jane looked dumbfounded. "I understand where you're coming from. I do. Luca and I had dreamed of raising our children off-grid and away from societal influences, but things have changed. I'd rather my child not starve to death."

Savanah raised and lowered her eyebrows and tossed her braid over her right shoulder. "Then you better teach her to hunt, gather, and fight to keep her food."

FIVE

Will

Texarkana Refugee Center
Texarkana, Texas
Event + Nine Months

"You guys decent?" a familiar voice called from the door to Will and Isabella inside the shelter.

"Are we decent?" Isabella asked, pulling a white terry cloth robe around her. Will groaned. He and Isabella had only been married for a little over two months, most of which had been spent training with the military. They'd barely had any time alone together, except for stolen moments between road marches and weapons training. This one-week furlough before their return to Little Rock was important to both of them.

Will pulled on a pair of shorts, grabbed a T-shirt, and headed for the door of the octagon-shaped, soft-sided shelter his family called home. He hated to use the term "home." Any way you put it, it was still a tent in the middle of a sea of tents used to house families at the Texarkana Refugee Center. But he was grateful for it. The single men still slept on the ground under flimsy tents. His shelter was luxurious in comparison. Soon, he was told, all the refugees would be moved to the cities where the power had been restored. But clean up and providing security had hampered the government's efforts. Who was to say when refugees would be relocated.

"I thought you went to Fort Hood," Will said, opening the door.

"I was. Now I'm back," Stephens said.

"What's up?"

"I can't just call on you two without you thinking something's amiss?" Her smile seemed forced.

Will slid his shirt down over his head and pulled it over his chest. His clothes fit a little better each day. The food at the shelter wasn't great, but it was filling and these days that was all that mattered. Everyone was putting on weight—even Savanah, who no longer felt the need to starve herself in order to provide her four children enough to eat.

"You don't do small talk, Stephens. What's happened?"

Stephen's smile faded. She looked past Will into the shelter. "Is Isabella around?"

Will stepped back and held his hand out gesturing for Stephens to step inside. As she did, her gaze perused the small sitting area just outside the two small bedrooms.

"Is Cayden home?"

"No. He's in school," Will said.

Stephens bobbed her head in acknowledgment.

"Stephens, I'd say it's good to see you, but I have a feeling I'm not going to like the news you've brought us," Isabella said, stepping from the bedroom she shared with Will.

"I'm sorry to crash your honeymoon. This couldn't wait."

"What is it?" Isabella asked, motioning for Stephens to take a seat in one of the folding chairs flanking the small round table where they ate their meals. They weren't supposed to take food from the dining hall, but they'd rather eat alone, as a family. It was difficult to have a conversation at a table of strangers, and the noise volume in the large dining tent made it hard to hear without shouting. Mealtime was about the only time they had with Cayden. He volunteered on one of the clean up crews in addition to his job in the kitchen. Will was quite proud of his son. He was a hard worker who never complained.

Stephens exhaled slowly as she lowered herself onto the chair. Will could tell she was not her normal, confident, and in-control self. She was nervous. He'd never seen her like this. He found it unsettling.

"As you know, Pete and Tank's teams were sent north a few weeks ago—"

"Are they dead?" Isabella interrupted.

Stephens looked to Will. "We don't know yet. All we know is they failed to check in."

"How long?" Will asked, his voice flat.

"Two days. It could be weather-related or—"

"Or they got caught," Isabella spat.

"We won't know anything until Charlie Team reaches them."

"How soon will that be?" Will asked. A pit had formed in his stomach. Pete and Tank had volunteered for the mission and the military had been eager to have them due to their prior military training. He knew they were tough and could handle themselves in difficult situations, but infiltrating Dempsey's transportation unit was risky. One mistake and they would be caught and interrogated. Something everyone trained for when they were assigned missions in the north country.

"A week," Stephens replied.

Will closed his eyes. He'd need to tell Savanah that their cousin, Tank, and friend Pete were in trouble. Worse yet, he'd have to tell Tank's sister, Gabby, and Pete's family. Gabby, Tank, and others from the casino back in Vincent had only just arrived at the shelter one month ago. They'd barely settled in before Tank lit out with Alpha Team on the intelligence-gathering mission. Their job was to find out where Dempsey's work camps were and how many prisoners he held. They were to travel west, by Humvee, across Arkansas to the Mississippi River, then north to St. Louis. From there they would have been on foot while making their way deep into Illinois and General Dempsey's territory. Other teams ventured into Iowa, Nebraska, and Wisconsin mapping the extent of his reach and control.

Isabella slid her hand into his. Their eyes met briefly before Will looked away. He shook his head.

"Charlie Team will be at the extraction point in three days. If they aren't there, they'll travel to the camp just outside Jacksonville, Illinois, and attempt to make contact. Let's not give up hope yet," Stephens said, standing and pushing her chair back.

Isabella stood and opened her arms to give Stephens a hug. "Thanks for coming to tell us yourself."

"I didn't want Smith doing it," she said.

Will thought he saw Isabella shiver at the mention of the CIA analyst, Brad Smith.

"Thank you," Isabella replied. "Thanks for sparing us that unpleasantness."

Will was still unsure what had transpired that had caused Isabella's visceral reaction to the man. He'd asked, but Isabella only said she disliked him and refused to provide a reason. From what he'd seen around the Little Rock military base where they'd all been the previous month, Brad Smith had a way with women. Just not Isabella and Stephens for some reason.

"Let Savanah and Pete's family know we're doing all we can to get to them," Stephens said as she approached the door.

"Thanks, Stephens. Let me know as soon as you hear anything?" Will said, nodding.

"Sure thing," Stephens said, pushing open the door.

"And you guys should be ready to move out. We might all be called back to Little Rock sooner than planned."

"So soon?" Isabella asked. She glanced at Will.

"There might be an important mission coming up soon. It's classified so I can't go into it now, but I've asked Colonel Sharp to assign you both to one of the teams."

Will wasn't used to Sharp's new title. He imagined that in ordinary times, being promoted would be an honor, but these days, it came with being in charge of very high-risk missions. He respected the man and was happy to have him as his commander, but he was still nervous about being sent out on their first real mission.

They had done patrols and escorted refugees from central Arkansas back to Texarkana. They'd encountered the same types of bandits and thugs they'd run into on their way to Texarkana prior to joining the military. But on this mission, they'd be up against Dempsey's army. Dempsey's people were well trained and equipped, unlike the new recruits of the 1st Cavalry Horse Detachment Unit. Most of the new recruits still had trouble even mounting their horses, let alone hitting a target while on horseback. At least he and Isabella knew how to ride. Stephens made it sound like they'd be sent out before their training ended. If that was the case, they could expect to see a great number of casualties. Will's gaze turned to Isabella. Although he was grateful that they were training together, he wished she had been assigned to a support unit where she'd be safer.

"We'll be ready to head out, but do you think the unit is ready for something this important. I mean…"

Stephens shrugged. "It will have to be."

Time seemed to not be on their side. Everything was ruled by time these days. The Rule of Three seemed to control their lives. You could survive three minutes without air, three hours in a harsh environment, three days without drinkable water, and three weeks without food. Their mission lately had been to survive and help others survive.

Stephens' missions were all time-sensitive. The enemy moved around a lot and anticipating their movements was critical. For that, the military leaders needed information. Stephens and Smith worked separately from the military intelligence officers. Will wasn't sure how they obtained their information. It was classified and above his pay grade.

Will and Isabella stood outside Savanah and Jason's tent. Will took Isabella's hand and knocked. He could hear Kylie's voice through the thin walls of the soft-sided shelter. "Mommy, someone's at the door."

The door opened and out popped his smiling six-year-old niece. She flung herself into his arms and wrapped her tiny arms around his neck. He felt a bump and then more tiny hands on his leg. He looked down to find Keegan attached to his left leg.

"Uncle Will," he squealed. "Mommy said we couldn't come visit you. I wanted to show you the toy horse that Jason got me," Keegan said.

"Well, hey, Will. We didn't expect to see you anytime soon," Savanah said, exiting the shelter.

Will forced a smile. Normally, he'd be happy to see his sister and her kids, but bringing bad news was never enjoyable.

"We need to talk," he said, peeling Kylie from his neck and placing her on the ground.

Savanah's mouth formed an "O" and she grabbed Keegan by the arm.

"Keegan, you and Kylie go back inside and color for a bit. Mommy has to talk to Uncle Will and Aunt Isabella."

Kylie stomped her foot.

"But I want Uncle Will to take me to the park and push me on the swing," she said and turned toward him. "You said you would when you got back."

Will tousled her hair. "And I will. Just let me talk to your mom for a minute and then we'll go. All right?"

Her shoulders slumped and she turned to go.

"All right, but don't take all day."

"Kylie," Savanah said. "Watch the mouth."

"Sorry."

Will waited for Keegan and Kylie to go inside and shut the door before giving Savanah the bad news about Tank and Pete. She took it better than he'd expected and even offered to go tell Gabby and then Pete's family alone. He was relieved. He hated being the one bringing bad news.

"Where are Kendra and Karson?" Isabella asked.

"In school."

That was unexpected. Savanah had homeschooled them prior to the lights going out. "You're not homeschooling anymore?" Isabella asked.

"Not allowed."

Will shot her a double-take. "What? Homeschooling isn't allowed? And you stood for that?"

"They're being taught skills needed for this new world. Things I might not be able to teach them at home. They have college professors instructing them on specific skills that will be needed in the recovery." Savanah looked over both shoulders as if she were expecting someone to come up behind her.

"Even Karson? He's only ten. Are they going to put him to work as well?" Isabella asked.

"Eventually. He's very bright for his age and tested out of high school already." She was beaming with pride and then her smile faded. "Did you know they're estimating that there are less than thirty thousand people still alive in all of Texas?" Her eyes grew wide. "Out of twenty-nine million people."

From all the death and destruction Will had seen, he imagined the figure was even lower. They'd had the hurricane the day of the EMP. Residents of Houston were on the roads evacuating. The loss of life would have been catastrophic.

"I can see where they'd need to train everyone in order to

achieve their goal of rebuilding the cities and restoring services," Will said.

"I'm supposed to go to classes two nights a week. I talked them down from four. I work at the laundry facility two days a week. I can't leave the little ones alone. With Jason and the rest of you away with the military, there just isn't anyone I trust to watch them."

Or anyone who could handle Kylie, Will thought.

"Have you seen Walker today?" Savanah asked.

"Nope. We came straight here after Stephens left. Why?" Will asked.

"I was hoping that he might…" She nodded toward the shelter. "He's so good with the kids. I don't want to take them with me to tell Gabby."

"I'll do it, Sis. I'll go let them know. I can't put that off on you," Will said.

"I'd like to go with you, at least. She's going to flip and we might have to talk her down from running off to find him herself."

Will looked skyward. She was right. Gabby was impulsive and likely to go off the rails when it came to family. Troy was back at Fort Hood assigned to the 504th Military Intelligence Brigade. They were readying for a mission to St. Louis, Missouri. He could be on a plane heading there now for all Will knew.

Maybe I shouldn't tell him until the mission is complete, Will thought.

It sounded like an extremely important mission. With only a few planes left operable, for them to use one, it had to be of vital importance to the military commanders and the president.

"How about I run to go get Walker and the three of us go tell Gabby. We can stop on the way and inform Pete's wife. We'll let her tell Beau and the others in their family."

SIX

Stephens

The 303rd Military Intelligence Battalion Tactical Operations
Center
Texarkana, Texas
Event + Nine Months

Stephens studied the map laid out on the long conference table in the 303rd Military Intelligence Battalion's Tactical Operations Center. When she'd entered the room, Stephens had been displeased to see Brad Smith seated at the table. She hadn't been informed that he'd be joining her team—if it were still her team. It wouldn't be the first time he'd stolen a mission from her.

For the last two months, she'd had people out trying to locate former FEMA Region Five director, Reginald Harding, and his deputy director who'd been last seen in Columbia, Missouri, and Smith had convinced the president to pull the plug on the mission. They would need to send more spies into Dempsey's region, and they'd be going in without the benefit of decent intelligence information.

"The Brazilian government has offered to sell us millions of dollars in weapons and equipment. Considering the wealth of the United States virtually disappeared when the internet went down, it was no small feat for President Latham to get them to agree to send the ship from Brazil to pick up the payment."

Stephens nearly jumped from her seat. She wanted to pump her fist and shout, "Hooray!"

"That's good. We'll have enough weapons to take down Dempsey and his army," Stephens said, bringing her emotions under control.

"It's only good if we can have the payment there when they arrive," General Waltrip said.

"I have a feeling that's what this mission is for," Sharp said.

General Waltrip opened a folder and held up a report. "Our people in St. Louis intercepted a gold shipment bound for Springfield, Illinois. They were headed back to the airport with it when they encountered significant enemy forces. Most of the unit was killed in the ensuing firefight. The survivors were forced to abandon the gold. Fortunately, they were able to get it to a concealed location. We need to retrieve it."

"Dempsey's army will be scouring the countryside in search of it," Sharp said.

"No doubt," Waltrip replied. "We're going to send in two teams."

"Both with the same mission?" Smith asked.

"Same mission. Retrieve the gold and get it to Fort Leonard Wood for transport to the Port of Houston. The Brazilian ship will be there in less than a month."

Sharp shook his head. Waltrip raised his hand in an effort to hold back Sharp's incredulity. "I know. I know. That's not much time, but we have to make this work, Sharp. We lost a plane in St. Louis. I'm going to need you to take control of the gold when our people get it to Fort Leonard Wood. I'm sending you to Fort Leonard Wood on the C-17. We can't afford to lose another plane.

If something happens to that aircraft, we can't get that gold to the Port of Houston in time."

Stephens knew what Sharp was thinking. He'd want to be leading the teams retrieving the gold. But the general was right, the safety of that plane was critical to the mission.

"How's the intel on the movement of Dempsey's forces in Missouri?" Stephen asked.

"Spotty at best. That's why I want you and Smith to accompany each of the teams. I need your expertise to work the locals and find out where Dempsey's army is and how many people they have in the area. You'll need the assistance of residents there for intel and to identify who's who."

"I'd think that would be easy enough. They'd been the ones driving vehicles and carrying rifles," Smith said.

"You'd be wrong. They have people in plain clothes scouring every barn, warehouse, and back yard."

Smith shrugged. "What makes you think the locals will help us over them?"

Waltrip glowered at him. "Because I'm told you're good at your job."

"What about the 303rd. Isn't that their mission? Don't they work human intelligence assets?"

Waltrip let out an exasperated sigh. Since the director of the CIA was in DC when it was wiped off the face of the map, along with most of the government, the few intelligence community assets who remained now fell under military command—at least until the president could appoint a new cabinet. There seemed to be a shortage of qualified volunteers. Stephens thought Smith had been vying for the job until he showed up back at Fort Hood, assigned to this task force.

"They are tasked elsewhere at the moment," Waltrip said.

Stephens supposed that was why they were using their secure TOC for this meeting. Otherwise, the 303rd commander would be conducting this briefing.

"The members of Sharp's 1st Cavalry Horse Detachment Unit will be split into two teams for this mission."

"We're going on horseback?" Smith asked.

"Humvees and transport trucks attract too much attention. Besides, the president doesn't want to lose any more military equipment to Dempsey."

"Guess he doesn't mind losing personnel," Smith said.

Smith was crossing the line. His animosity toward the president was on full display. He'd been passed over as the new director of intelligence and apparently didn't make the cut for director of the Central Intelligence Agency either. Stephens wasn't surprised. Smith and Latham had a tumultuous history—likely concerning a woman. Stephens couldn't think of anyone more qualified in Texas and wondered who the president had appointed for the positions.

The veins in Waltrip's forehead bulged. He'd had enough of Brad "the Cad."

"They're ready, sir. The new team members just completed training and are out on patrol as we speak. I can have my two platoons ready to deploy in forty-eight hours," Sharp said.

"New recruits? Well, that's just great," Smith said.

Sharp glared at Smith. "Not all are new recruits. They're just new to the team. This is a joint task force with varied skill sets. Their training here was to learn how to perform their skills mounted—on horseback. It's not as easy as just climbing into the saddle, as you're about to find out." Sharp said. Sharp knew what he was talking about—he'd had to go through the same training when he assumed command of the unit.

Stephens had been impressed with the level of competence and professionalism displayed by the previously ceremonial unit. Of course, they'd all been in other parts of the military before being assigned to the unit. Well over two-thirds had combat experience in Afghanistan, America's longest war. They'd seen their share of combat.

"1st Platoon—Team Razorback—will be commanded by Lieutenant Burns, and Lieutenant Bronson will command 2nd Platoon, Team Lonestar."

"We're riding horseback for three hundred miles. How long will that take?" Smith asked indignantly.

"Team Lonestar will travel by vehicle to Fort Leonard Wood, make sure the former base is secure and that the runway is operational. From there, they'll proceed to Iron County. While Team Razorback will head to a forward location by vehicle where they'll unload their horses at the dropping-off point and then ride to Iron County, Missouri. The idea is to get as close as possible by vehicle without risking drawing the attention of Dempsey's forces," Sharp explained.

"Why two separate routes? What if the other team needs assistance?" Smith asked.

"We need a team to recon the military base and make sure it's safe to land the C-17, and we need a team to get into Iron County and work the locals—find out how many of Dempsey's forces are in the area, if any. We don't want to retrieve that gold only to lose it. If there's an overwhelming number, Team Razorback will hold off and wait for Team Lonestar's assistance, if possible."

"I'll go with Team Razorback," Smith said, turning his gaze to Stephens.

Stephens scowled at him. He wanted all the glory for himself. Typical. He'd get there, secure the gold, and take all the credit for the success of the mission.

"Stephens will go with Team Lonestar, then. I want you to report the condition of the runway back to Sharp as well as any security issues surrounding the post and the airfield, and then get to Iron County as fast as you can in case Team Razorback runs into difficulties."

"Difficulties?" Smith asked. He crossed his arms over his chest. "We're going to make it and secure that shipment. You can count on that."

Stephens shifted in her seat and sat up straighter. "I'm sure both teams will make it. We'll get that gold on the plane at Fort Leonard Wood. The survival of the nation depends upon it."

"That's what I want to hear," Waltrip said. "All right then. Sharp, get your platoons headed toward Missouri, and prep the C-17 to go retrieve that gold."

Waltrip stood and the military personnel stood at attention until he left the room. When Waltrip was gone, Sharp pointed to the map. We're going to need a recon mission to find out what local gangs pose a threat to our mission. He nodded to the 303rd's Alpha Company commander. "Find out where the trouble spots are on our route. We need to be able to move as swiftly and silently as possible."

"I'll get you the intel and send a team out to clear the way for you," the captain said.

"No. I don't want anyone knowing we're even in the area. You start moving in with kitted-out soldiers, news of military presence will spread far and wide. It could alert Dempsey's forces. We want to move through without detection. Just give us a route around any trouble areas you're aware of."

"Yes, sir."

Stephens waited until everyone but Sharp had cleared the room. Surprisingly, Brad had been one of the first to leave. Normally, he'd linger about to see what she was up to. He must have had more important things to do—like getting back to that cute Hispanic chick she'd heard he'd hooked up with.

"How do you feel about his mission?" Stephens asked.

Sharp hesitated as he stared down at the map. "I'd feel a lot better if half of the Horse Detachment had seen real military combat."

"Will and Isabella can handle themselves pretty well. They've seen combat—just not as military soldiers. They survived the attack on the base back in Houston. Will fought the Chinese down near Fort Polk."

"Yeah, I know, but the rest of the new volunteers have barely left the shelter since the lights went out. The president thought we could pull people who'd ridden a pony as a kid and make an effective mounted unit."

"You've done a great job getting them ready. I've watched them. It's impressive."

"You'll need to be trained too, you know."

"And Smith," Stephens snickered.

"And Smith," Sharp said. "I'll have you work with Lieutenant Burns, he'll lead Team Lonestar

"He'll want that chick, Martinez, included on his team. You just watch."

"Martinez? Simone Martinez?" Sharp looked liked he'd been slapped. "She won't be joining his team."

"How long do I have to train?" Stephens asked, abruptly changing the subject. She didn't want anything to do with the love triangle she figured she'd just discovered.

SEVEN

Will
___

Texarkana Refugee Center
Texarkana, Texas
Event + Nine Months

Gabby took the news much better than Will and Savanah thought she would. Will watched her for signs that she was lying and secretly planning something. She sat erect in her chair with her hands in her lap and stared off toward the ball field where the younger kids were planning a game of soccer.

"You don't seem surprised, Gabby," Savanah said, breaking the silence.

"Troy told me already."

Will shook his head. Of course. Troy knew already. He was with an intelligence unit.

"Did he discuss the plan to find Tank?"

"No. He just said there was one and that the best team in the unit had been sent in. He recited that 'no man left behind' bullshit."

"He sounded confident?" Savanah asked.

"Yeah. He drank the kool-aid," Gabby said, a bitter bite to her tone. She had come to the shelter reluctantly and had exhibited a high degree of mistrust of the officials there. She'd refused to follow their rules and been penalized for it. Her house arrest had only made matters worse.

"Troy wouldn't lie, Gabby," Savanah said, reaching out and touching her arm.

Gabby stared down at Savanah's hand. She looked up and met Savanah's gaze. Will saw the tears in her eyes and his heart wrenched.

"I know he believes all that "hoorah" bullshit the military's been feeding him, but no one knows how powerful that general is up there in Illinois, or how extensive his network is. He's had seven months to get established. Look what's been going on here. They haven't had all that." She glanced at Will and then back to Savanah. "Did you know they have drones up there?"

Will had heard about the drones. He'd hoped they were only rumors. Drones would make getting anywhere near the camps without being spotted nearly impossible.

"Stephens said we have contact with satellites," Isabella said.

Will's head snapped toward her. "What? That's the first I've heard of it."

"She said they had satellite footage of troop movements in St. Louis."

"When did she say that?" Will asked.

"Last week when she stopped by the stables. We were talking while you, Jason, and Walker were saddling your horses."

"And you didn't tell me about this?"

She shook her head. "I forgot. I got distracted when that horse ran you into the fence."

Will's face flushed. Even though he'd ridden horses as a kid, training them to become cavalry horses was something altogether different. His new horse was especially obstinate, and he bore the scars to prove it.

"If they have satellite surveillance, why do they need boots on the ground to tell them where the labor camps are?" Savanah asked.

"I imagine from the air they look no different from any other buildings. The fences could be for safety." He pointed to his right. "We have one."

The twelve-foot-high razor-wire-topped fence surrounding the refugee center was there to provide security and to control access. It would be a safe bet that Region Five, as it was called, would have something similar to protect people. It wasn't likely they had control over everyone in their region. They would have escapees and others who could pose a threat.

"We might be heading back to Little Rock early, but as soon as I hear anything about Tank, I'll let you know," Will said.

"And I'll do the same," Gabby said.

"How is Troy getting information to you?" Isabella asked.

"I can't say. I don't want to take the chance of burning my source."

Gabby wasn't the only skeptical resident of the camp. She'd found several like-minded individuals before she'd been placed on house arrest. Some were nothing more than conspiracy theorists spreading rumors that the shelter was an enemy reeducation camp disguised as an American refugee center.

"We'll stop back by before we ship out to Little Rock. I hope there's good news before then, though," Isabella said, as she rose to her feet.

Will wasn't sure that they'd hear anything. At least not anytime before they were called back to base. Stephens had made it sound like they'd be leaving soon. He and Isabella needed to get back and make sure their gear was squared away. He wanted to find Cayden and spend the day with him, just in case. The worse part about joining the military was that he wasn't there for his son. He had to rely on Savanah and Gabby to look after Cayden, not that he needed much supervision. He was very mature for a thirteen-year-old. The shelter was the safest place in the country, as far as Will knew. But it still concerned him that he wasn't able to protect Cayden himself.

Will, Isabella, and Savanah met up with Jason on his way back to their place. He and Savanah were newlyweds as well, but with four children in the household, there hadn't been a way to fit in a honeymoon. Will felt a pang of guilt. He should have offered to watch the kids—at least for one night. He'd been so concerned about getting quality time with Isabella and Cayden that it hadn't even crossed his mind. He'd need to talk to Isabella about it first, but he intended to remedy that mistake.

"We had a visit from Stephens a little while ago," Will told Jason.

"She's back already?"

"She said we should be prepared to be called back to Little Rock. Something's come up."

Jason took Savanah's hand. "It figures," Savanah said.

"Listen," Isabella said. She looked at Will. "How about Will and I come over and stay with the kids while the two of you stay over at our place tonight."

"That would be great!" Jason blurted and then turned to Savanah. "I mean…"

Savanah was blushing. "That would be nice. You sure you can handle them?"

"You got duct tape, right?" Will laughed. Savanah's brow knit. "I'm kidding. We'll be fine. Cayden will love spending the night with his cousins and we've been wanting some quality time with them as well."

Jason couldn't conceal his ear-to-ear grin. It was a big responsibility being a parent and Will respected Jason for stepping up to the role.

The door opened and Walker filled the doorway. "Howdy, Will.

Hello, Isabella. I was hoping to see you two before you shipped out again."

Isabella walked over and threw her arms around the former lawman. He still sported his Texas Ranger's Western hat but had retired the white shirt and tie. Will wondered if he still had his gold star badge.

"We may be heading back out in the morning. We're waiting for word from Stephens."

"I know. I spoke with her shortly after she left your place."

Will's eyes widened. "You did? Did she tell you about Tank and Pete?"

"She did. She has full confidence in the team going in to extract them," Walker said, stepping outside and closing the door behind him. Will wondered where his niece was. She always tried to put herself in the middle of adult conversations.

"So what was the reason for Stephens' visit to you?" Isabella asked.

"She wants me to join her team. She's put in a request to have me reassigned from the security team here."

"Would you have to go through the training we just completed?" Isabella asked.

"I guess so."

"I didn't know we had enough horses to add personnel to the unit. Anyway, it'll be nice to have you with us."

"It'll be nice to be outside this fence and see what the rest of the countryside looks like," Walker said.

"I'm not sure what is going on, but I have the feeling we're about to see more of the countryside than we'd like," Will said.

"Looks like nearly everyone is getting to join the party," Savanah said, putting her arm around Jason's waist.

"I know it's hard to stay back here when we're all out there. Soon we'll get our home base moved out of the shelter. At least you and the others can get started on a garden and maybe get some meat put away for winter."

Savanah sighed. "That's going to be hard with most of you away all the time."

"You still committed to living off-grid?" Isabella asked her.

"For now. Having modern conveniences is nice, but they come at a high price. I just don't know."

"They have to have all those rules to keep their communities safe. There just aren't enough people to police the towns," Jason said.

"But not allowing us to have weapons to defend ourselves with is over the top," Savanah replied.

"You sure it's worth it to you?" Isabella asked.

"I lived without all this before the EMP. I chose to live off-grid and homeschool my children so I had some control over our lives and well-being. This..." She waved her hand toward the rows of refugee tents. "This is making me stir crazy."

An image of the compound where Corey had died flashed into his mind. There had been many heated discussions between Will and the members of their group who were adamant about not being relocated to Dallas or Houston. Isabella was so concerned that she'd spoken to Stephens about it. Somehow, she'd managed to wrangle an exemption for families of military members. Essentially, that exempted almost everyone at the shelter as nearly everyone had family serving, and with no way to verify this, Will had briefly considered listing everyone from Vincent as a relative.

The government permission to resettle outside a safe zone did not, however, come with protection. They would be on their own. They had not received an answer as to whether their weapons would be returned to them. Even if they were, ammunition was nearly non-existent. It would be a monumental task to secure a compound of their own.

Will had proposed moving to the abandoned compound at Williams Junction. The folks there had been doing fairly well, it had seemed. They'd been forcefully relocated after the firefight that had killed Corey. The place was within a day's ride from Little

Rock. Savanah was hesitant to be that far away but was willing to take a look at the farm. Will had hoped they could make the trip during this furlough, but if Stephens was correct about being called back early, it may have to wait.

EIGHT

Will

Texarkana Refugee Center
Texarkana, Texas
Event + Nine Months

Stephens led Will and Isabella to the east gate of the FEMA shelter facility and then turned to face them, an ear-to-ear grin spread across her face. She extended her arm and jiggled a set of keys in front of Will. "Who's your best friend now?"

"What is that?" Will said, pointing to the rusty old Chevy pickup parked along the curb just outside the double gates.

"That is your ride to Williams Junction."

"I thought we were being called back early?" Isabella said, swiping the keys from Stephen's hand.

"Colonel Sharp has to travel to San Antonio so we have a few extra days before we have to be back in Little Rock."

"Seriously?" Isabella said. She spun around to face Will, placing a hand on his arm. "Does this mean we're taking a road trip?"

Will smiled. "I guess it does, but that truck will only hold three people."

"We could fit maybe eight in the bed," Isabella said.

"I'll leave you guys to work out who's going with you. Don't forget to stop by headquarters and get passes for everyone. I don't want to have to bail you guys out of the pokey again," Stephens said as she turned to go. Stephens was referring to Savanah and Gabby. They had ventured outside the fence to attend an unauthorized meeting with persons deemed troublemakers. If not for Stephens, they both could have been sent to the camp in West Texas where they would have been held as domestic terrorists.

"Thanks, Stephens. I owe you—again," Will said.

"Oh—and there are four rifles in the bed of the truck under the blanket. Try to be safe out there." Stephens waved over her shoulder as she walked away. They both knew Will could never repay the debt he owed her. He wasn't sure who Stephens owed to arrange for his sister and cousin's release, but it must be someone very high up the chain of command. It was good to have friends in high places.

"Let's go tell Savanah. She's going to freak," Isabella said, tugging on Will's arm.

Reluctantly, Savanah had asked Jane to stay with the kids while she and Jason joined Will and the others on the trip to Williams Junction. Will convinced her that between Jane, Kendra, Karson, and Cayden, the little kids would be fine. For some unknown reason, Kylie was better behaved when Jane was around.

Walker drove the pickup. Pete's wife, Kathy, and Rob's wife, Erin, rode in the cab with him while the others rode in the back. Some members of their group had made the decision that they would move to one of the safe zones in Houston or Dallas instead of to the wilds of Arkansas. Jane was one of them. It was understandable. She was going to be a first-time mother. She wanted all the comforts and protections the safe zone would provide for her child.

August's wife, Pam, sat next to Isabella. She was on the fence about moving to Williams Junction. August was in Houston working on a construction crew assigned to the multi-faceted mission of rebuilding the country's infrastructure. He didn't want her and the kids there with him. He said the places he worked were nowhere near safe. The toxic waste from the hurricane alone was enough for the city to have been abandoned.

August and his wife had teenagers. The safe zones had advantages and disadvantages for teens. The lucky ones could live at home and continue their education before being assigned jobs. Others would just be assigned a blue-collar vocation rebuilding the nation—at least the Texas part of the country. The disadvantage was that they would give up some freedoms, like the freedom to choose where to live, where to work or travel, who they could associate with, and they couldn't own firearms. They had been assured the restrictions were only temporary. After security was established and the services restored, the freedoms provided in the Constitution would be restored—or so they were told.

Will leaned his back against the cab of the truck as Walker pulled onto Interstate 30 and headed northeast toward Little Rock. This was the first time Will had been this way in a civilian vehicle. It had been months since he'd seen a running truck that wasn't military. No one else had fuel these days.

As they passed by a highway sign for Hope, Arkansas, Savanah tugged on Will's pant leg. "We should move there."

Will nodded. "Maybe we could rename Williams Junction."

"Maybe. If it's everything you said it is," she replied.

"Or we could call it New Hope," Pam said. She moved closer

to Savanah. "It's kind of exciting to be the founders of a new town."

"I never dreamed I'd be a pioneer woman," Isabella said.

It had been two months since Will had been at the compound. Anything could have happened in that amount of time, but he hoped they'd find it much as it was when he'd first seen it. The fox holes and bunkers might need some work after Will's unit had attacked the place, but the houses, barn, and shop could all be pretty well the same.

They passed a sign indicating a rest area ahead and Isabella tapped on the back glass to get Walker's attention. "I need to use the restroom. Can we pull into the rest area?"

Walker nodded and exited the interstate. Will was surprised to see so many vehicles abandoned there. He hadn't been with the teams that had cleared the northbound leg of I-30. Walker drove past five tractor-trailers and a row of cars before stopping at the restroom facilities.

The men watched as the ladies cautiously cleared the tiny outhouse meant to handle the large number of visitors each day on the interstate. When the ladies all went inside, Walker, Jack, Will, and Jason checked out the cargo still inside the semi trucks.

"There's some useful stuff in here," Jack yelled from inside a Walmart truck.

"There's nothing but junk in this one," Jason called out. He hopped down and headed toward the next trailer. "Unless you need a printer or a sixty-inch flat-screen television."

"What we need is a grocery or grain hauling truck," Will said.

Walker pointed to a home improvement store box truck. "How about construction materials."

"We could definitely use those," Will said.

"How would we get it to Williams Junction?" Savanah asked as she approached.

Will pursed his lips and looked skyward. It would probably be pushing it to ask Stephens to get them a bigger truck.

"It would take a few trips and use some fuel, but we could use the Chevy," Jason said, pointing back to the pickup.

"I don't think there's enough in the tank for an extra trip," Walker said.

Will shrugged. "Oh well. We'll figure something out. At least we know where to find it when we do have a way to haul it."

"Who is that?" Erin yelled, spinning around.

Walker rushed to her side. "What did you see?"

"A woman or kid. I just saw the back of them as they ran that way." She pointed toward the trees behind the restrooms.

"Let's go, people," Jack said, doing a circle in the air with his hand. "We need to get the heck out of here."

Will liked Jack. The forty-something-year-old man had been injured trying to save his family. Both his legs had been broken, but he'd never given up. Now, even though he walked with a substantial limp and must be in constant pain, he was always the first to volunteer to help the group. Will hadn't known him long, but he trusted the man.

Isabella looked around toward the back of the restroom. "Shouldn't we check it out?" Isabella said.

"It's too risky. We only have four weapons," Will said, moving toward her.

"They could need help."

"Or, they could be trouble," Jason said.

Walker had the engine running before Will and Isabella reached the pickup. Will held his hand out to help Isabella into the bed.

She stiffened and her eyes grew wide. "Will!"

He spun around, raising his rifle as he turned.

"I got them," Jack said, unslinging his rifles.

"Everyone with a rifle, just hold it at the ready so they can see we're armed—but don't point it at them unless we get fired upon. We don't need a confrontation right now—we're on a mission."

"What are we going to do?" Isabella asked.

Will counted five men and three women. All were armed with bats and clubs, walking toward them. At least they weren't carrying rifles. If they had been, Will and the others could be dead by now.

"We're leaving," Will called to them. He pushed Isabella back behind him. "And we won't be back."

"Right on," Kathy said, brandishing her rifle at the ready.

The group said nothing but continued advancing.

"Get in, Will. Hurry!" Savanah said.

Jason reached down and grabbed the back of Will's shirt. "Let's go, man."

Will made sure Isabella and the others were all inside and then hopped onto the tailgate. Jack slapped the side of the bed and Walker hit the gas. The advancing group stopped in the parking slot they'd just occupied. Will studied their blank expressions. He saw no fear. Not like when the military rolled through. He also saw no desperation. He considered that as the rest area got smaller and smaller in the distance. Then it dawned on him. They'd likely been living off of the supplies in the trucks at the rest area. They'd been watching Will and the others as they rifled through the trucks. The group knew they weren't armed and therefore not much of a threat.

"There are likely other places with trucks filled with stuff we could use," Will said.

"And they all likely have people guarding them just like the ones back there," Jack said.

Will nodded. No doubt about it. The military had either missed this group when they did the sweep of the area or they'd arrived at the rest area later. That meant there could be far more people living in the countryside than they thought. That could put their new community at significant risk. It was unlikely the army would sweep through Williams Junction again. They had no reason to. Will and the others would need to thoroughly clear the area—and the area around the area. It was vital to know who their neighbors were, if any. There'd be no way he'd leave his family there without that information.

"Hey, Jason. We need to see if we can get some of our platoon to take a trip over to Williams Junction," Will said.

Jason nodded. "It'll cost us. You got anything we can trade for hooch? I got a source."

Savanah's eyes widened and she pursed her lips.

"Not for me. For the ole boy also trades in knives. He's a blacksmith," Jason assured her.

"I can find something. What will it take?" Will asked.

"He asked me about getting some grain."

"That would be tough," Will said. "They have the horse feed locked up tight."

"Robertson does enjoy moonshine, though," Jason said, and smiled.

"True. How much would we need for a trade."

"I bet a ten-pound bag would get enough to hire most of the squad."

Savanah threw her head back and ran a hand down her long braid. "What happened to military brotherhood and looking out for one another?"

"We'd be asking them to risk a lot, Sis," Will said.

Jason shifted his position on the wheel well and turned toward Will. "You thinking we'll run into trouble?"

"I'm thinking there are a lot more people out there in the countryside than we came across when our unit ran through the area. I'd like to take a second look before we establish ourselves and take our families there. We need to know if there are large groups or dangerous individuals to contend with."

"I hope there aren't from a security standpoint, but it would be nice to have established farmers and homesteaders with whom to trade," Savanah said.

"That would be nice," Isabella said.

"Not everyone out there is a threat."

"That's true, Sis, but the problem is, they don't wear uniforms with "Good Guy" or "Bad Guy" written on them."

Savanah rolled her eyes and waved her hand at him, dismissively. "You tend to see only the bad in people these days."

Will supposed she was right—for the most part. He had to acknowledge he may be a bit overly cautious these days—even of the soldiers in his unit. Most had been drafted like he and Jason, and not all were happy about it. He wasn't thrilled to be serving so far from his family, but he understood the need. He would have volunteered once he'd been able to get his family settled outside the camp, though. The military just couldn't—or wouldn't—wait.

NINE

Will
___

Walker stopped the old pickup truck a quarter mile from the junction of Highways 9 and 10. Will and Jason jumped from the bed and sprinted toward the crossroads store at the intersection. They stopped just as the building came into view and dropped to one knee along the edge of the road.

"See anyone?" Jason asked.

Will scanned the front of the convenience store through the scope of his rifle. It looked deserted, but it had the last time they were there, as well. An image of Corey popped into his head. She had lost her life, that fateful day.

"The weeds sure took over the parking lot quickly," Jason said.

"Is that the store?" Jack asked as he dropped down beside Will.

Will would have preferred for Jack to have stayed with the truck. He wasn't able to keep up with Will and Jason. He would

59

have been a better asset keeping guard on the truck and the ladies with Walker.

"Yeah. Stay here and watch the front of the store. Whistle if you see anything," Will said, motioning for Jason to follow him as he crossed the roadway and approached the side of the store.

After a thorough search around the outside of the building, Will and Jason cleared the inside. The smell was awful. Someone had been living there after the lights went out. The odor of human feces was overwhelming. They made quick work of their search and left quickly. Jason ran to the edge of the parking lot and bent over, emptying the contents of his stomach into the tall grass.

"I sure hope the buildings in the compound smell nothing like that," he said, straightening and wiping his mouth with the back of his hand.

"I think that group was smart enough to use an outhouse," Will said, crossing the parking lot and moving toward the roadway. He stood in the intersection of the highways and turned in a circle scanning through the rifle's scope. They'd been fired upon from the northwest corner last time they were there. Of course, that was after they'd engaged in a firefight with the store's occupants. They had been in uniform and driving military vehicles. It was obvious they were with the government yet the survivors had seen them as a threat.

Jason joined Will in the intersection.

"You okay to continue?" Will asked.

"I'm fine." Jason gestured with his hand for Jack to join them. When Jack finally limped up beside him, Jason said, "Run back to the truck and tell Walker it's safe to pull ahead. Tell him to stop the truck here in the store's parking lot and join us. You stay with the vehicle. We're going to continue west on Highway 10 another quarter mile. Listen for my signal and then pull down the road to meet us."

Without a word, Jack turned and walked as fast as his legs would allow. Will knew Jack just wanted to contribute and he'd be a great asset once the group got established, but this was no place for someone who could barely walk, let alone run. There were too many unknowns.

Will pulled a notepad and pen from the side pocket on his tactical pants and drew a diagram of the intersecting highways, including the store and boulders from which they'd been fired upon previously. He turned in a circle, looking for other positions of cover from which to monitor the intersection. The trees that lined the road were too thin to provide sufficient concealment. He turned to his left and studied a taller tree back away from the road.

"I'm going to check out that tree," he said, pointing.

Jason moved to the opposite side of the road and scanned the area as Will disappeared into the woods. Will slung his rifle around to his back and leaped, taking hold of a branch, then pulled himself up. A few seconds later, he was sitting with his back to the truck, observing the intersection. He could see only about fifty feet east of the store, but he could see at least a quarter mile in each direction along Highway 9. Will climbed down, marked the position of the tree on the pad, and labeled it with "OP" for Observation Post.

"Let's check out the north side of the intersection," Will said.

From the boulders, the compound's security forces would have had an unobstructed view of their approach. Observers would have been able to hear their vehicles for some time before their arrival. They would have had plenty of time to send word back to their compound, yet they had encountered no resistance so far. There were no physical obstacles to prevent anyone from approaching on foot or by vehicle. They had relied solely on a few firing positions from the boulders. They seemed to have been somewhat prepared for a small group attack. But they weren't expecting the Army. Their mistake and one Will's group wouldn't make.

When Walker had joined them, the three men pushed westward toward the compound, stopping as soon as the driveway came into view. They separated, with Will taking the north side of the road and Jason moving to the south. Walker remained on the pavement to watch for anyone exiting the driveway.

Will dropped to one knee beside a clump of bushes. He watched as Jason moved back into the undergrowth beneath a large oak tree. He was fairly well concealed. They waited, listening for manmade sounds that might come from an occupied compound. Will doubted the original occupants would have returned.

Will heard footfalls on the asphalt and spotted Walker approaching them in a jog. Will stood and waved Walker over to him. He pointed down the road. "The entrance to the compound is just over that rise. We're going to inch our way toward the drive and then move along the east perimeter fence to a clearing near the back of the property. A creek runs along part of the west side, and the property backs to a cliff that overlooks a valley with a view of a pasture below."

"Sounds like an easy place to defend," Walker said.

"Yes, but not as easy to escape from if you're overrun."

"You probably outnumbered and out-gunned them by a lot. We aren't likely to encounter the same numbers or anyone nearly as well armed."

"Let's hope not, but we'll be better prepared," Will said, moving back onto the roadway.

Will, Jason, and Walker cautiously moved to the corner of the compound. The trees bordering the place prevented a view of the grounds. Will stood still, listening. When he'd been there before, he'd heard nothing but gunfire. Had they approached them quietly, the unit could have heard children playing or some activity. He held his breath and cocked his head to one side. All he heard were crows and squirrels barking their alarms. No human noises. He exhaled and scanned the fence line. It was still intact. If they made the place their home, he'd want to make the fence taller and place perimeter defenses along it for early warning. They'd have OPs, of course, as well as LPs—Listening Posts—but their group wasn't large enough to cover a lot of ground. That was a problem he'd need to creatively solve. He pulled out his sketch and made a note to talk to his first sergeant about perimeter defenses.

They pushed on but stopped abruptly when Will recognized the small clearing where Corey had fallen. Even months later, the area was still littered with used gauze pads and QuickClot wrappers the medic had used to staunch her bleeding. Will swallowed hard and looked away. He pushed past the grief and continued east along the fence line to the back of the property where it abruptly dropped nearly two hundred feet straight down. Will stepped up onto a large rock and scanned the valley below. Across the field was another creek. They could grow crops or graze animals here if they could find an easy way to get up and down the cliff. He imagined deer and other animals came there to eat too. So far, it was looking like a very promising spot to build their new homestead. He drew the field and stream on his map and stuck it back inside his pocket.

Will, Jason, and Walker walked back to the road and approached the front of the property. The flimsy pipe gate lay in the ditch by the road, having been destroyed by his unit when they'd breached the compound. They'd need to construct something more substantial at the entrance. Will thought for a moment, trying to recall where he'd seen sheets of steel. He pointed at the crumpled gate. "Remember that shop about two miles from here on the highway that had those heavy-duty steel-pipe gates?"

"Yes," Jason said.

"What if we were able to get them and install them here? We should beef up the fence all along the road too if there is extra pipe there at that shop."

Jason stopped, looked down, and scratched his head. "It'll take time and muscle."

"I wish we had machinery, but we don't," Jason said.

"There might be an old tractor around here somewhere," Walker said.

"I thought of that. If there is and they still have diesel in them, the batteries might be dead."

"Maybe not. My grandad had an old 1970's Ford that he could go a year without starting and she'd crank right up and run all day long. It's worth searching for one," Walker said.

Will chewed on his bottom lip and glanced toward the barn. If there had been such a machine in the area, wouldn't this group have found it? If only they had more time. They couldn't count on getting another furlough for a while. Savanah and the others would be on their own to secure the compound. He didn't like it. He'd need to convince Savanah to hold off a while longer in hopes they could come back after this mission Stephens said they were about to take.

"These sandbags will need to be refilled," Jason said, moving toward one of the fortifications.

Bullet casings littered the ground. Empty rifle magazines still lay where they'd been dropped as the combatants had reloaded in the heat of battle. They had to have belonged to the compound's occupants. The army wouldn't have left their empty mags. Will stared down at a cluster of three AR-15 magazines. He wondered how many of his fellow soldiers this shooter had taken down to have gotten off that many rounds before falling himself.

Will, Jason, and Walker cleared and inspected the entire property. Most of the campers had bullet holes in them, but Will thought they could make a few of them livable again. The others could be moved to the edge of the property and used as cover and observation posts. An image of Dale from the zombie show, *The Walking Dead*, sitting in a lawn chair on top of his motor home popped into his mind.

The windows in the three-bedroom, two-bath house had all been boarded up by the previous occupants. The plywood had done little to stop the bullets from shattering the window glass. Savanah would want to be able to open the windows and let fresh air inside. But they would need window screens to stop the bugs from entering. He didn't look forward to having that discussion with her—again. She'd won the last time when it had been her house.

"What do you think, Will?" Walker asked. He leaned his rifle against a woodpile and took a seat on a log.

All around it were wood chips where someone had been chopping firewood. There was a huge stack of wood between two large trees just behind the house. They'd be set for cooking and heating water for a good while. But they'd need more before winter he imagined. It would be much colder there than any of them was used to. He had no idea how much wood it would take to heat a place in an Arkansas winter.

"Well, Walker, I think if we had all the time in the world, this would be a good place to put down roots."

"What if we had help?" Jason asked.

Will scoffed.

"Are you thinking of hiring somebody to help build fences and fix up this place?" Will said.

"Savanah has some friends who aren't too interested in being relocated to Houston or Dallas."

"Do you mean that group of troublemakers? They're all on house arrest. How are they even going to get passes to leave the camp? Besides, they'll just make us a target of the new administration. You and I both know they aren't going to be satisfied setting up here and letting Latham and his government do their thing."

Jason stood a short log on its end and sat on it, leaning his rifle against his knee.

"Not all of them are anti-government. Most just don't want to be forced into giving up all their freedoms. The government hasn't done such a bang-up job of protecting the nation so far," Jason said.

Will didn't want to argue with his sister about all this. In many ways, she was justified in her thinking. She had been forced from her home and thrust into an overcrowded FEMA shelter. But on the other hand, they had repelled the Chinese invasion there and were now working to restore modern services. Will didn't like their tactics any more than Savanah and her friends did, but he could see where some of the regulations would be necessary in the effort to restore the rule of law. As he recalled, the big cities had become more like the wild, wild west.

"I'm not comfortable with it, Jason. I don't trust them."

Walker nodded. "I agree with Will. Some of them are good, hard-working folks but others are more interested in fighting the system than rebuilding a country. They'll be trouble for sure."

"Honestly, I agree with you both, but Savanah and Gabby trust them. I respect them. Will, you know Savanah wouldn't put the kids at risk."

"I'll talk to her about it, but I have to tell you, I'm not trusting those asshats around my son."

It would be difficult to convince Savanah that they needed to take more time and secure the compound with her thinking the solution would be to invite strangers to join them. He'd need the others to agree with him. The last thing he wanted was to go off to battle somewhere and have to worry about Savanah and Gabby's friends bringing trouble down on them while he was away.

TEN

Savanah

Williams Junction, Arkansas
Event + Nine Months

At first glance, all Savanah could see was the devastation that had been brought to the prior residents of the compound. She stopped just inside the five-strand barbed wire fence and took in the scene. Families had occupied the campers and motor homes. Even from the road, she could see the children's toys strewn about outside camp. She shuddered to think they might have been killed in the gun battle with the military—Will's unit.

One minute they were going about their day—just trying to survive—and the next they're being fired upon by their own government—simply for disobeying the order to relocate to the safe zone. Will had told her they'd fired first, but they were just defending their home. What choice did they have? In the end, the survivors of that fateful day were forced off their land and moved first to Texarkana and then on to West Texas where they would be housed with still others deemed subversives.

"That motor home closest to the house doesn't look too damaged," Isabella said, stepping up beside Savanah.

"There are at least five that have minimal damage," Jason said. He nodded toward a forty-foot condo on wheels. "That one there is well worth repairing. It's super nice and big inside."

Savanah gestured toward the house. "Is it repairable?"

She had no interest in staying in a motorhome in the winter. She'd been told how cold it could be, and she had no idea how they could possibly heat the recreational vehicle.

Jason's smile appeared forced. "With time and supplies. The windows are all broken. There are holes in the siding that penetrate the walls. We'd need to seal everything up before winter."

It was obvious that he was still was against the whole idea.

Savanah lifted the bandana she wore around her neck and wiped sweat from her brow. In the late June heat, it was hard to think that in just a couple of months the ground could be covered in snow. Thankfully, Arkansas didn't get that much snow, but it would be cold and wet either way. She wasn't looking forward to the weather at all.

"What about food and water?" Savanah asked. That was the most important factor to consider. They had time to winterize the living quarters, but food and fresh water would be their immediate concern. They would arrive from the shelter with only a day or two of food and water, at most—and even that would be hard to sneak out of the camp. The guards performed regular checks when anyone left the shelter. Stealing food was a felony punishable by imprisonment and relocation to the prison in Lubbock, Texas. They would all be risking a lot to make this work.

"We found a cache of canned food under the floor in the kitchen. It's only enough for a week at most. Will thinks we should try to find more before settling here."

A week? It was six days more than they'd relied on before they left her homestead in Vincent. Somehow, every day they had found something to feed the group. Not this time, though. She couldn't do that to her kids. Not again. She hated it, but Will was right. They had to secure more food before taking the children up there. They'd have to hunt. Anything canned or packaged would have already been found and consumed by survivors from the area. She thought about the tractor-trailers sitting at the rest area along the interstate. All they needed was one truck with food inside, but that would take a miracle. She needed to be realistic. The lives of her children and all the others who would call this new place home depended on a more solid plan.

If they couldn't find sufficient game and fish in the area, this compound would not be a viable option—that was the cold, hard truth of the matter.

"When can we start looking for game?" she asked turning to face Jason.

"There's a nice field down the cliff behind the house. We can start there. We'll check the tracks along the creek and see if we can spot any game trails."

"Let's go," Savanah said.

She had never hunted in her life before the lights went out, but once it became the only way to feed her children, she'd been determined to learn all she could about it. She had a long way to go to be as good a hunter as Jason, but she knew how to tell a deer track from a wild hog, and where to look for rabbits. There were others in their group with better skills, and she'd observe them and ask questions until she was proficient and successful at putting consistent food on the table.

Jason, Savanah, and Pete's wife, Kathy, followed the creek as far as they could, then moved tree-to-tree the rest of the way down the steep grade toward the open field below. After searching for signs of game for two hours, they'd discovered three trails and a place where it appeared deer were bedding down during the day.

"Look!" Savanah said, picking up a turkey feather and holding it out. "That's a good sign, right?"

"Turkey would be amazing right now," Kathy said.

"I know, right?" Savanah said, licking her lips.

"We should cross the creek and check out that pond on the other side," Jason said.

Savanah walked close to the bank of the stream and peered through the trees. "Are you sure? There's a house over there."

"I'll clear it first," Jason said.

"You shouldn't go alone. We'll all go," Savanah said, looking to Kathy for confirmation. She doubted Kathy would object. Kathy was skilled with a rifle and quite confident in her ability to defend herself, though she wasn't trained to properly clear a building. Her husband and his family had been preparing for something like this for years—they were preppers. How they could have known, she didn't understand, but their forethought and planning had saved her and her children's lives, and for that, she was more than grateful.

"She's right. We should all go. I'll have your six," Kathy said.

Savanah still wasn't used to all the military jargon everyone seemed to be using these days. At times, she felt left out of the conversations as the acronyms and military terms flew over her head. She didn't want to learn it all. She just wanted her life to go back to something resembling normal, but that, she knew, would take a very long time.

The trio skirted the trees lining an overgrown field and made their way past a pole barn, stopping behind a woodshed to observe the house.

"The door's open," Kathy said.

"There's a screen door. The windows are open as well," Jason whispered. "Savanah, I'll clear left, you good clearing right?"

"Yep—I can do it," Savanah said.

"Kathy, you'll wait here. Let's go, Savanah."

Jason ran and pressed himself against the side of the house as Savanah followed behind him. They listened for voices inside or sounds of human activity but heard none.

"Ready—on three," Jason said and flexed his knees twice before bounding through the door and clearing left. Savanah followed and swept the right side of the room with her weapon, then followed Jason as he immediately walked toward the next room and quickly entered, clearing left again.

As Jason swept his rifle back to center, Savanah hadn't even begun her sweep from the right—she had barely entered the room.

"Hold it right there!" a young, female voice called.

Jason spun around, and his mouth dropped open as a young girl stepped into view from the right.

"No, Jason! She's just a child!" Savanah yelled, pointing her rifle in the air.

"The girl stepped into the room from a hallway, pointing a shotgun at Jason. Her eyes were wide with terror, but she didn't back down.

"Drop that rifle, mister, or I'll be forced to shoot this here scattergun atcha," the girl said, her accent thick with a southern drawl.

"Evie Dawn!" a male voice called from down the hall past the girl.

"Stay in bed, Papaw. I'm okay," the girl said with her eyes and weapon still on Jason. "Drop that rifle on the floor, ma'am."

Jason slowly placed his rifle on the floor and held up both hands, palms facing the girl. He stepped back, his size fourteen boot stepping on Savanah's toes.

"It's okay. We're leaving. We didn't know this house was occupied," Savanah said, still holding her raised rifle in the air while pulling her foot from under Jason's boot. "Is your grandfather all right?"

The girl's eyes darted down the hall and back to Savanah.

"I have some medicine with me. I have aspirin and some herbal remedies. I can take a look…"

"He's got a bad infection. He got his hand stuck in one of our traps and the wound looks nasty," the young girl said.

"I can take a look at it and see what I can do for him," Savanah said, taking a step closer.

Jason grabbed Savanah's arm as the girl turned the shotgun in

Savanah's direction. Savanah pulled her arm free of his grasp, slowly laid her rifle down, and let her pack slide off her shoulder at the same time. "What's your name?" she asked as she unclipped her medical pouch.

"Evie." The girl leaned slightly, eyeing the medical bag. "You got antibiotics in there. Papaw said he needed antibiotics."

Savanah met the girl's gaze. The terror had been replaced with concern.

"Who else is here with you?" Jason asked.

"Nobody," Evie said without looking at him.

"You're alone with your grandfather?" Savanah asked. She and Jason exchanged a concerned look. They both knew the girl was in a bad situation. If the grandfather succumbed to the infection and passed away, Evie would be left all alone to fend for herself.

Evie glanced back down the hall and nodded.

"Where are your parents?" Savanah asked.

Evie's gaze remained on whatever was down that hall. "Under the oak tree out back."

"I'm sorry," Savanah said, her tone full of sympathy.

Death had become so much a part of their daily lives, yet Savanah didn't think she would ever be used to it. For this child to have had to bury her parents was too painful to think about.

"How old are you, Evie?" Savanah asked, changing the subject.

"I'm nine." She looked past Savanah to the stove. "My papaw was going to make me a pie for my birthday."

Savanah grabbed the medical pouch and stood. "When's your birthday?"

"July twenty-fourth."

"Let's go have a look at your grandpa. Maybe we can get him back on his feet and the two of you can still celebrate your big day."

She tipped her head toward the far end of the hall. "He's in there."

ELEVEN

Will

Williams Junction, Arkansas
Event + Nine Months

An inspection of the house and shop had confirmed Will's suspicions; anything useful had been taken. But who could have cleaned the place out? It was now obvious the military had failed to round up everyone. Of course, his unit would have taken any weapons they found here, as well as ammunition and food. But they would have no need for the other supplies that the residents would have used for day-to-day survival. He found not a single canning jar. Even the cast iron cookware they would have used to make meals on the wood cookstove was missing.

"Isabella? Did you happen to see any laundry supplies? Clothespins, washboard, tubs—anything?"

She turned in a circle, looking toward the all-season creek running along the west side of the property where the onerous task of washing clothes by hand would have been accomplished. "No." A concerned look flashed between them.

"They could have taken them and moved on. They obviously

didn't stick around here," Isabella said, waving her hand back and forth.

"That just confirms we need to do a broader sweep before we bring the others up this way," Will said. He walked to the edge of the cliff and looked out over the pasture below. There just weren't enough people to secure this place. As much as Savanah had her heart set on leaving the shelter, it just was not safe to do so. He had to convince her. He must get Jason on board and the two had to put the brakes on this planned move.

He was staring off toward a distant farmhouse when a shout roused him from his thoughts.

"Will!"

It was Jack. He was moving toward Will as fast as his damaged legs would allow.

"Trouble!" Jack said, breathless.

"What? What is it? People?" Will shot back.

Jack nodded as he bent over to allow air into his lungs.

"Where? How far?"

"At the gate," Jack said between gasps.

Will ran. He rounded the house and weaved between travel trailers and collapsed tents until the gate came into view. His heart stopped. Walker had his hands in the air. In front of him stood a giant of a man dressed in hunting camouflage and a boonie hat holding a rifle pointed at Walker's chest.

Will stopped, dropped to one knee, and yelled. "Drop the weapon! Do it now! I will shoot you!"

"You do and I'll drop you before your friend hits the ground," a female voice said behind him.

Will's heart skipped a beat—or two.

"Just lower the weapon and put your hands in the air," she said. Will felt someone brush against him as he complied. He never took his eyes off Walker. His mind raced as he wondered where Isabella and the others were. Did they have guns trained on them as well? Where the hell was Jason?

"Unhook that sling and let your weapon drop to the ground."

Will hesitated a second too long and he felt a rifle barrel press into the base of his skull. A shot there would kill or paralyze him. He'd be no use to his group. He complied, lowering his rifle to the ground.

"Who are you people?" the woman asked.

"What?" Will replied.

"Where did you come from?"

"We're..." Will was about to tell her the truth that some of them were with the military but thought better of it. "We've been living at the FEMA shelter down in Texarkana, but we wanted to find someplace less... um... restrictive to survive this thing." He thought that explanation would make them seem less threatening— and it was partially true.

"You with the group that used to live here?"

"No, ma'am."

"How'd you know about it, then?"

Will hesitated. He couldn't tell her the truth that he'd been with a military unit that had run the folks off their land and forced them into the shelter.

"Ham radio," Will lied. He'd seen a radio tower in the back of the steel building there. He took a leap. "Before all this. We heard they were preparing."

His cousin, Gabby, had told Will about some prepper groups up that way. After the lights went out, they were still able to communicate with one another for several months. They'd worked together to alert each other to the government's movements. Will's unit had been ordered to look for communications equipment.

"I got one over here," the woman yelled.

The man gestured for Walker to head toward Will and the woman. He kept his rifle trained on Walker as they slowly approached her.

"Are we going to take them back or drop them here?" the woman asked.

Will tensed waiting for the answer. He desperately wanted to turn to see where Isabella was.

"How many are in your group?" the man asked.

Will did not want to answer that question. Firstly, he had no idea if Walker had already given them a number. Second, he wasn't going to give away that his wife and sister were with him.

He stalled. "In our group?"

"You're scoping out the place to possibly move here. How many of you will be living here?"

Will tried to read Walker's face. He wasn't making eye contact. His eyes were on the woman behind Will.

Will stammered, trying to think of something to say.

Walker looked at the man. "About twenty or so, I'd say. It's a fluid number."

Will held his breath. He respected Walker and hoped he knew what he was doing.

"We have some whose family members are adamant about going to Houston or Dallas. Of course, they don't want to split up their families, but they also know how stupid that move would be."

The man nodded. His features softened some. Will saw his shoulders relax. They'd found a common topic.

"So, it sort of depends on who leaves with us the day we pull out from Texarkana. Honestly, we'd like to have as many as we can get. It's gonna take a lot of people to make this place work," Walker continued.

"Ain't that the truth," the woman said.

The man lowered his rifle to the low ready and took a step back. "When are you planning on moving up here?"

Walker looked to Will. "Soon."

"They're talking of closing the shelter and moving everyone to the cities soon," Will chimed in.

"They're gonna just let you and twenty of your friends just walk off from there? I mean, they went to great lengths to round everyone up in the first place," the woman said, stepping around Will and joining the man.

"We have a connection," Will said. He didn't think that fact would cause any issues. It was true. They didn't need to know that it was a colonel and a CIA agent.

The two looked at one another. The man shrugged and stuck out his hand.

"Welcome to the neighborhood!"

TWELVE

Savanah
———————

Williams Junction, Arkansas
Event + Nine Months

Jason led the way down a short, dark hallway to a bedroom in the front of the house. He drew in a quick breath as he entered the room and moved to the opposite corner, his rifle pointed at the man in the bed.

The smell hit Savanah long before she entered the room. Curtains billowed in the breeze from the open window.

Savanah stepped walked to the window and held the curtains away. "Kathy, you can come in now."

A bead of sweat rolled down the side of Savanah's cheek. Her face flushed and bile rose into her throat. She fought back nausea as Kathy stepped into the room.

"Kathy, this is Evie and her grandfather," Jason said.

The man was lying with his head facing the windows. His purple, massively swollen hand was propped up on pillows. Necrosis extended past his wrist. If gangrene had set in, there would be nothing she could do for him. Savanah's heart broke.

How was she to tell Evie that her papaw was going to die? She said a silent prayer for the girl and the man and moved to the side of the bed.

"Hello. I'm Savanah Fontenot." She looked to Jason. "Blanchard." Jason gave her a slight smile. It was the first time she'd had occasion to use her new last name. "Your granddaughter said you had an injury. I have some medical supplies with me. Do you mind if I take a look and see if I have anything that might help?"

The grandfather slowly rolled his head to face her. She watched as his chest rapidly rose and fell. He was pale and weak. Sweat beaded on his brow. Savanah placed her medical kit on a chair next to the bed and removed a cotton cloth. She looked at Jason and pointed to his pack. "I need water."

Jason removed a canteen of water and moved toward her. The man tried to sit up. "It's okay, Papaw. They're here to help you," Evie said from the doorway. The man settled back onto the bed. His eyes met Savanah's.

"I'm just going to wipe your face and then take your temperature. Is that all right?"

His mouth opened and then closed without making a sound. Savanah took that as a yes. After pouring water from the canteen onto the cotton cloth, Savanah wiped the sweat and grime from his face and then placed the back of her hand against his forehead. She didn't need a thermometer to know if he was burning up with fever, but he felt really hot. Gangrene had set in and there was nothing that could be done for him.

Savanah glanced over her shoulder at Evie. What could she do that wouldn't do more harm than good. If she attempted to cleanse the wound, all she'd be doing was causing the man more pain. Could his heart even take it? She reached into her bag and removed the jar marked "white willow bark" containing the inner green layer of willow bark she'd cut into small pieces, dried, and then crushed into a powder. She turned to Evie. Do you have a way to boil water?"

The girl nodded.

"I need to make a tea. Can your papaw sit up to drink?"

"I have to hold him up for him to drink water."

"Jason, can you help Evie boil enough water for a cup of tea. I need at least two cups."

Jason glanced down at the man and then to Savanah before turning and following Evie out of the room. Savanah was confident the man wasn't a threat, but Jason was either leery to leave her alone with him, or he knew nothing could be done for the man and she was just trying to get Evie out of the room to figure out what she was going to do.

Dishes clanged in the kitchen as Jason and Evie went about their task. Kathy stood next to the window, her rifle in the low ready.

"I told her to leave me," the man said. His voice was hoarse and barely audible.

"I'm sorry, I can barely hear you," Savanah said.

He turned to face her. "I tried to get Evie to leave and go to Lake Sylvia."

"Alone?" Kathy asked, judgment in her tone.

His eyes moved to look at her then back to Savanah. "You can take her with you." It was more of a statement than a question. He was giving them permission.

Savanah touched his shoulder and nodded slowly. Tears welled in his eyes. "I have four children. One is Evie's age."

He closed his eyes. "Bless you."

"I'd like to try to clean your wound. Would that be all right? I have some herbal pain relievers."

He opened his eyes and glanced down at his hand. "I think we are well past that now."

"Maybe not," Kathy said. She took a step toward him and leaned forward to study his hand before turning her gaze to Savanah. "We might try maggots."

The image her words brought made Savanah's stomach turn.

She'd heard of larval debridement, but laboratory-bred maggots were used in the medical treatment. After being placed on the wound and covered in a dressing, the maggots would feed on the dead tissue; leaving healthy tissue alone.

"It's worth a shot," Kathy said.

"Where are we going to get them," Savanah asked, fighting back the bile rising in her throat.

"I'll be back," Kathy said and turned toward the door.

While Kathy went in search of the larva, Savanah turned her attention to what she could do to make the man more comfortable. She avoided looking at the wound. Instead, she focused on the man's face. His beard was salt and pepper colored, but his hair was still dark brown. Despite the grimace of the pain, he had relatively few wrinkles for a grandfather.

"What's your name?" Savanah asked him.

"Mark."

"You're Evie's grandfather?" she asked, pulling on a pair of surgical gloves.

"Her mother was my stepdaughter, but I raised them both. My wife and daughter are buried out back. They went last winter. Food was scarce. I made a trip to Lake Sylvia to trade for food and brought back a nasty virus. My wife and Evie's parents didn't survive."

"Evie said you got your hand caught in a trap."

"I was trying to set a beaver trap. I thought I had it set but it closed on my hand. I had to have Evie get it off. It took a while. The skin wasn't broken, so I thought it was okay until it started swelling."

Savanah examined his upper arm for red streaking, a sign of severe infection that can lead to sepsis and death. She saw none, only the black, necrotic looking tissue on the top and palm of the man's hand. The swelling caused by the trap crushing his hand must have led to the necrosis.

"Here's the hot water, Savanah," Evie said, brushing past her and placing it on the table beside her grandfather's bed.

Savanah stirred in the white willow bark powder and Jason helped Mark sit up to drink it.

"Thank you," Mark whispered as Jason lowered him back onto the bed. "Get her out of here."

Evie's eyes grew wide as her mouth dropped open.

"Get Evie out of here. Take her away from this place."

"No, Papaw," Evie said and ran to his side. "No. I'm staying with you."

Mark turned to Savanah. "Please!"

Evie began crying uncontrollably.

Savanah wrapped her arms around the girl. "We won't abandon him, Evie. We'll do everything we can. Okay?"

"Promise?" Evie said between sobs.

"I promise. We'll do our best," Savanah said.

Savanah didn't know how much time the man had left, or how long they could wait. Will would, no doubt, throw a fit. He, Jason, and Walker were all due back on duty at Little Rock soon. There would be no way any of them would leave without her.

"There are doctors at our shelter in Texarkana," she said, looking at Jason. She hadn't mentioned it before because she didn't think there was anything a doctor could do for Mark, and the trip there would only cause him excruciating pain, but there was a chance she could be wrong. Evie would believe it was worth a chance.

"Let's go, then," Evie said, her eyes brightening. "How do we get him there?"

"No," Mark said. He waved his good hand in the air dismissively. "No. I can't ask you to…"

"We live at the shelter. We came up here to see if we could find land to settle on and make our new home. My children are back there. We have to go back anyway. We can just take you with us," Savanah said, forcing the corners of her lips into a smile.

Mark scanned the room, his eyes landing on Jason who was looking at the floor. Savanah knew what Jason was thinking. The man would likely die on the road. She'd considered that but at least Evie would know they'd done everything they could. She could move on without guilt or hatred toward them. Savanah could also move forward without regret. Somehow, they'd just need to convince her brother.

While they were discussing how they'd move Mark from the house to the truck, Kathy returned with a bucket in hand. She held it out. "I found blowfly larva. Not as many as I'd like, but enough, maybe."

Once again, Savanah's stomach turned at the thought, but what harm could it do at this point. She took the bucket from Kathy and placed it on the bedside table.

"This might be painful, I don't know. It's dead tissue so you shouldn't feel it. If you do, let us know and I can flush them out."

Mark nodded his acknowledgment and turned to face the windows once more. "Evie, I need more boiling water. Would you mind?" Savanah didn't need the water, but she didn't want to traumatize the girl any further.

"I'll go with you," Kathy said.

"Jason, you want to help me?" Savanah asked.

Jason shook his head but said yes as he moved around the bed and stood beside her. After placing the larva in and around the open sores on the top of Mark's hand, Jason held the man's arm up while Savanah wrapped it. It had to have hurt like hell, but Mark never complained. While she removed her gloves, Jason helped Mark drink the last of the willow bark tea. What he really needed was morphine or a good bottle of Scotch.

"Now we need to go explain this to my brother," Savanah said.

Jason smiled. "Yep. I'll be right here when you get back."

"That's how you're going to be?" Savanah teased. She stood and addressed Mark. "Fine, then. I'll take Evie with me, if that's okay with you, Mark."

"You can take her. It's okay to leave me."

Jason placed a hand on Mark's shoulder. "We're going to take care of her, sir. Savanah is going to go get the rest of our group and bring the truck back. We'll be at the shelter in a jiffy and the docs there can get you fixed up. You won't have to worry about Evie. There's tons of food there and kids her own age. She'll love it there."

"I'll be right back," Savanah called to everyone over her shoulder as she left through the front door, followed by Jason. One way or another she'd have to convince Will that it was the right thing to do.

THIRTEEN

Savanah
_____

Williams Junction, Arkansas
Event + Nine Months

Will placed both hands on top of his head and inhaled deeply. Savanah waited for the reaction she knew was coming. He looked to the ground and shook his head.

"We can't just leave this child and her dying grandfather out here alone. You know it would be a death sentence for the girl too."

"Why would you ever think I'd leave an old man and a child out here to die?" Will asked, his tone low and soft.

"We don't know them or who they're with. but..."

Will lowered his hands and crossed his arms over his chest. "It's not that, Savanah."

"The government wants people brought to the shelter. What's the issue here?"

Will shifted from foot to foot. He uncrossed his arms and ran a hand over his close-cropped hair. There was something he wasn't telling her.

Savanah put her hands on her hips. "Spill it, big brother."

Will's eyes darted from Jason to Walker and then back to Savanah. He hesitated.

"Well?"

"Well." Will cleared his throat and stuffed his hands inside his pant pockets. "You see, it's like this…"

"We don't have permission to be here, do we?" Savanah asked, finishing for him.

"Not exactly." He gestured to Jason as if asking for his help.

Jason took Savanah's hand in his. "We thought it would be better to ask forgiveness than permission. Getting authorization to reside outside the safe zone would require a lot of wasted effort and paperwork, and the higher-ups don't want to start granting exemptions."

"But Stephens…"

"She agreed. It's unlikely that anyone from the government will be patrolling this region again. Unless…"

"Unless there is a need to," Savanah said.

"Exactly. If we bring in civilians from this region they'll be questioned, and if they reveal that there are still people living up here, they might feel the need to revisit the area."

"Missing two people would cause them to send out the military? I don't see that. You guys are much too busy to retrace the area you've already cleared because of two stragglers."

"Because of Lake Sylvia," Will said.

Savanah cocked her head slightly and narrowed her eyes. "Lake Sylvia? What about it?"

Will and Walker shared a knowing glance. "There's a community there. A thriving community."

Savanah's mouth fell open. "How? How do you know this?" She thought it odd when Mark said he'd wanted Evie to leave him and go there. He hadn't revealed that there were people there. People. A community. Free people.

"We just received a visit from their welcoming committee," Walker said.

Savanah threw her hands into the air and spun on her heel to face Jason. "Did you know about this community?"

Jason held his hands out, palms out, and took a step back from Savanah. "Not until this moment."

"Are they friendly or are they a threat?" Her mind was racing, but she was pretty sure, if they were a threat, Will would have wasted no time getting them all the hell away from there. She just needed to hear him say it before her mind could believe there was an actual community with which they could trade and provide mutual defense of the area.

"They seemed pretty friendly, but..."

"So we could establish a mutually beneficial relationship with them. Do they have children?" Her eyes widened. "A doctor—do they have a doctor or nurse—even a medic?"

"They said they have an Army medic—with combat experience," Walker said.

Savanah grabbed Jason by the biceps and jumped up and down. "We can take Mark there. He wanted Evie to go there, remember."

"I don't know if they're accepting people, Savanah," Will said. "I never asked about that."

"But they implied. Why else tell you they had a medic."

Will shrugged his shoulders.

"It's worth a try. If not, we have to take Mark and Evie back to the shelter with us. We can tell them not to reveal where they came from. They'll do that for us."

Will placed both his hands on top of his head and huffed.

"Let's go ask them," Savanah said, tugging on Jason's arm.

Evie squeezed Savanah's hand tight every time her grandfather cried out in pain as they moved him into the bed of the pickup.

They sat him back against the cab of the truck and placed pillows around his hand and arm trying to stabilize it so it didn't move as they drove through the rural Arkansas countryside from Williams Junction to Lake Sylvia. Mark seemed to be doing his best not to let Evie know just how much pain he was in, but Savanah could see it all over his face. She hoped he would survive the trip.

Six miles southwest of Williams Junction they encountered a roadblock just before the turn to Lake Sylvia near a little cabin in the woods. A well-worn path led from the cabin to the road where nearby trees had been cut and dragged across one lane of the roadway. The other lane was blocked by an old truck.

Jack stopped the truck near a gravel drive about four hundred yards from the roadblock and Will hopped down from the bed. Jason raised himself up to go, but Savanah grabbed his arm. "Are we sure they're friendly? It could be a trick."

"Only one way to find out. If it goes to shit, Savanah, Jack will get y'all the hell out of here. Don't even look back."

"What? No, Jason."

He pulled her into an embrace and whispered, "You have a responsibility to these people, Savanah."

Tears welled in her eyes. The thought of having to choose between her family and the rest of the group was more than she could fathom. She had to trust Will's instincts and that he wouldn't put them all at risk. "Okay, but please be careful. Don't take chances. I need you."

"I won't. I love you and those kids."

"I love you, too," she said as Jason threw a leg over the bed and climbed down.

"Hey there!" Will yelled. "It's Will Fontenot. We met Bryant and Lisa over at Williams Junction. They said to stop by."

Savanah twisted around and watched as the truck blocking the road pulled behind the logs, opening the right lane of the highway.

"We didn't expect you so soon."

A big man dressed in cut-off shorts and Western boots came

into view. He waved his arm, gesturing for them to pull through the roadblock. Will and Jason climbed back in and Jack pulled ahead. Savanah's pulse raced as they drove past the checkpoint. She prayed they weren't driving into an ambush.

Motor homes and travel trailers were visible from the road and the lake came into view as they reached the parking lot for Lake Sylvia Recreational Area. Women and children appeared to be bathing near the shore. Everyone turned to stare at them. No one seemed overly alarmed at their presence. No one ran or brandished weapons. A man and woman ran toward the truck and Jack stopped.

"I'm told you have an injured person," the man said.

Jack nodded.

"Drive down to the last RV on the left. I'll meet you there."

Savanah sat with Evie on a wooden bench outside the motor home as Tom, the medic, and Alice, the nurse, examined Mark. Evie swung her feet and nervously chewed her fingernails as they waited for news. Meanwhile, Jason, Will, Walker, and Jack received a tour of the camp's grounds and the improvements the group had made there to make it a more sustainable community. Savanah could hear August's wife, Pam, talking as she and another woman approached them.

"Aren't you worried for your daughters?" she was asking. "In Houston or Dallas, they could have the possibility of a normal life."

"We've discussed it. Right now, we're not willing to risk it. If they're able to get life back to normal there, then we'd consider it. We're not willing to take the chance that we won't be allowed to leave once we got there, if you know what I mean."

Savanah understood perfectly. That had been her concern, as well. She was well aware of the precarious nature of rebuilding a nation. At any moment, laws could arbitrarily be changed based upon the whims of whoever was in charge. Basically, whoever controlled the military was the one making the rules. The rules could help people, or they could hinder them. It could go either way because no one was holding those in charge responsible for adhering to the constitution. Dictators had no desire to be controlled. The change in policies at the shelter after its change in leadership had only solidified this belief in Savanah's mind. She was unwilling to risk her children's futures unnecessarily, but so far, the new government was providing for her children better than she could at the moment.

"That kind of makes sense," Pam replied. "I really hadn't thought about it that way. I like the idea of having the option. If things didn't work out here, we could always move to Dallas or whatever city they add to the safe zones."

Pam was assuming her boys would choose to go to the city. Savanah wasn't sure the choice would always be there. Pam's children would be drafted long before they settled into some apartment and were assigned jobs. Savanah was grateful she and Jason had a few years before any of her children reached the age of the draft.

As the door to the RV opened, Evie jumped to her feet and raced toward the medic. Tom slung a white towel with which he was drying his hands over one shoulder and descended the steps. The corners of his mouth turned up slightly. "He's resting comfortably. I've examined his hand and I think there's a possibility it can be saved. I've started him on a strong antibiotic. We'll know more in the morning."

Savanah was shocked and wondered if Tom was just trying to not upset Evie. From what she'd seen of the man's hand, she'd been certain he'd not only lose his hand but his life too. Sepsis in the apocalypse was one hundred percent fatal in her opinion.

"He's not septic?" Pam asked as she approached the RV.

Tom shot her a look.

"I don't think the infection has reached his bloodstream yet.

We will see what twenty-four hours of antibiotics do for him."
Tom placed a gentle hand on Evie's shoulder.

"You should go get cleaned up and eat something, then you can come back and sit with him for a while. It will ease his mind to see you."

"Can I bring him something to eat?" Evie asked, her tone soft and low.

"You could, but we're giving him soup right now with his meds. He might like something refreshing to drink. Margie makes the best raspberry tea."

Evie's eyes lit up. She nodded and then turned toward Savanah.

"I'll go with you, if you'd like," Savanah said.

Log benches encircled an extra-large fire pit where the Lake Sylvia residents apparently cooked and ate their meals. Cast iron pots hung by hooks from a steel campfire cooking rack. Steam rose from the pots and the aroma caused Savanah's stomach to growl. A middle-aged woman dressed in a long, floral print dress handed Evie a bowl and a spoon. A pretty teen girl scooped some stew into another bowl and held it out to Savanah.

"No, I couldn't," Savanah said, holding her hand up. "I can't take your food."

"We have plenty," the teen said. "My brother shot a bear that had wandered into camp two nights ago."

"What a blessing," Savanah said, reaching for the bowl. She still felt uncomfortable taking food that they might need to survive but didn't want to appear rude either. She'd repay the favor when she and her group became established and had food to spare.

"How long have you lived here?" Savanah asked, spooning the delicious stew into her mouth. She closed her eyes and savored the flavor. It not only fed her body but also her soul. These folks weren't starving as she and the others had been back at her homestead in Louisiana. In fact, from their appearance, they looked fairly well fed. They weren't overweight by any means, but they sure weren't skin and bones like most folks living outside the safe zones these days.

"We've been here since the cars died and the lights went out," the woman replied.

"Really?"

How had the military missed them?

"Most of us were here at the campground when whatever happened, happened," the girl said.

"It appears you've done pretty well here. Game must be plentiful in the area," Savanah said.

As the two looked at each other, Savanah noticed the girl hesitate. If these people were going to be her closest neighbors and they were to establish trade with them, she needed to put all doubts to rest.

"Hunting has been good here, right?" Savanah probed.

The girl looked away and the woman turned her attention to the fire.

"If there's a problem here, please tell me. I don't want to bring my children and friends out here if there is little chance of making it."

"Hunting isn't really a problem," the girl said, still facing the fire.

"But?"

"It's just that some of us are concerned, with more people moving into the area, hunting might get harder. We'll have to travel farther for game."

"Oh, I see," Savanah said. She did see. More people would mean more competition for the same resources. Over-hunting could lead to less food for all of them.

"We could work something out. We could divide our territories into sections. We could take north and east of our camp. Would that help?"

The woman slowly turned to face her. She shrugged one shoulder. "It might. You'd be risking running into the military. You willing to take that risk?"

Savanah didn't want to reveal that her husband and brother were part of the military stationed at Little Rock. She smiled.

"I think we would be."

"They can be brutal, we hear."

"I don't think they're patrolling and rounding people up like before. They believe everyone is already at the shelter."

"Not the military at the Army base," the woman said, returning to poking the fire. "The others."

Savanah swallowed hard. She struggled to open her mouth and form the words. Her stomach turned and almost rejected the stew as she spoke.

"The Chinese?"

The woman looked over her shoulder at Savanah.

"No. They ain't Chinese. They're Americans. I'm sure of that. They speak perfect English and drive Department of Homeland Security vehicles."

Savanah choked.

"What? Department of Homeland Security?"

FOURTEEN

Will
___

Lake Sylvia
Perryville, Arkansas
Event + Nine Months

From the moment Will heard of the presence of Department of Homeland Security officials in the area, he was ready to pack up and head back to Texarkana. He had a duty to let his superiors know this information and should have headed straight to Little Rock to report it, but he wasn't supposed to be where he was. Secondly, he wanted to hear what Stephens had to say about the presence of DHS forces first. Stephens was CIA, and he knew there was much about what the government was doing that she couldn't tell him. But why had she not revealed the fact that they could run into DHS officials around Williams Junction?

Isabella and Savanah were quiet on the ride back to the shelter. Will could hear Pam and Erin talking up in the cab of the truck.

They weren't yet aware of the news about the DHS presence. They were discussing the pros and cons of moving to Williams Junction. Will wished Pete, Rob, and August were there. It would relieve Will of the enormous responsibility he felt for their families.

Kathy leaned in toward Will.

"You gonna talk to that lady agent about those DHS goons hanging around north Arkansas?" Kathy asked.

She'd obviously overheard his conversation with Jason and Savanah on the topic. He should have told her himself. She was a smart lady—not much slipped past her.

"I am."

"I'm hoping she has a satisfying explanation."

Will had thought after the ladies saw how rough life would be back out on their own, they'd opt for the safety and security of the shelter—at least for the near future. But after coming upon Evie and Mark and then the Lake Sylvia camp, they seemed to be emboldened in their choice to move to Williams Junction. Even after learning about the DHS presence in the area, Savanah was still entertaining the idea. Whatever they learned from Stephens would likely sway their decision one way or the other.

Jack parked the truck in the garage of a house four blocks from the shelter, stashed the rifles in the crawl space of the house across the street, and the group walked to the gate. After showing the guards their passes, Will and Isabella said goodbye to the others and headed straight for Stephen's office.

"I don't think she knows, Will," Isabella said.

"How could she not. She's in on all the intelligence briefings," Will said.

"Maybe they don't know. They didn't even know Lake Sylvia was still occupied," Isabella said.

Will stopped outside Stephens' quarters. If Isabella was right, what else didn't they know? The Chinese could be occupying the countryside and they wouldn't know if they didn't institute regular reconnoitering.

The door to Stephens' building opened.

"We're about to find out," Will said.

"She said the decals on the vehicles definitely said Department of Homeland Security?" Stephens asked. She poured herself a glass of water from a pitcher in the middle of the conference table.

"That's what the woman told Savanah. She asked her to describe their vehicles and they weren't anything we've been using out there. They must have been MRAPs or something else we don't have," Will said.

"So, you didn't know about this?" Isabella asked Stephens directly. Her tone wasn't as accusing as Will's would have been. It was obvious to him by the concern on her face that she was as unaware of this as he had been.

"I didn't."

Isabella poured Will a glass of water and then one for herself. "What do you make of it?"

"I'm not sure," Stephens said.

From her tone, Will could tell she was holding something back. Something likely way above his security clearance.

She stood and pushed in her chair. "I'll pass this information along to Little Rock. They can check it out." She moved toward the door and turned. "I'll leave your names out of it."

"And the Lake Sylvia group?" Isabella asked. She didn't want to cause them trouble. She didn't think Stephens would either.

"I'll claim it came in on radio chatter," Stephen said.

Radio chatter. There were still people out there with working ham radios?

"So, we should hold off moving up to Williams Junction? At least until the military finishes their sweep?" Isabella said.

"I wouldn't plan on leaving the shelter for a while, Isabella. Let me find out what I can."

"What about the Lake Sylvia folks. The military might decide to search there now."

Stephens looked skyward and pursed her lips. She returned her gaze to Isabella. "You said they saw this DHS convoy due north of Little Rock heading east. That's where I'm going to recommend they search. If something changes, I'll let you know, and you can alert them to break camp and move south until the recon team has finished their search of the area."

"I guess that will work—I hope," Isabella said.

Will's thoughts went to Lake Sylvia and the community the folks had built there. If it were him, he'd want to know well in advance and not have it sprung on him at the last moment. Telling them would likely destroy any trust they might have gained with the group. The animosity from not being honest about their military status in the first place could make it difficult for Savanah and the others to make a home at the compound in Williams Junction and have a good neighborly trading relationship with them.

Will held the door open for Isabella as they exited Stephens' office. "I think we should give the Lake Sylvia folks a heads-up. I don't know how they avoided detection the last time the military searched the area, but they deserve to know so they can prepare."

"I agree. We've brought this upon them. We have a duty to alert them."

"Savanah won't like the consequences."

"That's a bridge we'll have to cross when we come to it," Will said.

Isabella shook her head.

"You know your sister. She had her heart—and more importantly, her mind—set on moving to Williams Junction."

He knew how stubborn Savanah could be, especially when she

felt she was protecting her children. That was precisely how he was going to approach the subject with her. It wouldn't be safe to move to an area where you've already pissed off the neighbors.

FIFTEEN

Isabella

Texarkana Refugee Center
Texarkana, Texas
Event + Nine Months

Days had passed since Will and Isabella had informed Stephens about the movement of DHS vehicles in and around north Arkansas. Will had attempted to see her several times but was told she was out of the area. Isabella assumed she'd gone to Little Rock to lead the surveillance and intelligence gathering mission herself.

Isabella, Will, Jason, Walker, and the others from their unit had received orders to report back to the base in Little Rock. It was unlikely they'd be part of the teams going out searching for the DHS vehicles. They were more likely to be sent out on the mission that had been planned prior to the discovery, the nature of which they'd still not been briefed on.

They all hated goodbyes. In this new world, everyone was keenly aware that each goodbye could be their last, so they made sure to leave nothing unsaid, and they expressed their deep love for those they left behind.

"You need to stop growing, young man," Isabella said, tousling Cayden's out-of-control hair. "And get a haircut."

She smiled and kissed him on the cheek. She noted he'd had another growth spurt, and she could no longer kiss the top of his head. In a few months, he'd be fourteen and old enough to begin training in the Reserve Officer Training Corps, or its equivalent. Cayden had scored high in testing and might be assigned to a civilian program instead of ROTC to train as an engineer or something else to aid in the recovery effort. Of course, that was Will and Isabella's hope, if they weren't able to get everyone moved out of the shelter by then.

Savanah was determined to keep her children with her. She was adamant that no one force her to send her "babies" off to war or to unsafe cities to finish their education. "I can teach them everything they need to know about how to survive," she'd insisted. After the stories Isabella had heard about the crime still plaguing the cities, she understood Savanah's position.

"You look out for my dad out there. He's kind of accident prone," Cayden said.

Isabella chuckled. It wasn't that he was accident prone, he'd just had the misfortune of being stabbed—two separate times. At this point, they all wore their own battle scars. Some were visible, like Will's, but others were hidden, like Savanah's.

"I will," she said.

They all knew the risks. There was a very real possibility that either she or Will, or even both of them, might not return to Cayden. Isabella refused to think about that. It wasn't productive. Instead, she'd focus on the after—when this mess was finished and they were all together again—hopefully at the farm. Maybe even back in the Fontenot homestead in Louisiana. That was what she was fighting for these days.

After giving Cayden one last hug, Will stepped forward and pulled him into an embrace. Isabella fought back tears. She knew how much they would miss each other, and how much Cayden would worry about them. Will would struggle with concern for his son, but necessity required him to put those thoughts aside so he could do his job out there. As she often did, Isabella cursed the enemy who'd brought all this upon them.

"You know how much I love you, son," Will said, giving Cayden one last squeeze.

"I love you too, Dad."

Will lifted Kylie off the ground and spun her around. "You try to be good for your mom, okay?" She giggled as he placed her back on the ground and tickled her belly. He said goodbye to each of his nieces and nephews and then hugged his sister. They held the embrace for a long moment. Isabella could tell Will was whispering something in her ear. She looked away, not wanting to pry into their secret conversation. Isabella closed her eyes and said a silent prayer for her own sister, far away in Oklahoma. She also prayed for her parents, although she doubted they would have survived this long—not with their health issues. Pushing the grief down and locking it away for another day, Isabella climbed into the back of the Humvee.

Savanah's tear-streaked face ripped new wounds in Isabella's heart as Will and the rest of the unit loaded into their Humvees. Savanah's arm was draped over Cayden's shoulder. They continued to wave as the convoy of military vehicles pulled away. Will sat across from her with his head down. Jason was fiddling with something attached to the rucksack at his feet, looking bored but she knew they were all preparing their minds and making the transition back to badass fighting machines on a mission.

Tapping the pack at her feet, Isabella attempted to make the same mental shift. It was difficult because she had no idea what they were going to be called upon to do next. They'd spent months preparing for some sort of important mission. The Horse Cavalry Detachment had been out nearly every day patrolling the seemingly unoccupied countryside surrounding the military base in Little Rock. They'd drilled and run training missions, but none of it gave her any indication of what they were really going up against. All she knew was they were meant to move silently and strike quickly—the who, what, and when, no one in her unit knew. It was all the uncertainty that bothered her the most.

Fortunately, Isabella didn't have to wait long for the answers she and the others had so long sought regarding their mission. When the unit arrived back at base, Stephens and the other CIA agent, Brad Smith, were waiting for them. Gathered around a table in the tactical operations center, Isabella and the others listened as newly promoted Colonel Sharp described the role the two teams would play in the covert mission into Missouri that they were about to depart on in search of the US government's lost shipment of gold.

Will and Isabella exchanged glances as the significance of the mission was explained. Isabella was sure Sharp was holding much more back than he was revealing.

"General Dempsey's men are spread out across southeastern Missouri looking for the shipment. They are better armed and supplied than you will be. It is important that we slip in, get the gold, and get it to Fort Leonard Wood on time. That's why we're sending two teams."

Isabella waited for him to say it—she chuckled a little whenever he did…

"Two is one and one is none," Sharp said. He used a telewhip, a telescoping lunge whip used by riders to make a horse go faster, to point to a pin on a map hung on the wall.

"Our gold is here."

He moved the whip to another pin.

"This is the airfield at Fort Leonard Wood. The base is supposed to be unoccupied. The military left the base shortly after the event and moved north along the borders between Missouri, Illinois, and Iowa." He pointed to a large area outlined in red. "All of this is Dempsey's territory. He controls everything east of

Wyoming and Colorado. North and South Dakota, Iowa, Wisconsin, Michigan, Illinois, and the northern parts of Indiana."

"If he doesn't control Missouri, why the stealth?" Jason asked.

"The last time we sent in teams, we flew them into St. Louis and sent them out in Humvees and cargo transport trucks. Dempsey's army was immediately on them like flies on shit and they were overwhelmed in number. Even though they don't 'control' Missouri..." Sharp made air quotes with his fingers when he said "control." He cleared his throat. "They have a significant presence there around St. Louis. There has been intermittent fighting for control of the city for months. Being a port city along the Mississippi River, it's strategically important to both sides."

"Team Razorback, you'll be transported to within fifty miles of Iron County. You will do surveillance around the cave where the shipment is held and report back to headquarters. Team Lonestar will be transported to Fort Leonard Wood. They will report on the condition of the base and airfield before moving to meet up with Team Razorback, at which time, both platoons will retrieve the cargo and transport it the fifty or so miles west to Fort Leonard Wood in time to meet the cargo plane."

Isabella's stomach churned. How were they going to transport a large shipment of gold fifty miles along rural roads without detection? This sounded more like a suicide mission to her.

"Smith will be attached to Team Razorback and Stephens will be with Team Lonestar. Lieutenant Burns and Team Razorback will set up headquarters to receive and relay information as Staff Sergeant Fontenot and 1st Squad gathers it."

Isabella sighed. She would have much preferred to be with Stephens. Brad "the Cad" gave her the creeps. With Stephens along, they'd at least be told something of the dangers they faced. Smith would just brief the first sergeant, and the first sergeant would brief the platoon sergeants, and the soldiers wouldn't get any information about what was going on or what was coming up until the last minute. If they were headed into a dangerous situation they may not even know where they were or where they were going—they'd just have to follow basic orders and execute Rules of Engagement on the fly. That meant if they were told not to fire their weapons—even if they were fired upon—there would be no room for discussion when the bullets started flying. They would just have to take cover and wait for someone to tell them it was okay to protect themselves, their fellow soldiers, or anyone else who was being fired upon.

"Okay, troopers. Let's mount up," Sharp said.

SIXTEEN

Savanah

Texarkana Refugee Center
  Texarkana, Texas
  July 4th
  Event + Ten Months

The children seemed thrilled with the announcement that there would be fireworks at that night's Fourth of July celebration. The commander of the shelter wanted to make everything feel as normal as possible and observing holidays as they used to was one of the ways he felt was necessary. His job wasn't an easy one, Savanah would give the man that. Residents of the camp had grown increasingly displeased with being in the shelter, especially those who'd been forced to come there.

Many families were separated due to mandatory military or civilian service. Savanah doubted they'd known that would happen when they registered at the gate and signed up to serve their country. The place on the form that asked for previous employment, training, and skills wasn't optional—they were looking for workers.

Most were eager to be assigned a job and Savanah could see how getting back to work would feel like a return to a somewhat normal life. The engineers, electrical workers, doctors, and others with the skills necessary to get the country back up and running were treated like royalty. Savanah didn't begrudge them that. She was pleased for them. They could move to Houston and Dallas and enjoy their air-conditioned apartments. She didn't hate air conditioning, she just didn't want to give up all freedom in order to enjoy it.

"You want us to save you a seat?" Jack asked.

Savanah had kitchen duty. She'd be washing dishes well after dark. Kathy had offered to trade shifts with her so Savanah could be with her children for the festivities, but Savanah hadn't taken her up on the offer. She had plans. There was to be a meeting after dark, and while the others were watching the fireworks, she'd be talking to a few of the new arrivals about joining her at the compound in Williams Junction.

"No, thank you. I have to work tonight. Will you help Jane keep an eye on Kylie and Keegan for me, though?"

Jack looked reluctant. "Sure thing."

She felt bad for pawning her kids off on people all the time lately, and she knew full well what a hand full Kylie was, but she was working hard to keep the dream of their own home alive. She was moving forward, despite Will and Jason being away all the time.

"Kendra and Karson are both working one of the games."

"The little kids are sure to enjoy them. It's so good to see them happy and carefree for a change," Jack said. He turned to head toward the field where the night's events were to take place. "I'll save you a seat—just in case."

Did he know? Did he suspect something? No matter. Savanah trusted Jack to keep quiet.

Although the issues with his legs prevented him from fighting for the country, he would be a valuable asset when the group finally settled in Williams Junction. He had knowledge and skills far beyond being able to run and shoot. He'd survived on his own for months, living off the land, until he reached her homestead in Vincent, Louisiana. They would need that kind of knowledge to feed themselves until they could establish gardens and find game.

Savanah's thoughts turned to Evie and her grandfather. It was a miracle that Savanah and Jason had found them and for the medical personnel at Lake Sylvia to be able to help Mark. She felt much better about bringing everyone up to Williams Junction knowing how skilled their new neighbors were.

After finishing the last of the supper dishes in the mess hall, Savanah dried her hands on her apron and slipped out the back door. She found her cousin, Gabby, and the newcomers in one of the storage trailers near the back of the shelter grounds. They were in the middle of a conversation when she slid into a seat next to Gabby.

"I stashed what was left of my ammo in a plastic barrel and buried it under my deck before the military forced me to come here," a man in his late thirties said. He was thin, but not as thin as most in Savanah's group had been when they'd arrived at the shelter. Under his left eye was a healing bruise. His lip was split, and abrasions covered the knuckles of his right hand—he'd put up a fight.

"Ammo ain't no good without a weapon to fire it from," another man said. He ran his hand down the length of his long beard. His clothes hung loose on him. He'd not faired as well. His cheeks were gaunt and eyes sunken as were so many struggling to survive these days.

A woman in her late twenties raised her hand timidly. "I can get weapons."

Every eye turned to her.

"My daddy stashed all our rifles inside an old semi truck a mile from our house. He said he wanted them in case he ever did find ammo for them. He never did. I bet you anything they're still there."

"How far away is that?" Gabby asked.

"About thirty miles south of Little Rock."

"Doable," the thirty-something man said.

Savanah reached into the pocket of her dress and retrieved a small notepad and pen. "We need to make a list." She smiled and looked around the circle of her new friends. "Anything you think will help us set up and survive out there. We'll need nearly everything from axes to cast iron skillets. List the items and locations where we can find them."

Everyone nodded and Savanah handed the notepad and pen to the young woman sitting next to her. The short-haired woman looked to be in her forties, but looks were deceiving with what they'd all been through.

"I got seeds," she said. "I got seeds and jars for canning."

Savanah's heart swelled with joy and hope. There were still people out there who were willing and able to live self-sufficiently, not content to rely on the government that had failed them so miserably for the last ten months. She wasn't about to leave her children's lives in the hands of people who didn't even know their names.

"We'll have to act quickly. As soon as the docs declare you fit for duty, you'll be shipped to your new duty stations—likely in Houston where they need workers for their factories."

"Factories?" the woman next to Savanah asked, surprise in her tone.

"They're trying to manufacture parts to get the lights and things back on."

"I didn't know they were that far along."

Savanah worried they were going to lose this woman—and her seeds to the big city.

"I'd hate to be sent to sweat in some factory all day," she said, much to Savanah's relief.

"You know, there is nothing wrong with someone wanting to return to a normal job and normal life, right?" the ammo guy said.

Savanah's heart sank.

"Of course. That is perfectly fine for those folks. I just ain't going to be forced into relying on the man to take care of me. I've seen how that ends," the woman replied.

"No one here is bashing anyone for their choices. If any of you choose to take jobs or assignments instead of joining us, there's no judgment here. We just would like for you to keep our plan to yourselves," Gabby said.

A pang of conviction struck Savanah. Had she been judgmental against those choosing the comforts of the big cities? She'd never felt that way before. She, herself, had experienced such judgment from people when she'd chosen to live a self-sufficient life on her homestead in Louisiana.

"We're not asking for a commitment tonight, but you'll need to decide soon, before the choice is made for you," Savanah said, stuffing the list into her bra. "And whatever you choose, I wish you a blessed life."

No one spoke as the storage container cleared of people. Even Gabby was quiet as she and Savanah made their way back to where the festivities were occurring. Gabby finally broke the silence.

"Do you ever wonder…"

"No!" Savanah interrupted her. "No. I've heard first hand how they separate mothers from their children—for their good— and send them to schools far away. I won't be separated from my children. Being apart from my husband and brother is hard enough. I won't…"

"I understand, Vannie."

Tears welled in Savanah's eyes. Gabby had used the nickname their grandmother had given Savanah when she was little. She missed her now—so much. The world needed women like her now more than ever. She had no doubt what her gran would do. Family had been everything to her—and was everything to Savanah. Family first! It had to be that way.

Savanah slid into the seat Jack had saved for her and watched as her children delighted in the aerial light display. Soon, Kendra and Karson would be old enough to choose for themselves but she still had years before Kylie and Keegan would fly the nest. She had to make sure all of them were equipped to survive, no matter what they chose.

SEVENTEEN

Will

Little Rock Military Base
Little Rock, Arkansas
The Fourth of July
Event + Ten Months

They'd trained for this mission for most of the summer. The horses were all in great condition and the unit was as prepared as Will thought they could be for a trip north into Missouri. It had been two weeks since they'd been informed where they'd be going and the hurry-up-and-wait game was in full effect. They had loaded up the horses and all their gear twice, only to be told it was just a drill.

At morning roll call, First Sergeant Charles Webster informed them they had the day off.

"Stand at ease, troopers. Rest. Just in case you knuckleheads didn't know, today is the Fourth of July. Colonel Sharp has decided to give you troopers the day off from PT and the cooks are preparing something special for supper. I'd advise you to take it easy on the revelries. We want to maintain readiness. You never know when we'll get the order to pull out." He looked at Hogan, one of the heaviest drinkers in the 2nd Platoon. Hogan adjusted his black Western hat and grunted quietly.

Will was grateful Hogan wasn't in his squad. Like Will, Hogan hadn't been with the military long. He'd been assigned to the Horse Detachment due to his blacksmithing skills. He was great at his job, but he sucked at everything else.

Stephens stepped forward and stopped to talk to the two newest members of the company. Both were special forces soldiers. They knew what the hell they were doing, unlike much of the rest of the company. These two were highly trained and had been with the military prior to the lights going out. Will noticed Isabella checking them out and nudged her.

"What?"

"You're staring."

"So are you," she replied.

"Did Stephens say anything to you about them—what their military occupation specialty is or what they'll be doing for this mission?"

"She just said they were on loan from Fort Hood and part of the Joint Task Force. There will be two JTF soldiers with each platoon. The ones traveling with us won't be here until tomorrow morning."

"She told you all that?" Will asked, his eyes fixed on the man with the enormous biceps and a tattoo of a grim reaper draped in the American flag.

"They're special forces. They've got all that high-tech equipment and super-soldier skills to make sure we succeed."

"I'm sure they're thrilled to be babysitting the rest of us," Will said.

"At least we can stay on our horses."

"What? He's not an experienced rider?" Will asked.

"He's not the worst rider I've ever seen."

"Oh crap."

Will had been detailed to working with his fellow squad

leaders signing for equipment and gathering and packing more food and water for the last two days as Colonel Sharp and the platoon leaders were finalizing the mission and briefing the platoon sergeants. What else had he missed?

They ate something resembling hamburgers for supper while a band played patriotic songs. There were no fireworks to celebrate the anniversary of America's Independence from Britain. But when soldiers lowered the flag outside the headquarters building to signal the end of the official duty day lately, the ceremony had begun to really mean something to Will. He had begun to understand what it was to pay respect and honor the American flag. It took several minutes for the team of soldiers to lower and fold the flag and march off to secure and store it properly each day. As the bugle played "Retreat" and the flag was being lowered, all activity stopped on the installation and everyone was required to stand still and be silent. Everyone in uniform was required to salute and hold their salute as the flag was slowly lowered until Retreat was over and the flag was unhooked from its tether. If not in uniform, the requirement was to put your hand over your heart. When the song ended, everyone would go back to whatever it was they were doing. It had been strange and uncomfortable initially, but as time went on, the daily ceremony provided a time for reflection on what they were all a part of. It gave people time to consider the importance and seriousness of what they were doing and to remember those who had served and died to provide them the freedom he and his son had enjoyed but never really appreciated as Will now knew they should have.

Others on the base regarded Retreat as a nuisance and would hide inside the building to wait for the ceremony to end. It was wrong and it bothered Will, but what were they fighting for if not for the freedom to act immature and foolish if that was what they were? His thoughts about freedom were continuously evolving whenever he found himself outside and the bugle began calling.

The next few days went by in a blur of activity and preparation for the mission. They examined and reexamined the horses making sure each one was in the very best condition, knowing that once they dismounted their vehicles, the horses would be one of their most important resources. Each rider made sure their horse had everything it would need. The veterinarian looked them over daily to ensure they remained ready for deployment.

The two platoons ate and trained together over the next few days. Each trooper knew the mission inside and out. They each memorized the maps and various routes.

Will and Isabella leaned against a Humvee and watched what would be their final sunset before departing Little Rock, knowing that there wouldn't be an opportunity for such moments once the mission began. Will longed for the day they could relax and enjoy a nice dinner and sit outside to watch the sunset until the stars came out. Ever since they'd met back in Houston on the day of the EMP, they'd been in survival mode. After nine months of it, it was hard to imagine their old life or how easy they'd once had it.

Embracing Isabella, Will kissed his bride softly. She leaned into him and the kiss turned more passionate. His hand had slid down her back. He grunted when he heard footsteps approaching behind him.

"Sorry," Walker said, noticing he had wandered up at the wrong time.

Isabella pulled away. If there'd been more light, Will would have seen her blushing.

"It's okay, Walker. Join us." Will cursed under his breath.

"We should hit the rack. We could be shipping out at zero dark thirty," Walker said.

"Right behind you, friend," Will said. He was grateful to be heading into this with Walker and Jason by his side. He trusted them. It still bothered him that Isabella was going on the mission as well. Not that she was incapable—she was a very skilled mounted trooper. But she was his wife and he never wanted to see her put in harm's way.

Will yawned. Regardless of whether tomorrow was the day they headed out or not, they would still be up long before the sun, either packing up or marching five miles and doing physical training. Will detested early morning PT. Either way, they all needed their beauty rest. He took Isabella's hand in his. He was grateful to have her there with him. He hoped that what they were about to do might somehow help the nation come back together, allowing them to celebrate Independence Day with Cayden and the rest of their loved ones next year.

It seemed like a pipe dream most of the time. Like an exercise in futility. It had been nine very long months, and very little progress had been made outside of Houston, Dallas, and Austin— at least from the part of the country he could see. Stephens believed in this mission. She thought it to be the first step in taking on Dempsey—now their greatest enemy—besides the Russians who'd attacked the West Coast. To her, his vast resources were the key to pushing back against the Russians and making true progress in securing the nation. Will wished he shared her optimism. Maybe it was the fatigue or missing his family, but he felt like they were on a giant hamster wheel and never making true progress.

∼

After a fitful night's sleep, the 0430 bugle call was most unwelcome. Five days after their Fourth of July celebration, they were as ready as they could be to secure the gold and defend the once-great nation.

"Fontenot, get your squad ready, the mission is a go," Lieutenant Burns said, as he stepped outside the barracks.

As they loaded the horses into the trailers the third time, Will believed this would be different. Missing was Colonel Sharp and the team that was to be on the cargo plane. Even Brad Smith looked more solemn this time around. Gone were his crude jokes and wise-ass demeanor. As he checked his pack and secured the rest of his gear, the special forces soldiers arrived dressed in black and all kitted out in their expensive, high-tech gear, most of which Will had never seen. This had to be it. It was definitely go time.

Stephens pulled Will aside. "I have a contact with that group you met at Lake Sylvia. Even though our recon teams were unable to find any trace of DHS activity in northern Arkansas, that group brought me proof."

"Proof?" Will asked. How had they gathered proof when the military couldn't find anything?

"A body. A man carrying DHS official identification."

Will's eyes widened. "Fresh?"

"They killed him about a week prior. That was three weeks ago. So, within the last month, they've been in our neighborhood," Stephens said. "Of course, I'm not supposed to be telling you any of this. I'm sharing it with you so you'll be alert out there. They aren't out patrolling the Ozarks in search of survivors."

"So there will be teams out looking for them again? Will that mean trouble for Lake Sylvia?"

"We have teams out now. They're still coming up empty. I've alerted the folks at Lake Sylvia. They're safe."

"What are DHS goons doing down here?" Will asked. He was pretty sure he knew. They were doing reconnaissance on the Little Rock base. They were reporting back to their headquarters in Illinois about military movement in Arkansas.

"Recon. Same thing we're doing up north," Stephens said.

A pang of grief moved through Will. There had still been no

word about Pete, Tank, and the others they'd sent to spy on Dempsey's so-called shelters operating as forced labor camps.

Stephens stepped back and turned. Will touched her shoulder. "You think we'll encounter trouble from them before we reach Missouri?"

"I doubt it. They're not supposed to be here, remember."

"I guess we'll see you in Missouri," Will said, forcing a smile.

"I'll see you in Iron County," she said, calling over her shoulder as she walked away.

"Second Platoon, load 'em up," Lieutenant Bronson yelled.

Will took in a deep breath and exhaled as he moved toward the convoy of military vehicles readying to pull out from the base. Walker and Jason were already seated inside one of the vehicles. Will searched for Isabella, but she was already with her squad in the back of the convoy.

Will gave one last glance back at the horse trailers before climbing into the Humvee. He'd feel much more comfortable if they were leaving on horseback as they usually did. Driving down the middle of the road in the noisy vehicles made them too much of a target; at least with the up-armored Humvee and the M2 Browning machine gun mounted on top. He understood why they couldn't ride three hundred miles on horseback, but he would sure feel better once they reached Iron County and could get back on a horse.

Will shifted in his seat as they pulled through the gate. "They'll be fine," Jason said. "We're stopping in a couple of hours to let them drink."

"Some of them are pretty hard to get into the trailer."

"We'll water those inside the trailers," Jason said. "We won't push them too hard. We'll need them in top shape when we arrive."

Will turned back in his seat. "What about us?" he asked.

Will's and Jason's eyes met. After all the fighting they'd seen, they should be ready. They'd fought civilians with hunting rifles and the Chinese with military-grade weapons, and they were still here to talk about it. But this somehow felt different. Will couldn't explain it. Maybe it was the importance of the mission or the transition from a fighting force to a reconnaissance and recovery team. But either way, Will didn't like that he'd be so far from his family if things went bad. Three hundred miles was an enormous distance these days.

~

Their first stop was at a creek near Searcy, Arkansas along Highway 167. The trailer containing two of the draft horses was unloaded first and the horses were led down to the water to drink.

"I don't know why we're stopping so soon," one of the troopers said as he led the horse down the embankment.

"The heat, dumbass. How about you ride back there with them, Clemens. We'll see how often you'd want to stop for some fresh air," Specialist Cara Fisher replied.

Clemens flashed her a dirty look but wisely kept his smart remarks to himself. Fisher was not a woman he'd want to mess with. She could outshoot and outride almost everyone in the squad, not to mention kick his ass in hand-to-hand combat. Will was pleased she was in Isabella's squad.

The two special forces soldiers assigned to Team Razorback had ridden in the first vehicle with Lieutenant Burns. Will looked around for them as members of the platoon began spreading out to pull security. He saw a flash of black as the two men disappeared on horseback into the brush beside the highway.

After each of the horses was watered and allowed to cool off for a while, they were loaded back into the horse trailers and the soldiers got back into the vehicles. They sat in the middle of the highway for several more minutes just waiting—for what, Will didn't know. It wasn't until he spotted the two SPF soldiers cross the nearby field that he understood. They'd been scouting ahead. Will was in awe of their gear. The sci-fi-like goggles they wore on the top of their heads were like something from a movie. He was sure the military had had all kinds of gear like that prior to the EMP, but how much of it was still available and operational now? He couldn't wait to have a chance to talk to these guys and find out.

EIGHTEEN

Stephens

Highway 67
Bald Knob, Arkansas
July 10th
Event + Ten Months

Just fifteen miles north of Searcy, the vehicles carrying Team Razorback stopped near the exit ramp for Highway 167 in the community of Bald Knob, Arkansas. Stephens and the vehicles carrying Team Lonestar passed them and took the exit ramp, turning left and heading north toward Missouri. First Sergeant Charles Webster sat in the seat opposite Stephens. His eyes were closed, but she doubted the man was sleeping. From what she knew of the battle-hardened trooper, he was preparing himself for what they both knew lay ahead.

Stephens was feeling the pressure as well. This was perhaps the most important assignment of her life. She was under no illusions. Retrieving the gold, and making sure it made it to the plane, would take a miracle. She'd been skeptical of the plan from the beginning. Going in on horseback seemed preposterous. If, or more likely when, they encountered Dempsey's army, they'd be unable to evade them pulling a wagon full of gold coins. Their only hope was to be able to detect the enemy's movement in time to hide. What kind of tactical plan was that?

After going over and over the mission in her mind, she prayed Brad Smith didn't screw up his part and was able to gather the needed intelligence from any survivors in the area to know whether Dempsey's men were near the area of the cave where the gold had been stashed following the previously failed mission to retrieve it.

While the military worked on obtaining the shipment of gold coins, President Latham was working on convincing the Brazilian government to wait for payment for the military supplies and equipment Brazil agreed to sell him. So far, the Brazilian president had demanded to see the gold before agreeing to the contract. The US wasn't their only customer.

Having the distinction of being one of the few nations unaffected by World War III, and still able to manufacture the weapons those nations fighting it still required, placed the Brazilian president in the unique position of not having to negotiate. The gold would be there when the ship was ready to leave or the weapons would go to the enemies of the US.

With nearly all of the nation's resources being used to supply the military and hold off the invasion by the Russians and Chinese, there wasn't much left for procuring food to feed the survivors. It had taken two months for the South American ship laden with food to reach the Port of Houston. If Latham failed to delay its departure or the two teams failed to secure the gold and get it to the port in time, those weapons would go to the enemies invading the country. Stephens couldn't allow that to happen. Somehow, someway, they had to succeed by any means necessary.

While her convoy moved north, Stephens stared out at the countryside and thought of Will and Isabella. How unlikely their meeting again had been. When she'd said goodbye to them in Houston after their battle with the insurgents at Ellington Joint

Reserve Base, Stephens was certain she'd never see them again. She wondered what cosmic plan had brought them together at the FEMA shelter in Texarkana, and now put them all on this mission together.

They'd all survived Houston and succeeded in securing the flash drive containing information that had been key to thwarting China's plans and aided in stopping the full invasion along the southern border. Stephens hoped they could prevail again against Dempsey and his goons. Will and Isabella were battle-tested this time around and better armed. She just hoped Brad "the Cad" Smith didn't do anything to screw it all up.

"Have you ever been to Fort Leonard Wood?" Webster asked.

Stephens shifted in her seat. "No. I was in St. Louis a year before the event, but never made it to the base."

"It's been years since I've been there, myself. I trained there for about six months back in the early 2000s. There weren't many people living in the area off-base. I'm betting the base is deserted. With the military pulling out, there would be little reason for civilians to take up residence there."

"I hope you're right. I would hate to have to evict survivors," Stephens said.

Webster rubbed the top of his close-cropped hair and rolled his shoulders. "At any rate, the airfield is all we need. If we can secure the area from the airport to the south gate, that might be sufficient. The plane lands, we load up the gold, and take off before anyone knows we're there."

They both knew it wouldn't be that easy. Anyone in the area would hear their military vehicles from miles away. When they heard the plane land, having not seen or heard one in almost nine months, they'd come running to the base. Colonel Sharp would need a significant force to hold them off. The survivors would no doubt expect aid from the only government they'd seen in months.

"What we need is more like him." Stephens nodded toward First Sergeant Peterson. Dressed in black and kitted-out with every high-tech gadget that had survived the EMP, Peterson looked bored.

Peterson was one of the four special forces soldiers that Latham had pulled from the battle against the Russians out in California. Their job was to pull reconnaissance and help the teams avoid Dempsey's men and any other trouble that might prevent them from completing their mission. He was a rugged, good-looking man. In another life, Stephens would have contemplated asking him out, but now, no one but Brad had time for dating. She shuddered as she thought that she'd once cared for the man.

She'd been informed that Brad was having an affair with someone from Colonel Sharp's team. He'd tried his best to get her assigned to Team Razorback so they could be together on this mission. Not that Stephens cared, but she'd been pleased to hear Colonel Sharp had denied his request. He'd said her skill set was best suited for securing the plane. Stephens had her suspicions that there was a love/lust triangle going on between the two men and this Martinez woman. Stephens had known that Martinez was trouble the moment she saw her. She had no doubt Martinez was accustomed to using her beauty to get what she wanted.

Stephens leaned her head back against the seat and closed her eyes. She doubted there would be much time for sleeping once they left northern Arkansas and entered Missouri. They'd need to be alert and ready as they crossed no man's land and headed to Fort Leonard Wood.

NINETEEN

Will

Highway 67
  Walnut Ridge, Arkansas
  July 5th
  Event + Ten Months

The convoy suddenly came to a stop just outside of Walnut Ridge, Arkansas, near an agricultural airfield. They sat there with the engine idling for what seemed to Will to be an eternity before being informed of the reason for the unplanned stop.

Smith, the CIA agent, appeared next to the driver's door. "We're going to hold here for a bit. The scout team hasn't reported in yet."

"Copy that," the driver said before turning to relay the message to the rest of the team, as if it needed repeating.

"What does that mean?" Will asked.

Walker shrugged one shoulder. "Seal Team Six hasn't phoned in."

Will gave him a sarcastic look. "I got that. Why? What could be the hold up?'

"My guess?" Walker raised his signature Western hat and wiped sweat from his brow. "My guess is they have radio problems. Depending on the terrain out here, I'm not sure how good the signal is going to be or exactly how far ahead they traveled."

The recon team was supposed to be twenty or so miles ahead scouting for any signs of trouble—Dempsey's men in particular. A reconnaissance team had driven the route all the way to the Missouri border the day before. The scout's report had found no significant threats, which greatly relieved Will. Now, with their scout team failing to report in, all sorts of dark thoughts ran through Will's mind. He hated just sitting there on the highway. He wanted to get out, stretch his legs and go check on his bride, but he knew that would be frowned upon. He couldn't leave his squad.

Five minutes later, when there had still been no report from the scouts, Will ordered his squad to dismount their vehicles and open the doors on the horse trailers. The sun was high in the sky and beating down on them. It wouldn't take long for the horses to overheat in those conditions. He didn't want to have to get them out of the trailers, though. As soon as they did, that would be when they'd be called to move out.

Will spotted Isabella at the back of the convoy, using a road sign she'd obviously found along the roadside to fan one of the horses through the window of the trailer. "Are they all right?" he called to her.

"It's over a hundred degrees in there. We can't sit here much longer without unloading them."

Will agreed. Traveling with the horses in the middle of summer complicated things. He understood they needed to proceed with caution, especially with the report of Dempsey's goons running around up there, but the horses were an integral part of the mission and they'd be of no use to them dead.

Thirty minutes later, the order to pull out was given. "Did the recon team finally check in? What was up with the delay?" Will asked as he loaded back into the vehicle.

"We haven't heard from them yet. Lieutenant Burns said we can't wait any longer for them."

"We're proceeding then—and without intel?" Will asked. He was concerned. After Stephens' warning, he would sure feel more confident if he knew the recon team had given the all-clear.

"They likely just had radio issues. We'll probably hear from them the closer we get to their location."

Will's mind went through all the likely scenarios trying to find a plausible—not life-threatening—reason for their lack of communication. He imagined if they encountered someone, they would observe, maybe even follow them for a bit to assess the threat. Not hearing from them didn't necessarily mean they'd met with trouble. But it couldn't be ruled out either. They were proceeding forward on the planned route. They'd likely know sooner rather than later whether danger awaited them ahead.

The convoy came to an abrupt stop again just before the bridge going into Pocahontas, Arkansas. There was shouting and cursing coming through the radio and then the order to back up. Back up? What the hell was happening? The driver reversed the vehicle and then slammed on the brakes. "What's going on? Will shouted.

"One of the idiots back there jackknifed their horse trailer," one of the privates said.

When the order to dismount came through the radio, Will knew things were about to get real. He threw open his door with his rifle ready for the action he anticipated. Walker and Jason were right behind him. Will scanned from right to left but perceived no threat. He took the opportunity to glance back and sure enough, the middle horse trailer had taken out the guard rail and was in the ditch. Isabella was running toward it, her rifle at the low ready position. Her attention was on the horses, not whatever had caused the convoy to stop abruptly.

Jason ran back along the shoulder of the highway and took a covering position at the front of the vehicle. Will turned and moved toward the front of the convoy and whatever trouble awaited them.

A burning Humvee sat sideways in the middle of the bridge that crossed Black River—the recon team's vehicle. It appeared the driver had attempted to stop before running into an electrical cable that crossed both northbound lanes, blocking the roadway.

An order was given to fan out and look for whoever might have set up this ambush—and for survivors. The fire and smoke inside the vehicle were too intense to determine whether anyone was still inside. Will doubted they'd find the recon team alive now. If they had somehow managed to survive, they were likely in enemy hands and being interrogated by now.

A thorough search turned up nothing except evidence of someone entering and exiting the riverbank in a boat below the bridge.

"That took planning. This was no spur of the moment attack," Burns said looking down at Smith. The tall officer paced back and forth rubbing the top of his head. A moment later, the radio operator appeared at his side. "I have General Waltrip for you, sir."

From what Will could glean from the lieutenant's side of the conversation, it appeared the mission had been compromised. Someone had talked. The enemy knew their route and now they had the recon team.

Smith took a seat on the guardrail. His head hung low. Gone was the confident, sarcastic ladies' man. Smith looked more like he'd been kicked in the balls.

"The recon team won't talk," Walker said, walking up beside Will.

"I know." Will couldn't even think about what the special

forces soldiers must be going through at that moment, if they'd survived.

Smith glanced up and then looked away. Did he know something? All Will knew was that something was not right with the man.

TWENTY

Isabella

Highway 67
Walnut Ridge, Arkansas
July 10th
Event + Ten Months

After the incident on the bridge with the reconnaissance team's Humvee, they'd performed a thorough search and found nothing to give them any indication of who had attacked them or where the team had been taken.

Isabella had checked and rechecked her weapons and all her gear. She took deep breaths as the convoy turned around and got ready to head back the way they had come. They had to take an alternate route—they couldn't take the chance that the enemy knew where they were heading. It would mean the trip would be longer —maybe a lot longer. They had to take roads the recon team hadn't planned to use.

"I ain't looking forward to those bumpy-ass dirt roads," Specialist Fisher said as she shifted in her seat attempting to find a more comfortable position. Fisher rarely complained. She had trained harder and longer than any trooper in the platoon. She appeared to be on a mission to be the best at everything she did. Isabella was honored to serve with her. No one treated her like a fragile doll.

"I'm concerned about the horses. This is hard on them," Isabella said.

"They'll be fine. They're tough-ass fighting machines like us." She made a fist and flexed her bicep. She was a tough-ass fighting machine. Isabella wanted to be, but after months of inadequate food and the stress of surviving, she lacked the physical strength. She was a good mounted markswoman—put her on a horse and she could do some damage. Somehow, though, she had the feeling they'd never get close enough to the enemy to do any damage.

After backtracking to Walnut Ridge, the convoy headed farther east along Highway 412 to Paragould, Arkansas, before connecting to Highway 62. As they grew closer to the Missouri border, Isabella grew increasingly anxious. Their risk of encountering trouble only became greater. They hadn't patrolled that far north. Other units had traveled north, but Isabella didn't know which routes they'd taken.

"It's gonna feel nice to be inside a cave. It's damn hot and I could use some relief. How long do you think it might take to load that much gold?" Fisher asked.

"I don't know. Quite a while, I'd imagine." Isabella pictured the disabled truck loaded with crates of gold coins. The team that had hidden it had come up against perhaps the same forces that had hit their recon team. It had to have been some fight for them to abandon the gold in a cave. She'd heard they'd eventually died from the injuries they'd received that day. Too bad they'd had to destroy the truck. The truck would make getting the gold back to Fort Leonard Wood so much easier. She understood why General Waltrip had chosen the Horse Detachment to go in after the gold. The enemy wouldn't be expecting it, and people dressed in civilian clothes riding horses wouldn't attract as much attention as a military convoy. Dempsey's men weren't the only ones they'd need to guard the gold against.

"The next time we stop to water the horses, I'm getting in the water. I don't care if I have to strip down naked. I hate feeling nasty sweaty," Fisher said.

The guys seated around them raised their eyebrows but none said a word. They knew better than to make a comment. Fisher would kick their butts.

"A dip in a pond would be nice," Isabella said. She glanced out the side window. A nice cool stream would be better than a muddy, mucky pond.

They passed a sign indicating they were entering Pollard, Arkansas. Isabella had no idea where that was in relation to the destination in Missouri. The convoy came to a stop, but Isabella wasn't very alarmed. She thought they were preparing to turn and make a course change again. A second later, she discovered how wrong she was.

The driver put the vehicle in reverse and sped backward as rifle rounds struck the truck. Isabella held on as it veered right and left trying to evade the shooters. The driver somehow managed to steer around the vehicles hauling the horse trailers and got turned around down a side road. He stopped abruptly and the occupants jumped out, rifles raised and ready to return fire.

"What the hell was that?" Fisher said. What part of "always drive through an ambush don't we understand? Never stop—remember that one?"

It seemed they were being fired upon from every direction. The rest of Team Razorback were out of their vehicles and diving for cover. As Isabella ducked down beside Fisher behind a road grader parked along the side of the street, she scanned the vehicles ahead looking for Will. Had he made it out and to cover? Her heart raced. Her mind raced. All she wanted was to get to her husband and know that he was okay. A three-round burst slammed into the heavy steel of the machine just inches above her head. This was real. These shooters weren't locals with sling-shots and arrows. This had to be the army Stephens had warned them about. Fisher moved to her left and inched her head up above the front tire. A round barely missed her as she dropped to the ground face first. "You okay?" Isabella asked, crawling over to her.

"It's days like this that I regret having big-ass boobs."

Isabella didn't share that attribute, but she could see where it could be a problem in this instance.

"Did you see anything?" Isabella asked. She was hoping for a sighting of Will and the rest of his squad. Her squad was spread out on both sides of the street. She caught glimpses of them as they'd pop up to return fire and received the order from the squad leader to hold their position.

"I saw two at our ten o'clock," Fisher said, pulling and releasing the charging handle of her M4 rifle. She used the top of the road grader's blade for a steady firing position.

Isabella craned her neck to see. "Where? I don't see them?"

"Just wait a second. They'll reveal themselves. There—behind that white SUV." Fisher rose slightly, popped off a three-round burst into the Toyota, and dropped back down.

A man dressed in black and green fatigues stepped around the rear bumper of the vehicle and returned fire. Isabella squeezed the trigger of her rifle and the man dropped to the ground. A second man appeared and stepped around the front bumper. Fisher dropped him with one shot and then put three more in him. He didn't move.

As Isabella turned to scan to her right for more threats, an auto-matic weapon hammered the road grader right in front of them. The shooter had to have unloaded an entire magazine as if they could waste ammunition like they had an endless supply.

Conserve ammo—one shot, one kill. That had been drilled into her by her drill sergeant since day one of training. Make every shot count. They would not be getting resupplied on this mission. What they carried was all there would be. Once they ran out of ammunition and grenades, they were done.

Isabella had vowed she wouldn't allow the enemy to take her alive. She'd placed one 9mm round in the bottom of an ammo pouch to make sure she had one bullet left if she was in imminent danger of being captured. They wouldn't get information from her that would endanger her unit—her country. Isabella thought of Cayden, back in Texarkana. The enemy was too close to the shelter where he and the rest of her family and friends were. That was too damn close. How had they amassed in such numbers without being spotted by the patrols? How many more were out there? Were they attacking the base at Little Rock right now?

"Watch out!" Fisher yelled as she swung her rifle in Isabella's direction. Gravel cut into her knees as Isabella dropped to the ground and pivoted to defend herself. Fisher squeezed the trigger and nothing happened.

Isabella didn't have time to bring her rifle around to fire before the man was upon her. He grabbed her by the hair and yanked her head back. Fisher cursed, let the rifle dangle on its sling, and pulled her tactical knife from its sheath on her right thigh. With a guttural scream, she lunged for the man, knocking him backward. A second later, Fisher stood, blood dripping from her knife. She kicked the man in the balls before wiping the blade on his pants and sliding it back into its sheath.

"You okay?" she asked, helping Isabella to her feet.

Isabella rubbed the back of her head. Her scalp burned where the man had pulled her hair. She tightened the elastic band holding her hair tight to her head and looked down at the man. Sunlight glinted off the blade of a knife the man had in his hand that now lay two feet from his body. Her hand went to her neck. He'd intended to slit her throat. Tears welled in her eyes. "Thanks, Fisher."

More rounds came from behind them and hit to their right. Fisher moved to the back of the road grader. Placing her rifle on the machine again to steady her shot, Fisher took aim, exhaled, and squeezed the trigger. One shot—one kill. The gunman dropped to the ground. Another shooter ran from one vehicle to another.

Isabella took up a supported position like Fisher, exhaled, and squeezed the trigger, and the second man fell to the ground. As he did, an image of Will falling flashed into her mind. She pushed it away. She couldn't go there. She had to stay focused on the enemy in front of her and protect herself and her battle buddy. Will would be doing the same.

Isabella was concerned the enemy could work their way around the building behind them in a flanking maneuver. She felt exposed. and she'd never see them until it was too late. They needed to move closer to the rest of the squad. They needed better cover. They needed someone to cover their rear. She scanned the parking lot of a nearby building. It was filled with cars and trucks. If they could make it there, they could move from vehicle to vehicle and go around the back of the building to rejoin the bulk of their squad fighting from the cover of a concrete block building.

"We need to move," Isabella said. She pointed to a jacked-up pickup truck with oversized tires. "There—and then to the red SUV."

Fisher nodded as she dropped her rifle's empty magazine and replaced it with a fresh one. "I'll cover you," Fisher said, stuffing the nearly empty mag into a pouch on her tactical belt.

Isabella pressed her cheek to the stock of her rifle, tapped Fisher's shoulder, and said, "Moving."

TWENTY-ONE

Will

Pollard, Arkansas
July 10th
Event + Ten Months

Rounds hammered the side of the Humvee Will was riding in. They were under attack. The driver swung the vehicle violently to the left and the vehicle stopped abruptly. Will and the others quickly exited and began returning fire.

"Get the horses," Will shouted. "They're shooting at the horse trailer." The horses were a vital tool in their mission. They couldn't afford to lose even one. The way the enemy was targeting them, they had to have known that too.

The Humvee gunner was rocking the world from above them in the turret with the Browning.

"Lay down suppressive fire," Jason yelled to a soldier taking cover but not returning fire. The soldier was white as a ghost and shaking in fear.

"Get to that door and be ready to get the horses out. Move them behind that white building," Will shouted. He moved up beside

Jason, dropped to one knee, and began sending rounds across the street and to his right. Walker took up a position five feet from them behind a mid-sized sedan.

"How many?" Will shouted.

"I see six shooters at our two o'clock. There are at least four farther down just before that bridge. They've got Charlie Team pinned down tight," Walker replied.

"Do you have a shot?" Will asked.

Walker placed his rifle on the roof of the sedan, sent a round downrange, and worked the bolt. An enemy shooter at their two o'clock fired a three-round burst back at them into the car they had taken cover behind, sending Walker scrambling back to the rear bumper. "I got one. Three to go."

As Walker moved into position to take a second shot, Will and Jason laid down suppressive fire on the enemy shooter's position. "Two more down. Charlie Team is on the move," Walker said.

Will glanced behind him and saw that Alpha Team had been able to open the horse trailer and were unloading the horses. But one horse reared up and knocked a soldier to the ground before it bolted. Will cursed and hoped it wouldn't run far.

He took the opportunity to look for Isabella's squad. He spotted Fisher and noticed soldiers spread out on the south side of the road, but he couldn't see his wife. Rounds whizzed by him as the enemy began returning fire again.

"Will!" Jason shouted. "We need to move." Crouching low, Jason moved back behind the Humvee as it was being peppered with incoming rounds.

"There—that building," Will said, nodding to the adjacent concrete block structure.

Will covered Walker as he ran toward it. When Walker reached it, he dropped down behind it and laid down cover fire with his M9, allowing Will and Jason to reach the building.

"We need to get inside," Will said.

"On the roof," Walker said. They needed to be able to see

enemy movement and assess the situation to find out how many they were really up against—and Walker needed somewhere to pick them off with his Remington.

Jason nodded over his shoulder. "Back door?"

"I'll check," Will said, moving along the back of the building. He thought of Isabella. He should be able to locate her from up there. He hated being so close to her, yet so far away. He couldn't lose her. This had to work. They had to somehow get the advantage and end this.

Will turned the knob and it squeaked open revealing a musky-smelling dark space. He flicked on his weapon light and scanned from left to right. He saw no one and stepped inside, scanning the room in search of a set of stairs leading to the second floor or better yet, the roof. He found nothing. He looked up and searched the ceiling for a rope that might be attached to a pull-down ladder. "Yes!" he said as he ran around the boxes and other junk littering the floor of the space. He yanked on the dangling rope and down came a set of fold-up stairs. Will wasted no time climbing them to the second level as Walker and Jason entered and followed Will up the ladder.

The floor was rotted and non-existent in places and it was hot as hell in there. A grime-covered window overlooked the street below. That is where they needed to be. Will carefully walked over to the window, making sure to avoid the holes in the floor. He expected to drop to the floor below at any second and exhaled loudly as he reached the window. He unlocked the window and attempted to ease it open. It didn't budge. Examining it more closely, he discovered it had been painted closed. Walker reached over and slammed the butt of his M24 into the glass and raked it around the opening to remove shards from the window frame.

With a good cheek-to-stock, Will scanned to his left with both eyes open, looking for Isabella. He inhaled deeply when he spotted her and Fisher behind the massive blade of a road grader. Past them, at a grouping of parked cars, four shooters had taken cover and were firing upon Isabella's position. Will waited for one of them to step out to take a shot before he held his red dot on the man and sent a round his direction. It missed. Walker. He could make the shot. "Walker…"

"Fontenot, you got eyes on our position?" The voice of Isabella's squad leader crackled over Will's radio.

He did and it didn't look good. "You got about twelve to fifteen to the east of you on both sides of the street advancing," Will said into his radio, barely holding it together. He couldn't let them get overrun. He had to do something quick.

"Walker, can you take the ones firing on Isabella?" Will asked. "They're pinned down behind that road grader."

Walker leaned to his right and peered through his rifle's scope. He squeezed the trigger, looked back over his shoulder, and shook his head. "I don't have a shot from this angle."

Will shut his eyes. There was nothing he could do but pray as Walker concentrated on the six shooters who had the rest of Isabella's squad pinned down.

"Three down. Two on the move," Walker reported without taking his eye away from his scope. "They're retreating behind that steel building to our right." A second later, rounds peppered the building, with some whizzing by Walker and putting holes in the walls to his left. The enemy knew where they were. That would make things much more difficult.

"Can you see any of the horses?" Jason asked.

"Looks like Alpha Team has them gathered behind that red brick building at our eleven o'clock. They're safe for now. The enemy is concentrating on the area around our vehicles. They don't seem concerned about anything but keeping them from moving."

"What gives you that impression?" Jason asked.

"Smith and the lieutenant took off down that side street and no one gave chase."

Attempts to raise the lieutenant by radio went unanswered. "Hold your position and take out as many as you can, Fontenot," crackled Sergeant Brooks on the radio.

As everyone tried to dig in and find sufficient cover, the gunfire died down, except for an occasional shot when someone would move to a new position. "Why don't they advance and take us. They have to know they have us outnumbered," Will said.

"Not sure. Maybe they're as low on ammo as we are," Walker said.

"They have us outnumbered two to one. How did they get here undetected?" Will asked as he scanned the buildings and parking lots below, counting the enemy combatants.

"The rivers and creeks," Walker said. "The same way you move up and down the Bayou in Louisiana. We never searched the banks. We were looking on the roadways for vehicles."

"Shit!" Jason said. "They could move a hell of a lot of men that way."

"It looks like they did," Will said, stepping back from the window. Time was ticking. They were pinned down in Arkansas when they should have been in Missouri securing the area around the gold by now. Stephens was going to be pissed. She'd known and warned him that Dempsey's army was in the area. Had her warnings to the higher-ups fallen on deaf ears. Obviously. The patrols they'd sent out reported not seeing any sign of the rumored army. How was it that the folks from Lake Sylvia were able to find them when the United States Army could not?

TWENTY-TWO

Stephens

Fort Leonard Wood Army Base
Fort Leonard Wood, Missouri
July
Event + Ten Months

As Team Lonestar pulled through the gate of the Army base at Fort Leonard Wood, Stephens was taken back by the amount of deterioration that had occurred in just ten months since the military had abandoned the post. She was pleased to find it deserted, and thrilled to see the airfield was intact and suitable for landing the enormous cargo plane.

After a search of the base, Stephens and Team Lonestar began their part of the mission to meet up with the Team Razorback at the forward meeting location—the town of Boss, Missouri. The convoy headed toward Fort Leonard Wood's south gate, leaving behind only a four-man team to guard the airfield. Once the plane landed, Stephens prayed Sharp could hold off any attack until she arrived with the gold.

Under a normal state of affairs, Stephens would have found the scenery of southern Missouri spectacularly beautiful, but these circumstances were far from normal, and the motion sickness from the twisting, winding roads had her in a foul mood as the convoy made its way through the Ozark countryside.

At the tiny community of Boss, Missouri, they crossed a bridge over a creek and pulled the convoy to a stop in front of an old post office to wait for Team Razorback, who should have been there already. The troopers of Team Lonestar set up security and began unloading their horses and taking them to the creek for water

As the horses were being watered, the lieutenant was on the satellite phone with headquarters. Team Razorback had been delayed. Team Lonestar was to proceed without them.

Stephens and Team Lonestar saddled up for the ride to Iron County. Stephens was soaked in sweat by the time she climbed into the saddle. She felt sorry for the poor horses having to work so hard in the mid-July heat.

Crack! Pop!

Stephens dismounted her horse and hit the ground as round after round of rifle fire kicked up dirt near her. It sounded as if it were coming from every direction. The platoon sergeant was shouting orders, but she couldn't hear him over the noise. Peterson grabbed her by the arm and pulled her over toward a vehicle for cover. "Stay down," he said.

"Where are they coming from?" Stephens asked, pulling her rifle to her cheek.

"The creek," he shouted.

A second later, they were surrounded. MRAPs and Humvees blocked them in. It was an ambush. They had to have known they were coming. There was no way Dempsey and Region Five's army could know they'd stop on that stretch of road in the middle of nowhere, Missouri, by chance.

Peterson ran and grabbed the reins of Stephens' horse before it could get away. He pointed over his shoulder. "Stay low and follow me." She glanced back at the rest of the platoon returning fire. "Stephens—follow me," he repeated. She did as instructed and ran towards a red-painted building. Peterson jumped on his horse and pointed. "You're going take that gravel road until it ends and then pick up an old logging trail heading northeast."

"What about you and the others?" Stephens asked as she slid her foot into the stirrup and climbed into her saddle.

"We'll catch up."

Stephens held on as the horse took off in the direction Peterson had pointed as if it knew where it was going then waited for hours at the rally point for the rest of the platoon. Just as she was thinking she'd been the only survivor, Hogan and Collins came trotting down the old logging road; with them were the four draft horses and two young soldiers.

"Where's the rest of the platoon?"

"As far as I know, ma'am, we're all that's left," Hogan said, trotting past her.

Stephens slumped in her saddle. She was sick of war and death. She was tired of seeing great men and women die when they'd fought so hard to survive this long.

Will and Isabella? What had become of them and the rest of Team Razorback?

How were they going to accomplish the mission now, with so few soldiers and the enemy hot on their heels? How had Dempsey known where they'd be? He must have discovered where the gold was stashed. Why else would he attack them before they retrieved it—that wasn't smart—and Dempsey wasn't dumb. There would be no way of knowing until they reached the cave.

At least they still had the draft horses. They could still pull the wagon—if they had one. "We lost the wagon," she stated to no one in particular.

"Green Team left one for us as a backup about a mile from the cave. It's older and not as well maintained, but it should haul the gold," Hogan said.

The Green Team. The team that General Waltrip sent out to

scout the area the month before and who'd never returned. They'd lost communications with them before they'd reached the cave. Their intel must have been wrong. The area had to be crawling with Region Five soldiers. Had they known they were coming for the gold? Or was it a random attack?

~

Hogan led them straight to the wagon located in a barn on a long-abandoned farm. Stephens inspected the wheel hubs. They looked to have been recently greased. Green Team had thought of everything. "Let's hook up the team and go get that gold," Hogan said.

It was a hard ride down dusty gravel roads to reach the mouth of the cave. They stopped in front of an old wooden gate secured with a chain and padlock. The gravel road beyond it was barely visible with tall grass having taken it over. Hogan dismounted and used a pair of Channellock hoof nippers from his pack to remove the lock. In minutes, Stephens was staring at the thing they'd come to retrieve.

Hogan cracked open one of the top crates, opened one of the tubes, and poured out a handful of gold coins. "Honestly, I didn't think I'd ever see this."

Stephens had had her own doubts, but she'd refused to entertain them. Failure was not an option. Too much was at stake.

"Let's get this shit loaded and get the hell out of here before Region Five shows up—again," Stephens barked. She held no rank on this team, but it seemed it had fallen on her to make sure the gold made it to Houston.

~

As they rode, Hogan shared directions to streams where they could water the horses, safe places to hide if they had to hunker down, and trails that would get them where they needed to be. She wasn't sure she could recall it all if they were attacked again, and with adrenaline pumping, but she'd do her best.

They stopped to water the horses at a pond near the road.

"It's getting dark. It's going to be hard to find our way out there when the sun goes down," Collins said. Stephens studied him. He, like the rest of them, was dressed in civilian clothes—part of going low-key. He wore his baseball cap on backward, but it didn't seem to fit with his polo shirt and khaki pants. "What's your specialty, Collins?" she asked him.

"Communications, ma'am."

"Did the radio survive?"

He shook his head.

"What about the satphone?"

"No, ma'am."

"That sucks," Stephens said, exhaling loudly. They would have no communications with Sharp or Team Razorback.

Stephens let down her hair and ran her hands across her scalp. She needed a shower. She couldn't recall the last time she'd felt so sweaty and grimy. She walked over to the pond and splashed muddy water on her face. That was the best she could do at the moment.

"So, we wait here for the night? We have three days, Hogan. Three days to get this shipment to the base."

He shrugged one shoulder and took a long pull on his canteen.

~

After a restless night of no sleep, Stephens was pleasantly surprised they were making better time than she'd imagined, but they still had to make frequent stops to water the horses and give them rest. Just past Salem, Missouri, Hogan stopped in the middle of the road, held a fist in the air, and motioned for everyone to dismount.

"What is it?" Stephens called to him. "Locals, I believe. Get the wagon out of sight."

The young trooper driving the wagon attempted to pull onto the gravel drive to his left but dropped one of the wheels off into the ditch. As Hogan and Collins set up along the road to cover them, the two privates on the wagon jumped down and attempted to pull the wagon out and down the road out of sight. They pulled on the horses' reins with all their might, but they were unable to drag the heavily laden wagon from the ditch in time.

The first shot took out the trooper who'd been driving the wagon. The other private attempted to duck behind the wagon for cover, but a round struck him in the head. Stephens yanked on her horse's reins, spun to her left, and took off for the trees. She dropped down and crouched low, leading her horse behind a clump of trees before taking cover behind a fallen log. She propped her rifle on the log and watch for the enemy. She felt so defeated that she wanted to curl up right there and die. There was no way that the five of them could hold on to the gold against so many. They were outnumbered at least two to one.

They'd come so far and been so close. The loss was unbearable. Latham would now have to find another way to pay for the military supplies the nation desperately needed. She'd failed. Obviously, the other team had also failed. They'd never even made it to the rally point. She pushed thoughts of Will, Isabella, and the others in Team Razorback from her mind.

The firefight continued far longer than Stephens ever imagined it could. She was sure the wagon had been pulled from its stuck position and was well on its way somewhere. This group was too well armed to be just some locals. After the fighting died down, Stephens was anxious to get after them and retrieve the gold.

"I'm going after them," Stephens yelled, taking off after the fleeing bandits.

She jumped on her horse and tore through the woods toward the road. She rode as fast as she could, but there were just too many side roads they could have turned down. She stopped at each gravel track, hoping for any sign that a heavy wagon had turned there, but saw nothing. She was alone, in the middle of nowhere and now she'd lost them. She'd lost the gold. She dismounted, kicked the gravel, leaned her head against her horse, and wept.

"Stephens."

"Hogan?"

She hadn't heard him ride up. How could that have happened?

She stepped away from her horse to find him leading his horse along the grassy area beside the road. Slung over his horse was a man. At first, she thought it was Peterson, but he was too small to be the special forces soldier.

"Who is that?" she asked, approaching them.

"He was with that group that hit us and took the gold."

Stephens was stunned. She gave Hogan a double-take. She'd underestimated the man. She looked past them to see Collins. They'd both escaped the firefight.

"The privates?" Stephens asked.

Hogan just shook his head.

Stephens swallowed hard. They were good men. Their deaths were a great loss for the country.

"Get him down. Let's find out what he knows," Stephens said, pointing to the big oak tree at the edge of the road.

The man they'd strung up in the tree looked to be no older than a boy. His hands were bound with a rope and his feet barely touched the ground. Hogan questioned him for only ten minutes before the kid sang like a canary.

"We were heading to Phelps County Trade Fair in Rolla," the kid said. "They'll take Highway 63. They'll avoid Highway 72. It's crawling with Nelson's men. They'll avoid them."

Stephens wasn't concerned about Nelson or his men, whoever they were. She needed to get to Highway 63 and stop these bandits before they reached that trade fair with her gold.

TWENTY-THREE

Isabella

Pollard, Arkansas
Early morning hours of July 11th
Event + Ten Months

When night had fallen, the gunfire had ceased except for when anyone tried to change positions. The enemy obviously had night vision. Isabella and her squad were pinned down at the side of a building a block from Will and his squad. She learned that he, Jason, and Walker had made it into the second story of one of the buildings, and Walker had managed to pick off several combatants before the enemy had discovered their position. They had relocated twenty yards down the street in a two-story house. Walker was concentrating on gathering intel on their numbers and locating their leaders. No one had heard from the lieutenant or Brad Smith since the fighting began.

A few hours before dawn, Isabella and her squad were briefed on a new plan. They were to try to get to the horses while Will's squad covered them. A pit formed in Isabella's stomach. They were going to try to get away on horseback.

"When we reach the horses, we're going to ride northwest. We're going to cross the Missouri border and wait for the rest of the platoon before proceeding to Iron County," Fisher told her.

"What about Will and the others?" Isabella asked.

"They'll catch up. They will be right behind us," Fisher said.

Isabella knew that was a lie. How could they? They were outnumbered and would be on foot.

Everyone checked their ammo and secured their gear as they waited for the signal. When Will and his squad began laying down suppressive fire, Isabella's stomach lurched. The realization that she may never see her husband again was overwhelming. She'd known what they'd signed up for from the beginning, she just hadn't considered how unbearable it would be.

Fisher nudged her. "Move out, Fontenot."

Her feet refused to move. Fisher grabbed her arm and pulled her along as they crossed the street and ran toward the red brick building where the horses were supposed to be. She was in disbelief as they rounded the corner of the structure and Alpha Team, along with the horses, were there waiting for them.

Fisher ran and practically flew into the saddle of one of the horses like some trick rider from the rodeos Isabella had attended as a kid. Fisher grabbed the reins of another horse and steadied it while Isabella climbed up. In a haze of movement, they all took off down the street, away from the fighting—away from Will.

They rode hard, pushing the horses much harder than they should in the pre-dawn light. They were risking injuries to the horses and themselves. Branches slapped Isabella in the face as they traversed fields and crossed wooded areas, finally coming out on a gravel road by a small river. Isabella had no clue where they were. Had they made it to Missouri?

They continued north staying close to tree lines, only crossing open fields when absolutely necessary. Isabella glanced back every few minutes, hoping to see Will and the others following them, but they were alone. It seemed they had evaded the enemy. She prayed that Will and the others would do the same.

After riding for hours, they were finally allowed to stop to water and rest the horses, nestled in a clearing near the junction of Highways N and 51, just across the Missouri and Arkansas state line. The sun was climbing high in the sky and the mid-summer temperatures were nearly unbearable already. The horses couldn't keep up this pace much longer. She couldn't either.

"Are we waiting here for the rest of the platoon?" Isabella asked her squad leader.

"We lost comms with them."

Although she knew there was a myriad of reasons radios wouldn't receive a signal, Isabella fought hard not to think the worst.

"We'll keep trying and give them until morning," her squad leader said.

Sixteen hours. Will had sixteen hours to eliminate the enemy and drive to the rally point or somehow escape and get there on foot. It was doable, she told herself over and over. They'd make it. She couldn't lose hope. Will would find a way to make it to her—somehow. She slumped her shoulders and bowed her head. "I'll let my team know."

Everyone secured a perimeter from fixed positions around the horses and those taking care of them near a creek. Isabella listened hard for the sound of vehicles or anyone moving through the brush. Anyone approaching from either direction wouldn't be able to see the squad nestled back in the trees by the creek, but they weren't going to let anyone sneak up and get the drop on them.

"He'll make it," Trooper Jones said, making his rounds along the perimeter to ensure everyone was good to go whenever they got the word to "un-ass the AO," as he liked to call whatever "Area of Operations" they were in at the time. Jones was a great soldier, Isabella thought. In ordinary times, at age fifty, Jones would be considered too old to be on the front lines, but his skill on the back of a horse made him a prime candidate for this mission. The only problem was, they hadn't been fighting from horseback when they were ambushed.

TWENTY-FOUR

Will

Northeast Arkansas
July 12th
Event + Ten Months

After Isabella's squad made their escape, Will, Jason, and the rest of his squad battled for hours before they were able to take out enough of the enemy to retrieve their vehicles and call headquarters in Little Rock on their satphone. The remaining few enemy combatants had fled.

"We searched every building in town. Lieutenant Burns and Smith aren't in them," Will said into the phone.

Will had expected to find their bodies. Finding nothing meant the worst had happened—they'd been taken.

"Find them, Sergeant Fontenot," Colonel Sharp ordered.

"But the mission, sir."

"Retrieving Brad Smith is your squad's mission now."

"Yes, sir," Will said. "But what about the lieutenant?"

"Yes. Brad Smith and the lieutenant," Sharp said.

Everything in Will wanted to protest. His wife and her squad were out there proceeding with the mission without him and his squad. He should be with them, not rescuing Brad Smith. Will liked the lieutenant, he was worth saving. But Brad Smith wasn't worth the effort, in Will's estimation.

Will had his squad consolidate ammo, grab food and water for a week. They set out on their new mission in two Humvees. It was almost dumb luck that led them to finally picking up Region Five's trail across the border into southeast Missouri. They came around a sharp bend in the road and discovered one of their MRAPs flipped over halfway down a cliff. Two of the occupants were deceased. By the trail of blood leading back up the hill, others had apparently survived. Will retrieved a radio from one of the dead men, and after hours of monitoring their conversations, he had a possible location.

From a distance, Will and Jason observed the movements of enemy vehicles coming in and out of a farm west of the town of Piggott. It took them hours to get close enough to learn that this was not a headquarters or a location where prisoners were held.

After two more days of tracking their movements, Will and Jason still hadn't reached the enemies' headquarters or located the lieutenant and Smith. Will feared it was already too late for them. The interrogators would have extracted whatever information Smith had about their mission in a matter of hours after his capture, Will thought. If by some miracle he'd misjudged the man and they hadn't yet cracked him, they had to try a rescue.

Brad Smith had been with the CIA for over a decade and was close to President Latham. Who knew what government secrets the man held or what damage those secrets could do in the hands of someone like General Dempsey. Finding their headquarters could also provide Will and 1st Platoon with valuable intelligence about the enemy's movements in Arkansas and their reason for being in the area. Were they there only to thwart the mission to retrieve the gold or was there a bigger purpose? Were they preparing an attack on Little Rock or maybe even Texarkana? They had to know.

Colonel Sharp's orders to bring back Smith meant they'd be tracking and locating the enemy's area of operations and spending the time necessary observing their activities. That wasn't part of Team Razorback's original mission. Their mission had been to move to Iron County, Missouri, and secure the area around the cave where the gold shipment was located. Now, that would fall upon Isabella's squad alone. And Isabella's squad was on horseback. It could take days for them to reach it. So many things could go wrong, and he wouldn't be there to help her.

Will was having a very difficult time putting her out of his mind and concentrating on his new mission. He was so conflicted. Retrieving the gold was vital to repelling the Russians and securing the nation, but having Dempsey's army there in their territory made this surveillance and the recovery of Lieutenant Burns and Smith of great importance as well.

Colonel Sharp refused to report on Isabella and her squad. He also gave him no information about Stephens and Team Lonestar either. Will hated being kept in the dark. It wasn't personal—he understood Sharp didn't want any more information falling into the enemies' hands, but not knowing was killing him.

Will's squad followed the enemy until they pulled into a gravel driveway. After stashing the Humvees, Will and Jason proceeded on foot back to the gravel driveway and a shed tucked back into the woods.

Will inched close enough to a window to overhear a conversation between two officers. That conversation gave them the first lead they'd had in days. One of the officers had been summoned back to their headquarters. It was hard to hear, but Will was almost positive he heard him say that he resented being called back to babysit prisoners.

"That could be our guys," Jason said as Will relayed the conversation. The two made quicker time getting back to the rest of the squad. They'd need to be ready to pull out and follow that officer back to his headquarters.

Will found following the officer's convoy without detection challenging on the windy roads. The Humvee had to hang back so far, and there were so many bends that they could round a curve and be right up on them. The risk of losing the convoy was great if they fell too far back. Every nerve in Will's body was on edge.

When the convoy slowed and turned down a gravel drive north of Piggott, Arkansas, Will's heart leaped. This had to be it. It was go time. As amped up as Will was, the hours of surveillance it took to finally locate the lieutenant and Smith were torture. Will informed Colonel Sharp. He hoped Sharp might dispatch a rescue team so his squad would be free to continue on to the rally point in Boss, Missouri. His heart sank when he was told they would be the rescue team—no reinforcements would be coming. Of course, he'd known this would have to be how it went.

"We have no one to send—and you're already there to expedite the rescue. We need to get the cargo plane to Fort Leonard Wood and secure it until the gold is on board and we can't leave Little Rock unguarded," Sharp said.

Will cursed under his breath. They were spread too thin. They needed more soldiers, but it seemed that the rebuilding efforts and the continued fighting out west had everyone tied up. They were running the Little Rock base with less than a battalion-sized element, not including Colonel Sharp's unit that was on the mission to retrieve the gold.

Will and Jason kept an eye on the shed where the lieutenant and Smith were being held as they tried to form a plan based on various likely circumstances they would encounter when they made their move. As they hashed out their plan, no one came or went except a soldier who had arrived with food. The soldier stayed with them for less than a minute and left.

As Will and the squad readied to execute their plan, a truck pulled up to the shed.

"What are they doing?" Jason asked.

"Moving them?" Walker replied.

Will's hands balled into fists. "Shit. We are so freaking close."

"Should we take them now or wait until we're out on the road?" Jason asked.

"It's risky either way. If we attack now, they could kill them before we reach them," Walker said.

Will studied the truck. It was a civilian truck. The tires were bald and the windshield was cracked. They weren't going far. He doubted the truck would make it ten miles, the way it sounded.

"We'll wait and take them on the road. Hopefully, they won't send very many security vehicles with them," Will said as he picked up the satphone to call it in to headquarters.

Lieutenant Burns and Brad Smith were loaded inside the cab of the pickup, and in less than a minute, it and an older sedan were heading east along County Road 344. Will had his lead vehicle follow closer than would usually be prudent. They couldn't afford to lose them. If Brad Smith talked, Stephens and Isabella would be walking into a trap.

TWENTY-FIVE

Stephens

Highway 63
Phelps County, Missouri
July 12th
Event + Ten Months

"You can stop right there!" a man yelled as Stephens, Collins, and Hogan topped a hill.

Stephens pulled her reins and slowed her horse. Hogan leaped down and took cover behind his horse. Stephens and Collins remained mounted. Stephens scanned the area looking for others. No one else was visible but she could sense their presence.

"State your business in these parts," a big man dressed in dirty bibbed overalls and a boonie hat yelled.

Stephens looked him over. He'd survived this long into the apocalypse. She wouldn't underestimate him.

"That ain't none of your business," Hogan replied.

"We're making it our business," a second man said, appearing from behind a tree.

Stephens eyed the weapon in his hands. She wondered how

they still had ammunition for it. How was it that there were still so many people who still had ammunition?

"I'm looking for someone," Stephens said.

"And who might that be?" the big man asked.

A young woman appeared to Stephens' left. She couldn't have been more than nineteen or twenty. Her blonde hair was pulled back into a tight bun. She wore a holster on one hip and another on her opposite thigh. Was she military—or former military?

"Are you bounty hunters?" the blonde woman asked.

"No," Hogan shouted.

Stephens realized they weren't going to get past these locals without giving them some kind of answer to their questions. And this little girl—where was all this confidence coming from? In the old days someone this young with such display of confidence would turn out to be no more than a brash, cocky person. But there was something very different about this girl. Her confidence seemed to come from more than just experience. Stephens decided a little honesty wouldn't hurt. She may even get some help from these folks. Stephens turned to the man to her right. He too was dressed in dirty overalls, but his bearing said military—she guessed Army. "Are you in the military?"

The man straightened. "Hooah, 5th Engineer Battalion."

"Are you stationed at Fort Leonard Wood?"

"I was. It's no longer an active military base," the soldier said.

She knew that much. She'd seen how deserted it was when they'd inspected the airfield before heading to retrieved the gold. This guy was a trained military fighter. She could use his skills. Stephens glanced between Collins and Hogan. She needed the help of these people if she had a prayer of accomplishing her mission.

"Are you for hire?"

The question seemed to catch the soldier off guard. "Depends. Who's doing the paying?"

"Colonel Ryan Sharp," she said.

"Colonel? Military or law enforcement?" the soldier asked.

"Military," Hogan said.

"Whose military?" the big man asked.

"Colonel Sharp is with the 1st Cavalry Division out of Fort Hood," Stephens said.

Stephens tried her best not to reveal too much, but they weren't having any of it. They were smart—smarter than Stephens had given them credit for, initially.

"You're full of shit, lady. I don't know why you think that bullshit story will earn you safe passage out of here in flyover country, but you're sadly mistaken," the big man said.

After a tense exchange where rifles were drawn and pointed, Stephens was about to reveal the reason for their presence in the county when a man she recognized appeared from his hiding place behind the wagon. He offered her a nod, acknowledging he recognized her as well, but said nothing. She was shocked to see the FEMA Region Five director there in the middle of nowhere. They'd had a team out looking for this very man. He would prove invaluable in her effort to bring Dempsey's kingdom down. She almost couldn't contain her delight with her good fortune.

"You're with the government? Why are you out here without security?" He was questioning her loyalty. She could understand that.

"We were attacked. The rest of my team didn't make it."

"Attacked by whom?" Another male spoke from his hiding place.

How many more of them are there?

Stephens hesitated.

"Who attacked you and killed your team?" the blonde girl asked.

Stephens studied her. She wondered what her story was and how she fit in with the group of men. One thing that seemed clear to Stephens, that girl could handle herself.

"A group of well-armed and well-trained men," Stephens replied flatly.

Deputy Director of Response and Recovery, Gerald Aims stepped forward. If he recognized her, he didn't let on. Their meeting years ago had been brief.

"Whereabouts was that?" Aims asked, stepping away from their wagon.

"Iron County," Stephens said.

"Did one of your men have a tattoo of a grim reaper draped in the American flag?" the girl asked.

Stephens almost fell off her horse. "Yes. How did you know that?"

"Because we found him face down in a ditch yesterday," the young girl replied, flatly.

"He's dead?" Stephens asked.

"Yes. Shot in the back. It looked like he'd ridden some distance before dying."

"We got split up. Peterson and a few others were laying down suppressive fire so I could get away. I got cut off from them. They were surrounded." Stephens swallowed hard. "Hogan and Collins managed to escape. I met up with them at our rally point. We waited twenty-four hours as agreed. The rest of the team never showed. We ran into some trouble after that. We were stopped on the road by bandits. They took government property from us. We need to get it back."

"Bandits, you say," the big man said, turning to the soldier. "Nelson's men?"

"What did they take?" the soldier asked.

"That's classified."

"I guess you won't be wanting it back then," the soldier said.

"I need to know where to find those men. I need to reacquire our cargo."

"You're going to need an army to reacquire that cargo. What the hell were you thinking traveling with a wagon full of gold?" the big guy asked.

Stephens stiffened. Were they with the group that had stolen the shipment? Had she misjudged them? Her mind was racing. No, she decided. Harding and Aims wouldn't be involved with that. She decided to try to appeal to their patriotism—if any remained.

Stephens stared at Aims. Without answering the big man's question, Stephens pointed to a water tank in the back of their wagon and said, "Mind if I give my horse some water while I tell you what's at stake for the nation, Deputy Director Aims?"

"Aims," the blonde girl said, turning her gaze to him. "What's her story?"

"Let's hear her out, Maddie," Aims said.

For the next hour, Stephens filled them in on what had happened to the country and about the new government. She needed them on her side. She needed all the help she could get. They seemed surprised that there was a functioning government operating in Texas, and that there was an effort to rebuild the country.

"What is this President Latham doing to get the lights back on?" Maddie asked.

Stephens explained the purpose of the mission, divulging much more than she was authorized to share. Without their help, she was doomed to fail, but it was a risk she had to take. She could see a spark in Director Harding's eyes that told her he hadn't given up on the country or his duty to preserve and protect it. She felt confident that she could at least count on Harding and Aims, and perhaps the two could convince the others. There was still hope.

"That shipment is vital to our national recovery. I have to get it back." She shifted to focus on the soldier. "I can pay—if you know men for hire. I can pay well."

The soldier looked over his shoulder to the big guy and then to Aims and Harding. "I don't have any use for gold," he said.

For a second, Stephens felt defeated. She'd hoped that there was some shred of duty left in the man. She'd need to appeal to his human nature.

"What about MREs? Do you have use for food?" she asked.

The soldier's eyes widened. "Now you're talking. How many? I don't see how you could be carrying enough to make me want to risk my neck," he said.

"They aren't with me, but name your price. We'll make it happen," she said. "We have three days. I have to have that cargo back within three days."

"What happens in three days?" Aims asked, taking a step toward Stephens.

"The gold must be at the Port of Houston in three days to purchase desperately needed supplies for the nation's recovery effort." Stephens cleared her throat. "But it's far more critical that this happens than just recovery."

High-powered rifle fire cracked nearby. Everyone drew their weapons, fanned out, and took cover.

"Can you see them, Dustin?" the big guy called.

"Four. I see four, Larry," Dustin said, peering through his rifle scope.

Dustin and Larry began advancing toward the shooters. The others took up supported positions to secure the group from all directions. In minutes, the four shooters were down.

"Too bad we couldn't take any of them as prisoners," Maddie said.

"Yep," Dustin said. "We might have gotten some information about where your gold is stashed.

Stephens was impressed. These folks had excellent tactical skills. She was more convinced than ever they could help her. She just had to convince them.

"Let's get the hell off this highway and go get your gold," Maddie said, walking past Stephens. "Are the horses ready, Jacob?"

Another man stepped into view. "They're fine. A little spooked but they're good to go."

"Thank God," Stephens said under her breath. They were going to assist her in the search for the gold. "I need to get to a trade fair in a place called Rolla. I was told they were heading there."

"Told?" Larry asked.

"We interrogated one of their men," Stephens said. She shook off the image of the boy, who'd died from his injuries before they could find out more.

"We were heading that way ourselves," Aims said.

"Well, let's get after it," Larry said.

The trade fair was impressive. Stephens had never seen anything like it. Of course, the civilians down south weren't allowed to live outside of safe zones, and setting up anything resembling a trade fair would have alerted the government to their unauthorized activities.

After they passed through a security checkpoint and tied up their horses, Harding motioned for Stephens, Collins, and Hogan to follow him.

"Maddie, Aims and I will escort Stephens and her men. We'll meet you back at our booth," Harding said.

While Larry, Dustin, Maddie, and the others in their group went about their business, Stephens looked for the men who had hijacked her gold shipment or any evidence they'd been there. After hours of searching, they hadn't found the gold or the men who had taken it, but Dustin came through for them. He'd learned from someone there who knew a guy who'd paid a bar owner in gold. They had a lead. It was a good lead. They were back in business.

TWENTY-SIX

Isabella

Junction of Highways N and 51
Fagus, Missouri
July 12th
Event + Ten Months

Morning came and went without any sign of Will or his squad. Isabella was beside herself with worry to the point of being sick to her stomach. She turned her nose up at the breakfast MRE Fisher offered her. Even if she hadn't felt ill, she was no fan of Meals Ready to Eat.

"You can't lose hope, Fontenot. They'll take care of business and catch up with us," Fisher said, stuffing the MRE back into her rucksack.

"I just wish we would've heard something by now."

"We will. Comms are difficult out here in the Ozarks. There are just so many damn hills that it's hard for a signal to travel through this shit."

Fisher was right. The terrain was a challenge, not just for radio transmissions, but on the soldiers and horses. Climbing hills in ninety-five-degree heat with likely eighty percent humidity was going to be brutal on them all. She wasn't sure how the draft horses were going to pull a heavy wagon filled with gold. She just hoped the terrain flattened out between Iron County and the military base.

On the day of the twelfth of July, Isabella's squad made it only twenty miles before stopping for the night just south of Poplar Bluff, Missouri. They still had slightly over eighty miles to go. At their current rate of travel, it would take five days to reach Iron County and the rally point to meet up with 1st Platoon. They'd miss their deadline to get the gold to the plane. In all likelihood, Stephens' team would be forced to move the gold on their own, without the support from 2nd Platoon. Isabella prayed Stephens wasn't running into similar problems, and that by some miracle that gold made it to Colonel Sharp and onto the plane to the Port of Houston.

As the squad slowly rode onward toward the rally point in Boss, Missouri, on the second day since leaving Will and his squad back in Pollard, Isabella's thoughts drifted back to Texarkana and her new family. If she and Will didn't make it back there, what would happen to Cayden? Would Savanah be forced to relocate to Houston? Would that really be such a bad thing? She wasn't sure. With the lack of communication coming from the new leaders of the country, it was hard to know if the authoritative rules they'd implemented were what was truly needed to restore order and bring services back to the citizens.

It was early afternoon when Isabella's squad leader called a halt and they stopped to rest and water the horses. She sat on a rock, took her boots off, and let her feet soak in the cold water of a stream just south of Ellsinore.

"Grab your pack, Fontenot. We're going to sleep in a real bed tonight," Fisher said, holding her hand out to assist Isabella to her feet.

"What?"

"Summers and Russell found a house just over the hill. The squad leader said we could bunk there tonight, which means no sleeping on the ground. We don't pull security until midnight, so let's go, girl, before that raunchy Summers takes the master suite and stinks it up with his foot funk."

Fisher practically dragged Isabella over the hill and up the path leading from the creek to the back of a two-story white-clad house surrounded by trees. After climbing a steep set of stairs to a deck overlooking the creek below, Fisher dropped her rucksack on the floor just inside the master bedroom and plopped down fully dressed onto the bed. Isabella placed her rucksack next to Fisher's and continued down a short hall to check out the rest of the home.

The bedrooms all faced the front of the house. The back of the house overlooking the creek consisted of floor-to-ceiling glass. The view was spectacular. A door in the center of the wall led to the enormous deck. Summer and Russel were seated there eating MREs and laughing like they didn't have a care in the world. Isabella envied them. All she could think of was Will, Jason, Walker, and the rest of Will's squad. They should have heard something from them by now. It was also concerning that they hadn't been able to raise anyone from Team Lonestar or headquarters in Little Rock on the satphone. They were proceeding blind, with no way of knowing what they would be riding into when they reached Iron County.

"You better get some rest, Fontenot," the squad leader called from the kitchen. He was seated on a barstool drinking something from a flask. Isabella hoped it wasn't liquor. They all needed to be clear-headed for this journey even in their downtime because the enemy could be lurking anywhere.

"On my way there now, Sergeant," Isabella said.

She leaned her rifle against a chair in the corner of the master bedroom and stretched out on the king-sized bed next to Fisher. Isabella rolled onto her side and curled into a fetal position, listened to Fisher's soft breaths, and drifted off to sleep. Sometime in the night, Isabella was jolted awake by the sound of gunfire. Her feet hit the floor and she dropped to her knees, scrambling for her rifle.

"Which direction, Fontenot?" Fisher asked, grabbing her own weapon and moving toward the window.

"I think it's coming from the direction of the creek," Isabella said, peeling back the curtains.

"Do you see anyone?" Fisher asked as she checked her rifle's magazine and pulled on its charging handle, advancing a round into the chamber.

"I see nothing. It's pitch black." Savanah pulled her rifle up and scanned through her night vision scope. "I can't see where the firing is coming from."

Fisher scrambled back toward the door to the bedroom where she'd dropped her rucksack earlier. Isabella could hear her rummaging inside her pack. A moment later she was back at the window with a pair of night-vision goggles. She pressed them to her face and scanned the area behind the house all the way to the creek. "Holy shit!" Fisher cursed.

"How many?" Isabella asked.

Without a word, Fisher grabbed Isabella by her shirt and yanked her to her feet. "Grab your rucksack."

"Fisher?"

"We have to get the hell out of here, Izzy."

Isabella struck her collarbone on the door jam as Fisher pulled her toward the front of the house.

"What's going on?" Isabella asked.

Isabella felt her brush past. "There's too many of them. There's no way we can hold them off. No freaking way."

"Fisher, Fontenot, take the west side and go around where Summers and Russell are by that rock outcropping," the squad leader said, as he slid open the back door and began firing on the combatants below.

Isabella and Fisher made their way to a side door and down a short flight of stairs. Fisher had begun firing her rifle before Isabella even reached the last step. Isabella was blind there in the dark. She saw no enemy—only heard the rifle reports echoing through the hills as a fierce battle ensued.

Fisher dropped to one knee by the trunk of an old tree in the side yard and pulled the NVGs to her eyes. "Four combatants, one hundred feet to our two o'clock," she whispered.

Isabella scanned the area and gasped as the attackers came into view. Through the green haze of the night vision scope, she counted far more than four enemy fighters. They were crawling out from behind every tree and rock and moving quickly up the bank toward the back of the house. Isabella searched for her squad members and spotted two near a shed in the backyard. To the right of them, two more were crouched behind boulders. Isabella handed the goggles back to Fisher, pulled her rifle to her cheek, and fired at the approaching enemy.

"Fontenot, cover me. I'm going to try to get to the rock there on the edge of the clearing "

"Ready," Isabella said.

"Moving!"

Isabella opened up, sending rounds downrange as Fisher sprinted off to her left.

After she reached the large rock outcropping, it was Isabella's turn. When Fisher began firing, Isabella took off to join her. She heard the enemy firing back and ran faster. A couple of yards before reaching the cover of the boulders, Isabella felt a bullet graze her left hand. She dove to her knees and twisted to return fire. As she did, a round tore through her left bicep, knocking her off balance. She was on her back with one leg stuck behind her. Isabella looked at the stars between the treetops. She thought of Will and Cayden. Would she ever see either of them again? Would she die there in Missouri never knowing the fate of her husband?

"I got you," Fisher said as she grabbed Isabella by the plate carrier and dragged her to cover behind the rocks.

Once Isabella was safely behind cover, Fisher returned fire again. Isabella managed to somehow get her rifle braced on one of the boulders and her finger inside the trigger guard. Pure terror took over and she began firing in the direction of the enemy.

Summers slid in next to her. "You okay, Fontenot?"

Before Isabella could respond to him, a round struck the trooper in the neck and he slumped down behind the rock. His radio crackled to life with orders from their squad leader to pull back.

"Where's Russell?" Fisher asked.

"Gone," Isabella said, flatly. "Grab his radio. We have to run, Izzy." And her battle buddy headed toward the front of the house.

"What about the rest of the squad?" Isabella said, following after Fisher.

Fisher grabbed Isabella's injured arm and pulled. The pain caused her knees to buckle. "We're overrun and outnumbered at least three to one. We can't win this one, Fontenot. We have to drop back and regroup."

Retreat? What she meant was they were going to run for their lives and pray they weren't captured. "Save a round for me, Fisher," Isabella reminded her as they ran toward the dark woods to the west of the house.

"You do the same, Fontenot."

As the only two females in the squad, they'd promised each other they wouldn't allow the other to be captured by the enemy. It was common knowledge what happened to female prisoners. They both agreed it was a fate worst than death.

"This way, Izzy," Fisher said, shoving Isabella down into one of the spurs to the west of the house. They had to go down. There was no way to climb to the top of the ridge in the dark. It was too dangerous.

As Isabella dropped down into the rocky watershed, fear and adrenaline took over. She went somewhere else in her mind—to a time before all this. She escaped back to Houston and to her apartment by the bayou. She thought of Jaz and Gus for the first time in months. Fisher's use of the nickname that only Jaz called Isabella must have triggered the memory. Isabella wondered if they'd survived this far and if they were working in Houston somewhere now? Jaz should have given birth to their daughter by now. It broke her heart to think that she would likely never have answers to those questions. She might never know what became of Will. If she and Fisher weren't successful at evading the overwhelming force that had infiltrated their camp, her loved ones back in Texarkana may never know what happened to her.

Fisher tried several times to raise someone on the radio but the squad leader's order to pull back was the last transmission they'd received from any member of the squad. It appeared the two women were on their own—for the moment.

"Look what I found," Isabella said, producing the squad's satphone.

"Holy shit, Izzy! Where the hell did you get that?"

"Russell had it clipped to his belt along with the radio."

Fisher pressed the "Last Call" button.

"Colonel Sharp here," Sharp said.

Isabella's heart skipped a beat. They'd reached headquarters.

"Colonel Sharp, this is Specialist Fisher from Team Razorback. We were just attacked near Ellsinore, Missouri. Me and Specialist Fontenot escaped. There were dozens of enemy combatants that attacked us while we were sleeping—they outnumbered us—we shot a couple of them but Fontenot was hit and we had to drop back and regroup or they would have killed us both.

"Okay, okay, Fisher. Calm down. Are you hurt? Where was Fontenot shot—is she okay? Who else is hurt? Where is everyone else?"

"Sir, I'm okay. I don't know how we got out of there without being killed—I don't know how anyone could survive—I think everyone else is... We don't know for sure—there were so many enemy coming up the hill at us."

"Okay, Fisher. What about Fontenot? Where was she hit—is she okay?"

"She got hit in the arm—her left arm—left bicep, sir."

Isabella was wrapping a handkerchief around her bicep and was trying to tie a knot in it with one hand.

"How bad is the wound? Did you stop the bleeding?

"Yes sir, she seems okay. We're just now putting a dressing on it. There's a lot of blood but I think the bullet passed clean through. She has been holding pressure on it with her right hand until now."

"Okay, Fisher. Is it safe for you to be talking to me wherever you are? Is the enemy near enough to hear you?"

"No—I mean yes, sir—I mean I think it's safe—I don't see or hear anyone near us."

"What's your location? I need to know exactly where you are."

"Sir, I don't know. I don't know where we are exactly. We're in the woods."

"Okay. This is what I want you to do. When you think it's safe enough, I want you two to pick a direction and start walking—being careful to stay hidden. Remember your Escape and Evade training? Well, now you get to put that training to good use. I need you to get to a location that a rescue party can find—a location such as a highway with a mile marker or on a road near Elsinore with a landmark we can find, like a gas station or a restaurant. When you find a location like that where we can come get you, call me back at this number."

"Okay, sir."

"Fisher, stay hidden—escape and evade. Got it?"

"Yes, sir. Got it."

"And when you get there, hunker down and stay hidden. I don't know how long it may be until we can get folks in there to extract you two."

"Yes, sir. Got it, sir."

"Alright. Remember your training. Remember the SALUTE Report? What does the acronym SALUTE stand for?"

"Sir, that's Size, Activity, Location, Unit identification, Time, and Equipment."

"That's right. I want you to give me a good SALUTE Report when you call next."

"Yes, sir."

"Alright. Stay alert and quiet on your way. Sharp out," he said and hung up the phone.

When Fisher hung up the satphone, Isabella said, "What the hell was that, girl?"

"What?"

"Where was all that tough-ass confidence go? You sounded scared shitless."

"I don't like talking to officers. They make me nervous."

Isabella tripped and stumbled her way downstream in the dry creek bed following as close as she could behind Fisher. She didn't really feel much pain. She walked in a fog as her mind tried to grasp what had happened back there, refusing to accept that she was injured, they were on their own, and on the run from an over-whelming enemy force.

Fisher grabbed Isabella's shirt sleeve and yanked her from her thoughts. She pulled her to the right and they climbed over a hill and down another draw that led to the creek. They stumbled in the dark following the creek downstream as the sound of gunfire faded completely. The two women dropped down to the muddy bank and slid back under the roots of a large tree overhanging the creek. Isabella wrapped her right hand around her injured arm and wept.

Morning seemed to take forever to arrive as they hid among the tree roots along the bank of the creek. Fisher nudged Isabella. "I think we should follow this creek until it crosses a road. I can get a compass reading and see where we need to go from there."

Isabella attempted to stand. She was stiff from being in one position for hours, and her legs protested. Fisher steadied her as Isabella stepped back into the icy stream.

"Ouch!"

Fisher glanced down at Isabella's arm.

"Shit, Fontenot, you're bleeding again."

Isabella stared down at the crimson stain on her light blue button-up blouse. She stuck her finger into the hole the bullet had made in it and felt the sticky substance.

"Let's get that off and take a good look," Fisher said, unbuttoning the cuff of Isabella's right sleeve and then helped her out of her blouse.

Isabella couldn't look at it. Fisher wrinkled her nose as she cleaned the wound. Despite the pain, it felt better once Fisher had rinsed out the bandana and rebandaged her wound. She knew the risk of infection she faced without proper medical attention. She'd have to hold on and pray they made it back to Little Rock before gangrene or sepsis set in. Isabella picked up her blouse and gently slid her left arm into the sleeve and pulled the shirt over the top of her tactical vest. She held her left arm close to her chest with her hand resting just under her chin.

They continued downstream until reaching a road that crossed over the creek. "Any idea where we are?" Isabella asked as they climbed the bank.

"Let's look for road signs or landmarks."

Fisher chewed on her bottom lip as she placed her compass on the topographical map. "I think we're here." She pointed to a road running east away from Highway 60 to the east of Ellsinore.

Isabella studied the map. They were on foot, she was injured and they were maybe two hundred miles from Little Rock. She ran her right index finger over the map south along Highway 60. She stopped at the town of Pollard, Arkansas. "How far are we from Pollard?"

Fisher stowed the map and compass back into her pack and exhaled slowly. "Fifty miles."

~

They quickly discovered they would be unable to follow the highway. Thirty minutes into their trek, Isabella heard a vehicle approaching and they were forced to hop the guardrail and hide from a convoy of black painted military-style vehicles. "MRAPs?" Isabella asked.

"I counted five."

They waited there until the sound of the engines faded before climbing back over the guardrail and continuing south on Highway 60 heading toward the city of Poplar Bluff.

"We'll stay under there." Fisher pointed to a bridge on Highway 60 next to a gas station called The Wood Shed. She redialed Colonel Sharp, took a deep breath and, this time, delivered a proper SALUTE report, albeit still lacking her battle-hardened, tough-ass demeanor, just before her satphone died.

TWENTY-SEVEN

Stephens

Henson Farm
Texas County, Missouri
July 14th
Event + Ten Months

The wagon stopped at a checkpoint where the two guards made Stephens, Hogan, and Collins dismount their horses and then checked their weapons. After passing through another manned gate, the wagon stopped by a small barn. Stephens was impressed. This group seemed to be managing quite well. They had proper security, a seemingly working farm, and a group of knowledgeable people. A woman and girl emerged from the barn to greet them. The girl looked to be around eleven or twelve years old. She was a little thin, but not overly so. It struck Stephens how they now judged people based upon their weight. Thin and gaunt meant they were barely hanging on. A little thin, like these folks, meant they were doing better than most at surviving this awful time in American history.

"Is breakfast ready?" a tall man wearing a long black beard

asked, walking up behind the pair. "Hey, Lugnut. I'm glad you're back. Breakfast will be ready soon," the woman replied.

Maddie nodded toward the house. "Let's go in. We'll gather everyone, and you can tell us all what the government has been up to these last few months."

"Maddie!" a little red-haired girl squealed, running toward her. "You're back already?" When she spotted Stephens, her eyes widened, and she took two steps back, pushing rich auburn ringlets from her pale face.

"It's okay. They're with the government," Maddie told her. "They're here to help," she said with more than a hint of sarcasm.

～

Inside the house, there was a long oak table set just off the well-equipped kitchen. Another woman was at the stove, stirring something in a large cast iron pot.

Maddie pointed to the table. "Let's have a seat and hear your story."

Stephens repeated what she'd told Harding, Aims, and the others out on the road for everyone gathered to hear. There were many wide eyes and open mouths as she described what was taking place down in Texas.

"What are you not telling us?" Aims asked.

She was holding back information—that much was obvious. It was only natural that she'd only give them the information needed to enlist their cooperation in her plan to retrieve the gold. She'd need to up the stakes it appeared, so she told them about the Russian and Chinese invasions.

"It's important to stop their advance into the rest of the country. To do that, we need military equipment. To buy that equipment, we need that gold shipment. I don't have time to sit here and explain everything. I have to get that gold on the plane heading south

175

before the Brazilian government's ship leaves the Port of Houston."

"Just how are you planning on getting a shipment of gold all the way to Houston?" a bearded man wearing a shirt with a skull printed on it asked.

"I have a plane coming to meet me at the Fort Leonard Wood airport."

"You hear that, Lugnut? She has a plane."

"Just hear her out, Rank," Lugnut replied.

"What about General Dempsey? How do his forces figure into this?" Aims asked.

Stephens pursed her lips. "General Dempsey is not working with the federal government at this point. His forces are the ones that attacked my team and killed my men."

Rank turned to a third man with a long beard who was gripping a Marine Corps coffee mug in both hands. "What do you make of this, Ryan?"

Ryan lifted one shoulder. "Nothing surprises me these days." He studied Hogan and Collins before turning his attention to Stephens. "If it's all true, it looks like they might need some help."

Stephens smiled. They indeed needed help and from the looks of this group, they just might have the skills to pull it off.

"So, we have three days to get that shipment back?" Lugnut asked, turning the conversation back to the task at hand.

"If we have any hope of it reaching the Port of Houston in time," Stephens said.

"So, all you have to do is get the gold back from the outlaws who stole it, get it on the plane at Fort Leonard Wood, and somehow make it down to the Port of Houston? Simple," Lugnut said.

"Well, at least we have an idea where the Godwin boys are holed up," Dustin said.

Stephens pushed her chair out and stood, then rounded the table heading for the door. "Let's go, then."

"You're sure it was the Godwin boys?" Lugnut asked.

"Yeah. It's a pretty sure bet. The guy at the trade fair says Justin Godwin was flashing gold coins around Nelson's bar. Two and two adds up to those boys are the ones who took it," Dustin said.

"Let's round up some fresh horses and extra riders and see if we can't track down those Godwin boys," Lugnut said.

Stephens turned to Lugnut, who was already heading for the door. "We need to find this Justin kid."

"He'll be at his momma's place near Newburg," Lugnut said.

Ryan, Lugnut, and Rank led Stephens and her two men through the woods to the entrance of Carver Cave.

"Ryan, you guard the entrance. Rank and I are going in to confirm whether the gold is even in there."

A gunshot came from the cave. The three men dove for cover and waited a few minutes. Lugnut pulled a mason jar from his pack and stepped inside the mouth of the cave. He reared back and threw it as hard and far as he could. Rank buried his mouth and nose in the crook of his elbow and waited for the foul odor to fill the space.

"Oh my God!" a young male voice cried out. "What the hell, man."

A moment later, a kid of about fourteen years of age emerged from the cave, tears streaming down his cheeks and holding his nose.

"What? You don't like eggs?" Rank laughed while breathing through his shirt.

"How many more are inside?" Lugnut asked, grabbing the kid by his shirt collar.

"Nobody. Just me. The rest are all dead," the kid said.

Rank grabbed the boy's hand and twisted it behind his back. "What happened here?"

The boy looked up. "Some guys came in, guns blazing and shot everyone dead."

"Was it Nelson's crew?" Ryan asked.

The boy's head shot up. A look of fear faded from his eyes. "You're not with Nelson's crew?"

"No. I'll ask you again, who did this?" Rank gave the boy's arm a little shake.

"Jep will kill you if you hurt me," the kid whined.

"I ain't going to hurt you if you tell me the truth," Rank said.

"I'm telling you the truth."

"Was it Nelson?" Ryan asked.

"Yeah."

"Hogan, come secure our prisoner," Lugnut called out.

The three men went inside. When they emerged, they didn't look pleased.

"Is it gone?" Stephens yelled.

Lugnut turned his back to the mouth of the cave. "Yes. Locating it could take days. Nelson has dozens of men with an almost endless supply of ammunition."

"You backing out on helping me?" Stephens asked.

"No. We won't back out. We're Marines. I just wanted you to be clear about what we're going up against. With those odds, even if we get the gold, we may not make your deadline," Rank said.

"How long will it take to get to Nelson's place?" Stephens asked.

"I don't know. Maybe five or six hours. We can trot or canter on the dirt roads, but the gravel and blacktop will slow us down. The horses are already tired."

"What are you thinking?" Lugnut asked her.

"We're going to need more weapons, more ammo, and more men," she said, climbing into her saddle.

Rank and Lugnut looked at each other. "You're planning on

waiting for the plane to arrive and then go for the gold?" Rank asked. "What if the plane never comes?"

"We can't take them on with two shotgun shells and a few boxes of ammo. Didn't you say he had dozens of well-armed men?" Stephens asked.

"I agree. We should go to the fort and wait for our team," Hogan said.

"All right, then," Rank said, climbing into his saddle and turning his horse to face Stephens. "Let's go to the fort."

They had a plan. They'd go to Fort Leonard Wood and get reinforcements. Stephens wasn't ready to give up—not yet—not while there was still hope. They had another lead and she wasn't going to stop until she found the gold.

TWENTY-EIGHT

Will

Northeast Arkansas
July 14th
Event + Ten Months

Will had his orders. It was clear the enemy wasn't planning on taking Smith and the lieutenant very far from where they'd previously been held or they would have far more soldiers escorting them. It was now or never. Will's squad had to make their move before the pickup reached its destination. They may never get a better chance.

Will gave the order and Jason opened up on the rear vehicle with the M2 Browning Ma Deuce tearing apart the sedan. It skidded on the loose gravel, veered left, ran off the roadway and down a ravine. The pickup weaved back and forth kicking up a dust cloud and trying to avoid being hit by the rounds. As the driver veered to the left side of the gravel road, Jason fired at the front tire and the pickup flipped several times before stopping upside down in a ditch. Will and the squad raced toward the truck.

Dropping to his knees, Will reached inside the vehicle to check on the lieutenant. He looked at Jason and shook his head. Walker was on his knees on the other side of the pickup. "I've got a pulse." Smith had survived the crash. He was unconscious, so Will couldn't try to find out if he'd told the enemy anything about the mission at the moment.

After Brad Smith's and the lieutenant's bodies were loaded into the Humvee, they headed southeast across an open field and away from the scene.

Will pulled the satphone from his belt and called Colonel Sharp.

"Sir, we've got Smith and the lieutenant but Smith is unconscious and the LT is dead. We can't determine whether either of them talked."

"Roger that, Fontenot. Good work. Get your asses back to Little Rock, and call me back if Smith wakes up."

"Roger that, sir."

The dirt road eventually wound around until the squad emerged a few miles south of where the enemy had held the prisoners. Will chose to take Highway 62 back to Pollard. There he tried again to radio Isabella's squad without success. He decided to believe they had already made it to their rally point and met up with Team Lonestar. He had to do his best to think positively because he wanted to pull Smith out of the vehicle and pummel him.

Jason had climbed out of the turret and traded places with another soldier to babysit Smith on the way back. He kept prodding Smith with the barrel of his rifle trying to rouse him awake. The amount of blood seeping from the gash on the side of Smith's head worried Will. It could be that Smith might die before making it back to Little Rock.

"His pulse is pretty good," Walker said, letting the man's hand drop to his lap. Walker turned Smith's head from side to side studying his face. "He doesn't look like he was interrogated much."

Much? How much would it take? Maybe they didn't have to work him over very long before he sang.

"The lieutenant looks like he took a beating," Jason said, looking down at the dead officer lying on the floor of the vehicle. He didn't get all that from the crash. There's bruising under his left eye and his lip is swollen. That happened before the crash."

"Maybe they didn't know who or what Smith was. They might have somehow determined he was a nobody," Will said.

"Smith may have told them he was a private and didn't know anything," Jason said.

"Maybe."

Jason plugged his nose. "Some time or another, he shit his pants."

It was an unbearable smell in the enclosed space of the Humvee, and just one more reason why Will couldn't wait to reach the base and get rid of this guy.

Will studied Smith as they bounced over the pothole-filled roads back toward the post. They had to proceed as if Smith had talked and the enemy knew everything. Stephens and Team Lonestar needed to be informed. They'd need to take measures. They needed to get Smith back to Little Rock, find out where Isabella was, and somehow catch up with them. They still had a mission to complete. They would need all the help they could get to keep that gold out of the hands of the enemy, wouldn't they?

"They'll send us back out. I'm almost positive," Walker said.

"I'm not so sure." If Team Lonestar and 1st squad hadn't secured the gold by now, there was no way Will and his squad could do it and get it to Fort Leonard Wood in time to be flown the Houston by the deadline. "I guess it will depend on how things are going up there in Missouri."

∼

Will knew the moment they pulled up to the gate at Little Rock Military Base that something wasn't right. The guard stopped them and had everyone get out of the vehicle. Military Policemen and a civilian rushed from the guard shack to the gate and whisked Smith off toward the medical facility. Will and his squad were escorted to their barracks and told to sit tight.

"Has there been any word from the rest of our platoon?" Will asked. It was stupid. He knew the MPs either wouldn't know or wouldn't say even if they knew. He needed to know, desperately.

"You've been ordered to remain here."

Will stepped in front of the MP. The MP's right hand dropped to the pistol holstered on his hip. Will and his squad had been disarmed before they entered the barracks, but that fact didn't seem to make Will any less of a threat, it appeared. Who ordered us confined here?" Will asked, attempting to keep his tone non-threatening. It wouldn't help if he got himself arrested.

"Lieutenant Birch," the young MP said, squaring his shoulders. "You need to step back inside and stay put."

Birch? Lieutenant Birch was with the 504th Military Intelligence Brigade out of Fort Hood—the same unit that sent Troy and Pete, off to infiltrate the Region Five command and spy on General Dempsey.

Walker approached and placed his hand on Will's shoulder. "He's just concerned about the rest of our platoon," Walker said to the MP and pulled Will back a step or two.

The MP's facial features softened and his hand dropped to his side. He nodded an acknowledgment. "I hope you hear something soon."

Will turned and sat down on a cot. As the rest of the squad washed up and sprawled out on their bunks, Will paced, trying to figure out what was going on. His growing fear for Isabella was making him desperate for news. He had to risk it. He had to get out of there and find someone who would tell him what was happening with his wife.

TWENTY-NINE

Stephens

Fort Leonard Wood Army Base
   Fort Leonard Wood, Missouri
   July 15th
   Event + Ten Months

Getting to Fort Leonard Wood wasn't any easier than the rest of the mission. They'd once again come under fire and had to use valuable ammunition to defend themselves. Stephens was impressed with the professionalism of these Marines she'd somehow managed to hook up with. If anyone could get the job done, these men would find a way.

Once they reached the airfield at Fort Leonard Wood, soldiers stopped them two hundred yards from the plane.

Rank stood staring at the C-130 cargo plane with his mouth open. "It's all true. There really is a functioning military, and legitimate government officials running things."

"Where's the cargo, Stephens?" Colonel Sharp asked as he approached her. She gave Sharp the abbreviated version of what had happened and what they were needing in order to complete her mission. He immediately assembled a team and they were ready to head out.

Sharp turned back toward the Marines and smiled. "I was wondering what happened to ZZ Top."

Rank raised his eyebrows, and Ryan and Lugnut looked at each other not knowing what to make of the colonel's comment.

"They're Marines, Colonel," Stephens said. "They're some of the most competent guys I've ever worked with. And they're going to help us get that cargo."

"Is that right," Sharp said, looking them up and down. Your country will be grateful for your loyal service—even with impressive beards like those. You Marines ready for this?" Sharp asked.

Rank eyed Sharp's Ranger patch and smirked. "Ready? We're rough boys—"

"And we gotta get paid," Lugnut cut in.

"Not until you get your legs and tushes into those four Humvees and let's get 'er done—don't let me catch you sleeping inside your sleeping bags during this mission—stay alert, stay alive," Sharp said, turning toward his Humvee with a grin. "Consolidate your ammo on the way. Your vehicles are already loaded with food, water, and more ammunition. You'll have to deal with MREs—no TV dinners were available."

Let's get this show on the road," Stephens said, tiring of the ZZ Top song references.

"We were just waiting for the bus," Ryan said as they all turned to follow Sharp toward the Humvees.

The convoy slowed to a stop near Nelson's ranch and everyone exited their vehicles.

"We're assuming they have comms, right?" Sharp asked.

"Yeah. They have radios. Not long-range, but they can definitely communicate within the compound," Ryan said.

"And sentries? You sure they don't have lookout posts this far out?" Sharp asked.

"They may have lookouts in the farm on the right about mile from here. Leave them to Rank and me. Give us a twenty-minute lead. We'll clear the way," Lugnut said.

Sharp turned to the rest of the team. "Gear up. Just ammo. Nothing rattling. We need the element of surprise."

As everyone tightened up their gear, Rank and Lugnut took off toward the Nelson farm.

Thirty minutes later, Lugnut and Rank came running from down the drive chasing a box truck as it tore out of the driveway from the ranch.

"The gold is in that box truck," came through the radio. "Don't let it get away," Rank said.

Stephens and Sharp jumped into their Humvee and took off after it.

The Humvee driver stopped beside Lugnut and Rank. Stephens waved for them to get in. "Hurry. We need to catch that truck," she yelled.

Before Rank could get the door closed, Maddie appeared out of nowhere. "Scoot over," she growled as she climbed into his lap.

"What the hell is she doing here?" Stephens asked.

"They've got my brother," Maddie yelled, pounding on the driver's seat. "Catch them."

"When Nelson spotted us, he took off for the truck. He knew we were coming for him," Lugnut said as the driver stomped on the gas and they took chase after the Nelson. Two more Humvees had pulled in behind them.

"Bravo Team, you watch our six. Don't let any of his men catch up with us. Alpha Team, be ready. We don't know what all he had in there with him."

The box truck was a half mile ahead when it turned right into a subdivision and the convoy followed them. There was going to be a gun battle. There was no way Nelson was going to give up without a fight, and Sharp and Stephens were not leaving without their gold.

"Alpha Four, dismount and take the right side of the street. We'll go left," Colonel Sharp radioed.

"Gilbert, dismount the .50 cal. Brent, get over here. You're the gunner's assistant. You two take cover over there by that boulder and prepare to rock."

"Where are the guards?" Lugnut asked.

"Three guards took off around the beige house with the red door," Stephens said.

"Gilbert, cover us," Sharp said, disappearing around the boulder.

Gilbert and his battle buddy got up and ran ahead, crossed the street, and dropped into the tall grass next to the house on the east corner of the adjacent street. Sharp, Stephens, and Lugnut followed soon after.

Sharp smacked Gilbert on the back and Gilbert went to work firing at a house on the next street. Stephens couldn't see what or who they were shooting at.

Maddie slid in next to Stephens. "What are you doing here?"

The girl gave Stephens a dirty look. "Long story, but that asshole Nelson kidnapped my brother, Zach."

"He what?"

"Listen, I don't give a flying flip about your damn gold, lady. I'm here to get my brother back—alive."

"I don't understand," Stephens said. She was trying to make sense of it all. "Did they come to your farm?" Stephens asked but the thunderous noise of the .50 caliber weapon drowned out all other sounds.

"I caught shrapnel," Gilbert's battle buddy yelled.

"You bleeding?"

"I'm fine," Gilbert yelled as he charged the .50 cal. again and continued sending rounds down the block. It wasn't true—blood ran down the man's shirt, but he remained engaged in the battle.

Using a U-Haul truck parked at the curb for cover, Lugnut, Stephens, and Sharp slowly moved toward Gilbert. Stephens was returning fire. She felt a hand on her shoulder and jumped. Sharp pulled her back toward the front of the truck and stepped in front of her. He poked the rifle barrel through the jagged hole in the side window and sent three-round bursts of rifle fire at the advancing men.

Seconds later, Sharp's radio came to life. "Alpha One, Alpha Three is advancing on your position."

"Alpha Three, Alpha One is in heavy contact with six to eight shooters to the right front of the U-Haul truck. Gilbert's down," Sharp radioed.

As Alpha Three's team engaged the shooters to their right, Sharp pushed forward toward Stephens and Gilbert's position. The two men appeared ahead, throwing their hands in the air. "Whoa! Whoa there. You're with Zach, right?"

Maddie ran up to them and grabbed hold of one of the men's arms. She was asking about her brother when Sharp stepped between them.

"Which direction did Nelson and his men go?" Sharp asked.

The men pointed over their shoulders. "That way. There's a farm at the back of the subdivision," one yelled.

Everyone ran in that direction. The street ended at a tall steel gate. There was a wooden privacy fence surrounding the property. It appeared there might be explosives planted along it. They'd need to find another way in. Maddie and Rank went north along the fence while everyone else headed south.

After finally working their way around to the back of the property, Stephens stopped in her tracks. Nelson was running toward the shed at the back of the property. The back of the white box van protruded from the structure. If he made it to the vehicle, he could flee and disappear on the backroads and be out of the county before Stephens and her team could stop him.

The man was less than fifty feet from the van when Maddie appeared from around the corner of one of the outbuildings. She was running after the man. How had Maddie arrived there before them? Where was Rank?

Stephens cursed loudly as the man climbed into the van. He was seconds away from again taking off with her gold. Maddie raised a rifle and fired, and the man slumped forward in his seat. The van's horn sounded, and the vehicle lurched backward. Maddie scrambled to get out of the way. She took off running as fast as she could, diving over a stack of railroad ties as the vehicle plowed into the fuel drums and burst into flames. Rank appeared and ran over to rescue Maddie, pulling her to safety. Seconds later, Aims and Harding appeared with a teenage boy. How had all these people made it here before her? How did they even know where the gold had been taken? At the moment, the answers to those questions didn't much matter. All that mattered was getting that gold back to Fort Leonard Wood and on that plane to Houston.

"Who caused this mess?" Stephens joked as she approached Maddie. Looking down at her, she asked, "You okay, kid?"

"I'm good."

She didn't look good. She'd been shot. Blood covered her shirt.

"We have a doctor back on post. Follow us back and let him take a look at you," Stephens said.

Maddie looked to Rank. "You should go let them patch you up, kid," he said.

"We've lost a lot of good soldiers here today. We could use your help with security getting that shipment back to base and on that plane," Stephens said to Rank.

Rank scooped Maddie up into his arms and turned to face Stephens. "I can do that."

"I'll go with you and make sure the gold gets on the plane," Lugnut said. "We left our horses there at the airport, anyway."

They were too close to fail now. "Let's get that gold loaded then get you to Fort Leonard Wood and get you fixed up, Maddie," Stephens said.

"Alpha Two, move the truck over here and get this loaded up," Sharp called into his radio.

~

Forty-five minutes later, they were pulling through the front gate of Fort Leonard Wood. The soldiers wasted no time getting the gold loaded onto the plane while the pilots began their pre-flight checks.

Aims, Harding, and Stephens were huddled in the door of the hangar watching the flurry of activity when Aims drew a deep breath. "I'll be damned."

"What is it," Stephens said, raising her rifle, expecting another enemy attack.

"You got binos?" he asked.

She reached into her pack and handed a pair to Aims who pressed them to his face, and then lowered them slowly. He pointed. Rank pivoted to see what he'd been pointing at. "What is it?" Stephens asked.

"There's your spy."

"What? Who?"

Aims handed Stephens the binos. "The Latino female," he said.

Stephens gasped. Martinez! Brad "the Cad's" Martinez. If this was true, she'd infiltrated their intelligence team and Dempsey likely knew everything. Everything that Brad knew, anyway. And if she was right about Sharp, Dempsey knew absolutely every aspect of their mission immediately as it had all unfolded.

"You're sure?" Stephens asked. "You know for sure Martinez is one of Dempsey's spies?"

"Absolutely. I don't know what she's calling herself now, but that's Simone Perez."

"How can you be so sure? Maybe she just looks like someone..."

Aims cut her off. "We were lovers. I know every inch of her."

Colonel Sharp rode up on a golf cart. Stephens had to inform him—it may still be too late to complete the mission, depending on what Perez knew and what she had communicated to Dempsey. The damage may already be too great to recover from. She needed to tell Sharp now. Stephens pulled him aside as he dismounted his golf cart. When she had finished speaking to Sharp, Sharp approached Aims.

"Deputy Director Gerald Aims?"

"Former deputy director. I was relieved of duty," Aims replied.

"By whom?" Sharp asked.

"General Dempsey."

"By what authority?"

"By his order to have me murdered," Aims said.

"You know this for a fact?"

"FEMA Regional Director Reginald Harding, sir," Harding said, interrupting, and stretching out his hand. "Yes, Aims and I were both on Dempsey's kill list. We were forced to leave our posts and run for our lives."

"And you believe Dempsey has planted a spy within my unit?"

"I know he has, Colonel. Your Latino private over there is one of his top deputies. She's been working with him for over a decade. She's no soldier," Harding said.

The colonel's face paled and he reached for a radio attached to his belt. "I hope you're wrong, Harding. If you're right, our mission may be completely compromised." He turned toward the plane and pressed the mic, and radioed for Perez to be brought to him.

As Perez arrived under escort, rather than appearing surprised, the sultry spy dressed as a soldier smiled as if she still had the upper hand.

"How long have you been with this outfit?" Aims asked her.

"A while. A few months," Perez replied, placing a hand on her hip and cocking her head to one side. She looked him up and down.

"What's Dempsey up to?"

Perez threw her head back. "I wouldn't know. I'm enlisted down south with this unit."

Aims shoved his hands into his pockets. "You've been feeding him information about their missions." It wasn't a question.

Perez laughed.

Sharp's jaw clenched, his hands balled into fists. "I've heard enough. Harris, take her into custody. Make sure she gets nowhere near a phone or radio," Sharp said.

"See you around, Aims," Perez said as Harris grabbed her arm. She looked back over her shoulder as she was led away. Her cavalier attitude was foolish. Her looks wouldn't save her this time. She may have been able to charm Brad Smith and maybe even Colonel Sharp—Stephens wasn't sure, but she'd committed treason. President Latham wouldn't find that at all endearing. Treason was punishable by death—she had to know that, yet she wasn't the slightest bit concerned. Why?

With the gold loaded and everyone strapped in for the flight to Little Rock to refuel, and then on to Houston, Stephens was starting to relax. Against impossible odds, they'd accomplished the mission—so far—and they would meet their deadline, barring any additional unforeseen Perez-leveraged circumstance. The nation would be able to purchase the weapons and ammunition needed to continue the fight against the Russians on the west coast, and hopefully go after Dempsey. With Aims and Harding choosing to join them in making sure the gold made it to Houston, they'd provide great additional insight into Dempsey's operation. She imagined the chance to begin rebuilding the nation was what appealed to

Rank; why he had chosen to leave his friends—break up the band —and come along to deliver the gold to its final destination as well. The military could certainly use a man with his skills and knowledge. Aims and Harding looked deep in thought as they prepared to leave. Their knowledge would be invaluable to the new government. This could be the game changer the nation needed to get back on its feet.

THIRTY

Will

Little Rock Military Base
Little Rock, Arkansas
July 15th
Event + Ten Months

"Come on, McDougall. I know you've heard something. You can tell me. They're from my platoon. I know the parameters of the mission. I just need to know if Isabella's squad made it to the rally point. Can you at least give me that much?"

Private First Class Christy McDougall stared back at Will. She and Isabella were friends. It was a small base, the female soldiers all bunked together. She was aware that Will and Isabella were married. Technically, they shouldn't have been assigned to the same platoon, but Stephens had once again pulled some strings for them.

"We received word to expect Sharp's plane to land within the hour," McDougall said.

She backed away from the door and closed it in Will's face. She'd divulged all the classified information she was comfortable sharing. With the sensitivity of this mission, even giving out that much could get her a courts martial. Although the information hadn't given Will the answers he was seeking, he now knew where and when he might find some. He'd be there when the plane landed. He prayed that his wife was on it. All Will had to do now was evade the MPs and get close enough to the runway to see the plane when it landed.

~

All the activity appeared to be concentrated upon the east end of the runway where extremely large, wooden shipping crates made out of one-inch-thick oak planks sat on the tarmac. There was a flurry of activity as the crew prepared for the cargo plane to land. They wouldn't have long to recrate the gold and get it ready to be flown to the Port of Houston and loaded onto the Brazilian cargo ship.

Will observed for several minutes before moving closer so he'd have a better view when the plane landed. When he heard the plane's engines, Will's stomach flip-flopped. He was filled with nervous anticipation. In minutes, he could possibly see his wife walking down the ramp. Will couldn't bring himself to consider any other alternative. As he waited, he imagined their lives together, settling in at the compound in Williams Junction, establishing a home, and someday maybe even having children. Will smiled. Cayden would make a great big brother and Savanah was sure to spoil her new niece or nephew rotten. There had to come a day when bringing children into the world would seem more like a blessing again. They were all fighting hard to bring that day to fruition.

Will tensed as the plane came into view. His eyes followed the C-17 as its wheels touched down and eventually came to a stop at the end of the runway. Will's right leg bounced up and down as he crouched behind a parked vehicle waiting for the plane to taxi to the unloading area. Sweat poured down his face, and he wiped it away with his sleeve. A knot formed in his stomach as the plane began moving and eventually slowed to a stop to be unloaded. After an eternity, the rear cargo door slowly creaked open revealing two rows of Humvees.

As the loadmasters ran to the plane and began unloading the vehicles onto the tarmac, Will shifted positions trying to get a better view inside the plane. After several moments, the Humvees had all been unloaded, the K loader was moved to the ramp, and several pallets of small wooden crates were removed. When the K loader backed away, Will spotted Colonel Sharp and a man he didn't recognize approaching the ramp. Behind them were several soldiers from 3rd Platoon. The soldiers looked relaxed and relieved to be back on the ground. When Stephens appeared, Will stepped away from his concealed position. He wanted to somehow get her attention, but the pilot hadn't shut down the engines and there'd be no way she'd hear him over the noise.

Will craned his neck anxiously awaiting for the rest of the passengers to disembark the plane. He spotted Hogan and Collins from Team Lonestar but no one from Isabella's squad. Will's inside twisted. She had to be on that plane. If not, where the hell was she?

Stephens had gathered with three men Will didn't recognize and was walking toward the hangar. Will slipped out from behind the vehicle and ran toward them. Someone called for him to stop, but he ignored them and kept running.

"Stephens!" Will shouted. He was within fifty feet of her when he was tackled to the ground and his hands cuffed behind his back. Stephens saw the commotion and arrived just as two MPs pulled Will to his feet.

"Was Isabella with you? Did her squad make it to the rally point?" Will blurted.

The look on Stephens' face told Will all he needed to know. She hadn't made it. She wasn't on that plane. He hung his head.

It took some convincing and finally an order from Sharp for the MPs to release Will from their custody. As Sharp and 3rd Platoon prepared to re-board the C-17 and fly the gold the rest of the way to the Port of Houston, Stephens escorted Will back to his barracks and filled him, Jason, and Walker in on what she knew about Isabella, Fisher, and the rest of their squad.

"Their last transmission was from somewhere south of Ellsinore, Missouri. They're safe, but their satphone died when they were talking to Colonel Sharp."

"Where the hell is Ellsinore?" Will asked.

"Not far from the Arkansas border. They hadn't made it very far after separating from your squad. They also reported that the combination of heat and terrain had been taking a detrimental toll on the horses. They'd stopped for the night when the ambush took place. Isabella and Fisher appear to be the only survivors of the attack," Stephens said.

"How bad are her injuries?" Will asked.

"She's okay. She and Fisher had stopped the bleeding in her arm. Now, we know this because they have the squad's satphone— but it died during Sharp's last contact with them. That's all we know."

Will ran a hand over the top of his head. His wife had been shot and needed him, but he was stuck there two hundred miles away. He stood and grabbed his rucksack.

"Where are you going?" Stephens asked.

"I'm going to rescue my wife. It appears the Army is more concerned about getting the gold to Houston than going after two of its soldiers stranded behind enemy lines."

"Will, wait. You can't do this alone. Just wait a second," Stephens said.

Will spun on his heels to face her. "Every second we wait is a second longer she's out there alone without support or medical attention." He clenched his teeth. "You know what they'll do to them if they're caught."

Stephens reached out and touched his shoulder. "I'm not going to let you go it alone, Will. Just give me a few minutes. Okay? "Let me try to round up a team. We need to be able to slip in there, grab them, and get out before Region Five knows we're there." She squeezed his arm. "We'll be out there on our own. They won't be sending a rescue team in for us."

"That's screwed up," Jason said.

"With losing 1st and 2nd platoons, we're down to the bare minimum, and no one with the expertise to handle a mission like this is available anywhere near us. There's no one left to send."

"Who are you going to get to go with us, then?" Walker asked, sliding his arms through the straps of his own pack.

Will hadn't asked Walker and Jason to go. They all knew what it could mean. They'd been ordered to remain in their barracks. There were no orders to leave the base to rescue Isabella and Fisher. Will, Walker, and Jason would be declared absent without leave. Going AWOL these days was such a serious offense and they could face serious consequences when they returned—if they returned.

"Wait here for me. I'll make some arrangements and then send for you," Stephens said, backing out the door.

THIRTY-ONE

Stephens

Little Rock Military Base
Little Rock, Arkansas
July 15th
Event + Ten Months

Stephens found Rank, Aims, and Harding at the dining facility. Rank ran his hand down the length of his long black beard as Stephens explained what had happened with Team Razorback and Isabella's squad. She could see in the Marine's eyes that he understood the challenges of the mission.

"How many enemy troops did they report seeing?" Rank asked.

"Fisher said the force that hit them in the night looked to be an entire platoon, at least. Maybe even a company. They were completely overrun before anyone really knew they were under attack. They were wiped out in minutes. They didn't stand a chance."

Rank shook his head and pursed his lips. He glanced across the table to Aims and Harding. "That's going to be quite a shit storm you'll be driving into. You know that, don't you?" Rank said, turning his attention back to Stephens.

"I can't leave those women out there, Rank. Isabella's husband and two other men are going—I'm not going to be able to stop them."

"Well, shit fire, I just got here. I didn't even get to finish my strawberry shortcake." He spooned a scoop of it into his mouth, pushed his chair back and stood. "What do you say, Aims. Wanna go put some butt hurt on Dempsey's army—again?"

Aims lifted one shoulder and let it fall. "Why not? I'm free at the moment." Aims looked to Harding who sat stoically with his hands folded in his lap. "I know you need to go to Austin and enter your report on Dempsey. I guess I'll see you down there some-time." Aims pushed his chair away from the table and stood.

"Be careful out there, my friends," Harding said, standing and extending his right hand to Aims.

Stephens felt encouraged. Rank and Harding were a start. Six people were better than four.

"Who else you got going?" Rank asked as they walked toward the door.

"So far, myself, the two of you, the husband, and two from his squad," Stephens replied.

"That's going to be tough." Rank stopped outside the door. "How far is Poplar Bluff from Fort Leonard Wood?"

Aims scratched his head. "Two, maybe two and a half hours, I'd say. What are you thinking?"

"You know what I'm thinking. I say we find ourselves a radio."

While Stephens went to procure the vehicles, weapons, and ammunition they would need, Rank and Aims went to make a call to their friends back in Missouri. Stephens had no doubt that Lugnut, Ryan, and others from Rank's old group were loyal friends, but would they be willing to walk into another hornets' nest for more complete strangers? Their odds of success and making it out alive would sure be greatly improved if Rank's battle-hardened friends joined them. Perhaps they would have an interest in learning about the enemy army operating in their backyard. Dempsey's army would no doubt present a problem to the Evening Shade group sooner or later. Stephens thought she'd rather know sooner if it were her group.

Back at the barracks, Stephens found Will, Jason, and Walker going through their gear preparing for the mission. She handed Will a map. "I found a few more people to go with us, and I've got two Humvees waiting for us at the back gate. We don't have as much ammunition as I would have liked though. It seems you guys used up a shit ton out there already."

Will unfolded it and ran his finger up Highway 167 and Highway 67 north all the way to where she'd drawn the circle on the map. "Ellsinore," Will said. "Do they have a radio--can we reach them by radio and let them know we're coming?"

"Not unless you want Dempsey's men crawling up their asses," Rank said, appearing around the corner of the building. "They'll be monitoring all radio transmissions. If they learn there were survivors from that ambush, they'll scour that area until they find them. We have to go in quietly."

"And we don't know if they even have a radio," Stephens said. "Will, this is Rank. He has years of combat experience as a Marine serving in Iraq and Afghanistan prior to the EMP," Stephens said.

Will looked Rank up and down before giving the big man a nod. "Thanks for your help."

"This is Aims. He's very familiar with Dempsey and his tactics. He served with him back in Illinois."

"I'm sorry to be meeting under such circumstances," Aims said, stepping forward and extending his hand to Will. "We're going to do everything we can to help you get your wife and the other soldier back."

Will shook his hand. "I appreciate that."

"Are we ready then?" Walker said, exiting the barracks followed by Jason.

Stephens turned to Rank. "Are we ready?"

Rank nodded. "Lugnut and the guys will meet us there."

Stephens surpassed a smile. Their odds of success just went up. From what she'd seen of that group, they might just pull this one off as well. As they loaded into the Humvees, Stephens asked Rank how he'd been able to reach his friends so quickly. It wasn't like one could just pick up the phone and call someone these days.

"You remember Quincy, Nelson's Ham operator?" Rank asked.

Stephens didn't, she'd been too concerned about the gold and getting it safely back to Fort Leonard Wood to pay attention to who was who in Nelson's crew.

"Some of our group hung back at Nelson's ranch. I had your comms guys radio Quincy and he got a message to Lug and the group. They sent word back that they'd met us there. They'll come locked and loaded with plenty of Nelson's weapons and ammo."

"We can sure use the help—and the ammo," Stephens said. "Did they have any intel on Dempsey's army operating down in that area?"

"They didn't know a thing about them, just about Nelson's crew operating in the area. I'm sure Lugnut will be anxious to find out, though. That many traitorous bastards roaming the backroads is something they'll have to deal with. Best to take care of it before it reaches the home range."

"So, you've dealt with these guys before?" Will asked.

Rank chewed on his bottom lip. Stephens sensed a hesitation to discuss it. It could be that he didn't know Will enough to trust him yet. She'd informed him that Will and Jason hadn't been military prior to the EMP and that Walker had been in law enforcement.

"We've gone a round or two with their comrades," Rank said.

He stared down at his boots. As everyone grew quiet, Rank appeared lost in thought. She'd learned about his history with Dempsey's goons in St. Louis. Lugnut had given her the abbreviated version during one of their stops on the way to Fort Leonard Wood. He'd said it had changed Rank—made him more distant. Being captured and tortured would do that she imagined.

THIRTY-TWO

Will

Southeastern Missouri
July 16th
Event + Ten Months

Just south of Walnut Ridge, Walker turned their Humvee north heading back the way they had gone before days earlier. Will nervously twisted his gold wedding band around and around his finger and stared out the side window as time slowly ticked by. Walker was pushing the Humvee hard down Highway 67 toward the Missouri border. The second Humvee carrying Stephens and the two men she'd picked up in Missouri followed them. Aims was driving, with Rank wearing goggles in the turret manning the .50 cal, his long black beard hanging on for dear life, flapping in the wind.

There hadn't been time for Will to find out the details from Stephens about what had happened in Missouri, or how they'd lost their platoon, yet still retrieved the gold. The fact that she'd brought civilians back with her and the gold gave him an idea.

She'd somehow managed to assemble a team of locals to assist her. It appeared that among the few survivors there were in the world, Stephens had happened to come upon people with the skills needed to accomplish her impossible mission. The mission that had cost two platoons their lives and stranded his injured wife and her battle buddy behind enemy lines. The folks who had helped Stephens must be a bunch of bad asses to have pulled this one off. The strong survive, Will thought. His wife was strong—she'd survive this, he told himself.

Will had resented how happy the crew had been as they exited the plane after landing in Little Rock with the gold. He'd lost so many, and even though they'd secured the gold that would purchase the equipment and ammunition the country needed to stay in the fight, it had come at such a high price.

As they approached the bridge spanning the Black River in the town of Pocahontas, Arkansas, Walker slowed the vehicle to a stop.

"See anything?" Walker called to Jason, who was sitting in the turret manning the .50 cal.

"The bridge is clear from what I can see. Hand me the binos."

Will grabbed a pair of binoculars from his pack and handed them up to Jason.

"The cables are still there and the Humvee is in the left-hand lane where we left it."

Will leaned forward and strained to see for himself. The scene looked the same as they'd left it.

"Is it safe to proceed?" Walker asked.

"I say go for it," Jason said.

"What's the hold up?" Stephens called over the radio.

Will briefed her on the encounter on the bridge with their recon team. "Just making sure the bridge is clear now," he answered.

"Copy that," Stephens replied.

The Humvees crossed the bridge at speed and weaved through

the town before turning north onto Highway 115 toward Maynard and the Missouri border. They were fifty-five miles from Poplar Bluff. In one hour, Will could be holding his wife in his arms. He didn't know what their future held after that, and at the moment, he didn't care. He just wanted to get to her before Region Five's army did and get her back to Texarkana, far away from the front lines. He'd worry about his courts martial for going AWOL when they returned to base.

Not long after crossing the border, as they approached the town of Doniphan, Stephens instructed them to stop at a small convenience and bait store on their right. A Humvee sat in the parking lot facing the road. Walker pulled in next to it and the doors opened. A large man wearing a long beard stepped out, followed by three other men dressed in tactical gear.

The Humvee carrying Stephens stopped next to Will's vehicle, and everyone got out except Jason pulling security in the turret. Following fist bumps and man hugs, the group began discussing the rescue mission. Will and Walker stood by, listening in silence as the obviously more experienced men plotted their approach to the gas station where Isabella and Specialist Fisher were supposed to be holed up under the bridge.

"Twenty-five miles is too far to hump it in this heat carrying an injured girl. We need to risk it and get closer, Lugnut," Rank said.

"You said they called in that they were overrun by at least fifty enemy. That's a shit ton of combatants to evade. You know as well as I do, without being able to do proper recon on their position, we're flying blind. Those bastards can pop out of nowhere," Lugnut said.

Will was with Rank on this one, solely because he wanted to hurry and get to Isabella. She needed medical attention and they didn't know how much blood she'd lost.

"I don't think we have time, but we'll wait here if you and Ryan want to drive up there and check it out," Rank said sarcastically.

Will didn't know these guys' history with one another but he sure hoped they knew what they were doing and worked it all out in a way that saved Isabella and Fisher. That was what the men had come to do. They'd driven there from their homes to risk their lives for two strangers. That, alone, spoke volumes about their characters. They were part of Rank's group, and Stephens trusted them. Will had no choice but to trust them as well. He had to—Isabella's life depended on them now.

Lugnut and Ryan studied the map laid out on the hood of their Humvee, while the others listened.

"After we pass through this town coming up and then turn onto Route 21, the road looks pretty straight. We may be able to spot anyone coming at us. We could leave the vehicles there at the junction with Routes K and B. That's like five miles. That's doable—even for you." Ryan smiled showing a mouth full of bright white teeth. He was shorter than Lugnut and Rank but the three bearded men carried themselves with the same bold confidence.

Lugnut looked up from the map and flipped Ryan the bird. "Okay. Dustin, Jaxon, let's load up." The two men turned and sprinted back to their Humvee.

"How are you doing, Will?" Stephens stopped and asked on her way to her vehicle.

"I'm okay, I'm just anxious to get to her," Will said.

Stephens touched his arm. "I know. These guys know what they're doing. I trust them—you can trust them. We'll get her and be back at base in no time."

As she turned to go, Will grabbed her hand. "Thank you for this—for everything." Will knew that she'd stuck her neck out for them—again. She had called in favors or maybe even threatened someone to make this happen. He wasn't sure what it would cost her, but he appreciated her friendship immensely. It was such a strange world he'd entered since he'd encounter the CIA analyst back in Houston. They'd formed a bond through all they'd experienced together. He wasn't sure what would have become of them if they hadn't met her and Sharp.

"We're all in this together, Will," Stephens said, placing her hand on top of his. "Together, we have to get the country back on its feet. I'm glad there are still people like you and Isabella in the world. It gives me hope."

Will nodded toward the Humvee carrying Lugnut and his band. "People like that give me hope."

Stephens smiled. "Me too!"

After camouflaging the Humvees in the woods behind an old barn near the junction of Routes K and B, the group marched east in two columns, one on each side of the road, toward Highway 60. Will expected to encounter Region Five forces over every rise and around every bend in the road. He listened intently for the sound of engines. He scanned the fields and woods near the road looking for scouts or combatants, but he saw nothing.

No one spoke as they walked at a brisk pace. The two young guys, Dustin and Jaxon were on point and were several paces ahead. Stephens followed behind Lugnut and Ryan on the opposite side of the road from Will, Jason, Walker, and Rank. Everyone carried their rifles ready to engage the enemy.

Will noticed Ryan had a slight limp. He rubbed his own leg where he'd been injured. It had taken months to heal and still gave him problems. Nearly everyone he knew carried their own battle scars, both mentally and physically. His heart ached for his wife. He couldn't stand the thought of her in pain. He pushed himself and picked up his pace, ignoring his pain.

When they approached Highway 60, Lugnut ordered everyone to take a knee while Dustin and Jaxon ran ahead. Long moments passed while they waited hidden in the tall grass under the hot sun. Will started to take a sip of water from his canteen and then shook it. He'd save it for Isabella. She was likely out and needed it more than he. He made a mental inventory of the medical supplies he'd been able to gather for her. There was no morphine or any strong painkillers, but they could cleanse the wound and dress it for transport. The doctors back at Texarkana could do the rest. He thanked God for the two doctors and three nurse practitioners. Without them, a lot more people would have died over these last months.

Dustin and Jaxon returned. The taller of the two gave a thumbs up and the group all stood and proceeding toward the intersection of Route B and Highway 60. Will noticed how rundown the house on the corner had become. How quickly nature had reclaimed the space. The roof was barely visible behind the overgrown bushes and weeds growing in the yard.

The group crossed over to the northbound lane and proceeded south toward the convenience store. Rank was in the rear of Will's column walking backward at times watching their six. The road was straight and flat along this stretch of the highway giving them nearly a half mile of clear visibility. Will noted how quietly the group moved. They were much quieter than when his platoon did a road march. Nothing clattered or clinked as they walked. He could barely hear their footfalls on the pavement.

Will continued to listen for anything that might indicate the presence of enemy forces. Not that he was a pessimist, but the fact that they'd not had any sighting of the enemy made him suspicious. Were they waiting for them at the store? Were they holding Isabella and Fisher waiting for their rescuers to come for them, only to be ambushed—again?

The stretch along Highway 60 to the store was the longest mile-and-a-half Will had ever walked. When the sign for the store finally came into view, Will wanted to run toward it, but Lugnut stopped and gestured for everyone to take a knee. Dustin and Jaxon dropped back and the three had a hushed conversation. Will strained to hear what was being said even though he knew Lugnut was telling them how he wanted them to scout out the area around the store. The waiting was unbearable. They were so close. Will's stomach roiled, threatening to evacuate its contents. His chest tightened as all sorts of negative scenarios ran through his brain.

When the two men returned with smiles spread across their faces, a shot of adrenaline jolted through Will's body. It was as if every cell had awakened. He jumped to his feet ready to race to the bridge on the other side of the parking lot to get his bride.

Rank grabbed him by the pack and held him back. "We need to move in quietly."

Will nodded his agreement even though his insides disagreed immensely.

The group left the highway near a cell phone tower and metal building and entered the north side of the convenience store's parking lot. "Wait here," Rank said, and he and Lugnut disappeared behind the store. After a search of the inside of the store and every car in the parking lot, Lugnut sent Dustin and Jaxon to check the store for Isabella and Fisher.

"They'll find them," Walker said as he and Will leaned against the fender of a fairly new Ford F-150.

"They should be there. Sharp told them to stay put. Fisher said they would stay there at the store," Will said.

Jason had cupped his hands around his eyes and was staring inside the cab of the truck. Dustin appeared from the other side of the parking lot by the bridge and ran over to Lugnut. Will saw Dustin shaking his head.

They aren't there. Will's legs nearly buckled. He grabbed the mirror to steady himself.

Lugnut pointed at the auto repair shop on the other side of the creek and Dustin took off toward the building. Jaxon popped up near the bridge and ran to help Dustin clear the last building.

Long minutes crept by in the summer heat. Sweat poured down Will's face.

Dustin was suddenly crouching behind Will. He put his hand on Will's shoulder. Will turned to look at him and Dustin looked

Will in the eyes. "They're across the creek at the auto repair shop." "They're both good to go."

Will turned and ran across the parking lot toward the repair shop. He could hear Walker and Jason behind him. Dustin passed him and ran ahead. "Watch yourself when you cross the creek. Those stones are slippery."

THIRTY-THREE

Isabella

Wilson's Auto Repair
    Poplar Bluff, Missouri
    July 16th
    Event + Ten Months

When Fisher had shaken her awake to inform her that people were coming, Isabella's first thought was to run. They'd expected Region Five soldiers to catch up with them at any moment. They hadn't moved far from where they'd made the call to Colonel Sharp for extraction. If the enemy could somehow monitor the calls, they would have known right where they were, so Fisher had decided to move to the repair shop building.

Fisher shoved a rifle into Isabella's hands and went to look out the front window.

"Fontenot—two guys in tactical gear outside the building— hide and get ready to fire at them if they aren't our rescue party!" Fisher said.

Isabella scrambled behind a large crate and took up a supported position placing the barrel of her rifle on top of it. The door eased open. Fisher yelled, "Freeze! Who are you?" when the first man came through the door. The man ducked back just as Fisher fired.

"Are you Fontenot and Fisher?" the man yelled through to open door.

"Fisher—it's us—don't shoot!" Stephens yelled.

When Stephens poked her head around the door, Isabella thought she was dreaming. It was unreal. Help had finally arrived. She was safe. Isabella burst into tears, unable to contain all the emotion.

"It's okay. You're safe. We're going to get you back to base and get that arm taken care of now," Stephens said, coming inside. She dropped down beside Isabella and began pulling her medical kit from her pack. Isabella was speechless—a first for her. She was still trying to wrap her head around how it was that Stephens was there to rescue them.

"The gold?" Isabella managed to croak out between sobs.

"We got it. It's on its way to Houston now."

Isabella's eyes lit up. They'd done it. They'd somehow managed to accomplish their mission. She broke down again at the thought of what it meant for the nation—for their future.

A man Isabella didn't recognize suddenly ran up behind Stephens and Isabella stiffened and reached for her rifle.

"It's okay. He's with me," Stephens said, moving the rifle out of Isabella's reach. "Dustin, go tell the others we found them." The man disappeared and Stephens continued pulling things from her pack to attend to Isabella's wound.

"It was awful, Stephens. Enemy soldiers were everywhere. The squad was dropping like flies around us. The squad leader gave the call to un-ass the AO and then all hell broke loose. We hit the woods and didn't stop until we were too exhausted to go any farther. I don't know how the hell we made it here, honestly. It's a blur."

"You had to have been in a lot of pain."

The pain was the least of it. The fear of being caught was debilitating.

"Isabella!"

Isabella straightened. "Will?" She looked up at Stephens and broke into tears. Her right hand flew up to cover her mouth. "Will's here?"

Stephens smiled and nodded as she stood and stepped back.

Will dropped down, threw his arms around her, and held her so tight she could barely breathe, but she didn't care. She didn't care that he was crushing her injured arm. She was so grateful to be alive and be in the arms of the man she loved and adored. Isabella had nearly given up out there and resigned herself to the fact that she'd never see Will again. To be in his arms now was beyond fantastic—it was a miracle.

Will finally released her and allowed Stephens to continue to dress Isabella's wounds. He held her right hand as Stephens placed Isabella's left arm in a sling and helped her to her feet.

A man rushed over. "We have to go, Stephens. Can she travel?"

"What is it, Rank?" Stephens asked without answering him.

"We've got vehicles moving toward us from the south," Rank said.

"Oh shit!" Stephens scooped up Isabella's rifle from the ground as Will helped Isabella to her feet.

"Where's Lugnut and the others?" Stephens asked.

"They're going to buy us some time."

Walker appeared from nowhere, pushed Will aside, grabbed Isabella around the waist, and threw her uninjured arm around his neck. The sling around her left arm pulled on Isabella's neck as they moved quickly toward the highway. As they left the building, Isabella noticed Will wince as he walked. His leg was hurting again. Between both of their injuries, they would have slowed everyone down. Isabella admired the old Texas Ranger even more. She tried to move faster and not put too much of her weight on him. She had no idea how far they had to travel. Will followed them with his weapon slung, the toe of the buttstock in his shoulder with the muzzle pointed, ready for enemy contact.

"Rank said they saw a convoy of five vehicles moving quickly north," Walker said.

"They know where we are," Isabella said. "They were waiting just like I feared they would be."

"They're in for a big surprise," Stephens said.

"They won't be expecting it, that's for sure," the unfamiliar voice replied.

"Fisher?" Isabella called over her shoulder.

"She's not here at the moment," Stephens said.

"Where is she?" Surely they hadn't left her battle buddy behind.

"She's with a couple of Marines setting up a little surprise for the enemy," Jason said from behind them.

"Marines?" There weren't any Marines on this mission. In fact, she didn't know of any stationed at Little Rock.

"Don't worry. She's going to meet up with us back at our vehicles," Jason said.

Rank rushed past and across the north and south-bound lanes of the divided highway and disappeared into the woods on the other side. He reappeared and waved them over. Isabella kept her eyes peeled on the road to their south expecting the enemy to crest the hill at any moment. They entered the woods near a fence line and then veered north. Brambles tore at her pant legs and ripped at her skin as they pushed on deeper into the forest.

"Will, head to that big cedar tree," Rank said, pointing. "Jason, on me."

Jason ran up beside him and followed Rank down into a dry creek bed. Walker led Isabella forward toward Will. She looked back to see where Stephens and the other man were, but they were no longer back there.

Walker cursed and laid Isabella on the ground. "Stay down, Isabella."

Gunfire echoed through the valley and Walker dropped to his stomach. Isabella tried her best to crawl back toward a tree stump. Walker ordered her again to stay down as he placed the barrel of his rifle on top of a small rock.

"What's happening, Walker?"

Walker didn't answer. He pressed his eye to his scope and scanned from left to right. "Shit!"

"Walker, what's happening?"

"We have to go, Isabella. I can't carry you. You'll have to walk on your own."

"I can walk. It's my arm that's shot," Isabella said. "Where is Will?" she asked—she had lost sight of him.

The thunderous sound of automatic gunfire rang out. Isabella heard Rank shouting orders to Will and Jason. She crawled over to Walker, who helped her to her feet and pointed her north toward the wet weather creek bed. "We need to go."

"I'm not leaving Will and the others behind," Isabella said. There was little she could do to help her husband and friends, but she wasn't about to abandon them.

"Here." Walker handed her a pair of binoculars. "Be my spotter."

As she peered through the binos, Isabella's stomach lurched. It was like a repeat of the night her squad had been overrun. The forest floor was crawling with Region Five soldiers. They were behind almost every tree and boulder. How the hell were they going to get out of this shitstorm?

Rank ran over to where Stephens was positioned behind a large tree trunk. He pointed back toward Isabella and Walker then opened up on the two enemy soldiers as Stephens crouched and ran toward a rock jutting out of the ground. Isabella scanned to the left of Rank and spotted Will. He had taken a knee and was firing into what appeared to be a pile of brush. Isabella scanned back to the right of Rank. Jason was pinned down taking heavy fire from four combatants. Every time he moved an inch, rounds kicked up soil to the right and left of him.

"Jason needs help," Isabella said. "He's ten yards to the right of that large boulder. There are shooters near that group of cedar trees thirty yards in front of him. See them?"

He peered through his scope. "Got them." He fired and one enemy soldier fell to the ground. Walker continued firing and picking them off until they realized where the rounds were coming from and began returning fire. Walker shoved Isabella to the ground as round after round flew overhead. He clutched his rifle to his chest and they crawled from the rocks to a thicket of brambles. Walker continued moving west until they could once again see Jason and the others. Stephens was halfway down the hill, followed by Aims. Will had moved to the rock Stephens had vacated.

Isabella raised the binoculars and searched for Rank who was at the top of the hill and more and more soldiers were advancing toward them. Will and Jason were pinned down. There was no way for them to move without being fired upon. She had to do something. They were running out of time. They were going to be overrun at any moment.

THIRTY-FOUR

Will

Poplar Bluff, Missouri
July 16th
Event + Ten Months

Region Five soldiers were descending the hill like ants. They were everywhere. He couldn't move in any direction. He tried to make himself small behind the rock he was using for cover. Every few seconds he'd glance over to see if Jason was still okay. He was in the same situation. Will prayed Walker was getting Isabella the hell away from there and back to their vehicles. He had no idea where Lugnut and the others with him had gone but he doubted there was anything they could do for them now. It would take a miracle for him and Jason to make it out of this one.

Will heard more gunfire from behind him and the next thing he saw was a Region Five soldier tumbling down the hill past him. He leaned and looked toward the enemy soldiers who had been advancing on Jason's position. Two more soldiers were on the ground. Jason rose slightly, and seeing the same thing, he opened fire on the remaining soldiers.

Crawling to his left, Will peered around the rock. "I'll be damned."

Lugnut, Dustin, Jaxon, Fisher, and Ryan were standing on top of the cliff overlooking them and firing down upon the enemy at an angle to miss him and Jason. They were picking the enemy off with precision like they were shooting fish in a barrel. Will rose to a crouch and searched for his own target. Spotting a combatant attempting to reach the cover of a brush pile, Will aimed, squeezed the trigger, and watched him drop face first in the dirt.

"Will," Rank called behind him. "Let's go."

Will ran in a crouch to the cover of an old oak tree and pressed his shoulder against it. He fired at the nearest enemy soldier and moved downhill toward Stephens, Rank, and Aims.

Rank was picking off the enemy that had Jason pinned down as Jason ran downhill toward Will. When Will and Jason finally reached Stephens and Aims, Rank pointed toward the wet weather creek. "Get your wife back to the vehicles and get the hell out of here."

"We can't leave you guys," Stephens said.

"We'll see you back in Little Rock after we take care of these asshats," Rank said.

"But, Rank," Stephens stammered.

"Aims, get her back to the Humvee," Rank said, ignoring Stephens' pleas.

Will, Jason, Stephens, and Aims caught up with Walker and Isabella where the dry creek bed passed by a field. They stopped at the edge of the clearing. "How much farther is it?" Isabella asked. Perspiration poured down her face, dripping down her brow and stinging her eyes. She wiped it with the back of her hand but all that did was smear it around her face.

Walker pulled his handkerchief from his back pocket and handed it to her. "About two more miles," he said.

"Do you think you can make it?" Stephens asked her.

Isabella puffed out her cheeks and exhaled. "I can make it."

"Maybe we should carry her," Jason said.

"I said I can make it."

"You sure?" Jason asked.

She nodded, but Will wasn't at all sure she could. Her face was flushed and it was becoming increasingly harder for her to lift her feet up to avoid tripping on rocks, fallen tree branches, and brambles. As the sound of the gunfire faded behind them, Will felt less pressure to move quickly. Slowing down would make it easier on all of them.

Will grabbed Isabella's right hand and placed it around his neck. He slid his arm around her waist and pulled her close to his side. He wiped a stray strand of hair from her forehead and kissed the top of her head. "Ready?" he asked. Isabella nodded, and they began moving again.

It took them over an hour to walk the several miles back to their vehicles. Will could no longer hear the gunfire. That concerned him. It could mean the enemy was on the way and could catch up with them at any moment. When he spotted a bright red gothic arched barn in the distance. Will finally recognized where he was and he picked up his pace.

"Not much farther," he whispered to Isabella. "We're almost there."

She looked up and attempted a smile but it looked more like a grimace. He knew he was pushing her too hard, but they were so close to making it now. They had to stay ahead of the enemy.

Jason was the first to spot the vehicles. Will came into the clearing behind the barn and exhaled a sigh of relief. They'd made it. They'd somehow survived and made their way back to the Humvees. In three hours they'd be back to the safety of the base at Little Rock and Isabella would be able to get proper medical care for her wounds. Will imagined them relaxing with Cayden, Savanah, and the kids back at the shelter in Texarkana as Isabella healed…if he weren't in jail for going AWOL.

Stephens seemed to find a new burst of energy and stepped ahead of Will and Isabella. She threw a hand in the air as if she were greeting someone. "Hey there. Glad to see you made it."

"Who is she talking to?" Will asked.

Will and Isabella rounded the back of the barn and Will stopped in his tracks. Rank, Lugnut, Ryan, Dustin, and Jaxon were leaning against their Humvee. Fisher was seated in the driver's seat.

"How?" he asked.

"Let's just get loaded up and back to base. We can tell war stories around the table in the chow hall tonight," Rank said.

Will held his hand out to Lugnut. "I can't thank you enough for what you've done."

"It's what we do. Besides, I couldn't let my brother here get himself in trouble," Lugnut said, wrapping a massive bicep around Rank's head. Rank shoved him away and then gave him a fist bump. "Thanks, brother," Rank said.

Lugnut, Ryan, Dustin, and Jaxon did some more fist bumping, high-fiving with the others as Stephens approached them. "I need to get back and brief the President about Region Five's increased activity in this area. It's far more extensive than we'd known," she said.

"I'd be interested in any intel you could provide us. I don't like having them playing in our backyards without us knowing. It's unsettling," Lugnut said.

Stephens gave Rank a questioning look. "Maybe they should ride back with us," he said.

"I'm not sure General Waltrip will appreciate that, especially since I involved them in our unsanctioned mission."

"They're your best source of intel on what Dempsey is doing in

Missouri." He dropped his rucksack to the ground. "You want to know what they're up to before they reach Little Rock?"

Stephen pursed her lips and turned to Lugnut. "You got a couple of hours to spare?"

Rank held open the door for Stephens. She kissed him on the cheek as she bent to climb into the Humvee. Will sensed something more than friendship between them. He was happy for her. It was tough to be alone in times like these. He couldn't even imagine how lonely he would be without Isabella. He squeezed her tight and led her toward their Humvee. Aims opened the rear door and held his hand out to Isabella. "Thank you so much for coming to rescue me," she said as she lowered herself onto the seat.

"My pleasure," Aims said.

Will ran around and climbed in on the opposite side as Walker got behind the wheel. Specialist Fisher was sitting in the turret. She leaned down inside and fist bumped Isabella. "I told you they'd come, Fontenot."

Walker started the engine and pulled back onto the roadway.

"I love you, Fisher," Isabella shouted above the engine noise.

"I love you, too, Fontenot."

THIRTY-FIVE

Stephens

Little Rock Military Base
Little Rock, Arkansas
July 30th
Event + Ten Months

Two weeks had passed since the mission to secure the gold was completed, and much had occurred during that time. They'd rescued Isabella and Specialist Fisher. After nearly daily meetings between herself, Lugnut, Rank, Aims, and General Waltrip, she had briefed the president and his cabinet about the build-up of Region Five forces in Missouri. General Waltrip had sent a recovery company to northeastern Arkansas and Missouri to locate and bring back their fallen soldiers. Part of the recovery company's mission was to track and report on Region Five activities in the area and establish a secure forward area of operations. The US Army was finally focusing on Dempsey and his army. And all of the non-commissioned officers in Sharp's unit had been issued satellite phones, a sign of the times that indicated to every one that civilization and order in the country seemed to be on the upturn toward a new state of normal.

Despite General Waltrip's displeasure with her involvement in the unauthorized mission to rescue Isabella and Fisher, Stephens was allowed to be on the task force charged with planning their forward push against Dempsey and his army. As soon as the weapons and equipment arrived from Brazil, they would enact a massive offensive to liberate Region Five from his control, and free up enough resources to care for survivors and get the nation back on its feet.

Stephens pulled open the door to the dining facility and came face to face with Rank. He stepped back, smiled, and gestured for her to enter. "You've had breakfast already?" she asked.

"Yep. I could use a second cup of coffee though. If you're buying."

She smiled and pointed to a table in the corner near the back of the room where they could talk in private.

As Stephens leaned in to share some information she'd learned about Dempsey's activities, Rank took her hand in his then pulled it free and looked around to see if anyone had noticed. She placed her hands in her lap and continued. Stephens was intent on telling Rank about the increased build-up of Region Five military equipment in St. Louis, but Rank reached under the table and took her hand.

"Are you listening? He's planning something—something big."

"I heard you," Rank said, caressing her hand. "And you have a plan to stop him, right?"

"I do." A big grin spread across her face. "And you're going to stick around and help me."

"I'll have to check my schedule." Rank pulled a small notepad from a side pocket of his tactical pants and flipped it open. "Let's see. Tomorrow I'll be helping Will and Isabella move." He looked up from the notepad. "How about next week?"

"How's the compound looking?" Stephens asked. She hadn't

had a chance to go over there since Will had received permission to settle his family there. She'd been surprised how easy it had been to convince Sharp to overlook Will, Jason, and Walker's AWOL status, and to push for authorization of the Williams Junction as a safe zone.

Sharp had his own issues to deal with, having been compromised by Dempsey's spy, Simone Perez. Military Intelligence was still investigating the extent of the breach, who else she'd managed to successfully compromise, and how much total damage had actually been done, the extent of which might never fully be known—if Brad Smith didn't regain consciousness. According to Aims, another of her former "marks", she was a talented spy. They had to proceed on the assumption that Perez, and therefore Dempsey, knew everything Smith knew.

Protocols were changed and information sharing protocols were reconfigured to prevent similar incidents in the future. In many ways, this made Stephens' job much more difficult as she no longer received all the information she needed from each source. But she didn't need to know about operations on the west coast, or the efforts down south to secure the gulf, which were the major areas of information reclassification emphasis she encountered. Those weren't her focus, anyway. Stephens had her sights on Dempsey. As long as she stayed in the loop on what he was up to, she was good to go.

"They have a pretty good set up there at Williams Junction. Aims and I rode out there last week and gave them some help with physical security and met some members of the group from Lake Sylvia. Will's cousins, Tank and Troy, they know their stuff. I think, together, they'll be able to make that area fairly secure," Rank opined.

Will's cousins, Tank, and Troy had brought Stephens invaluable information regarding the inner workings of Dempsey's forced labor camps and how he coerced residents to inform on one another. The whole system reminded Stephens of how the Chinese operated, including the so-called reeducation camps discussed as "Vocational Re-Training" facilities. She wondered if Dempsey was the one in control or were the Chinese?She had another big mission coming up for Tank and Troy, but she wasn't yet ready to divulge it to Rank. He might feel obligated to share it with Will and she doubted he and the rest of his family would be keen to have their folks disappear for months again so soon.

Stephens' mind began to drift as Rank described the Williams Junction compound and the abundance of game and fish in the area. Her thoughts were on St. Louis and what Dempsey was up to there. She had assets reporting that they had better control of the ports in the region and were moving barges up river. She needed to get someone inside to find out what he was planning, and then convince General Waltrip to allocate military resources to help stop him.

"I may make a trip up to Branson in the next few weeks," Rank said.

That caught Stephens' attention, and pulled her from her thoughts.

"Branson? Why?" Was there something going on in that area she wasn't aware of?

"Lugnut and some folks from Texas County will be in the area looking for building supplies—windmill parts. I said I'd come up and visit."

A knot formed in her stomach. Rank obviously missed his friends back home. There hadn't been much for him to do there in Little Rock like he had imagined there would be. He was bored most of the time. Why General Waltrip was waiting so long to assign him to a unit, Stephens didn't understand. She feared they risked losing him if Waltrip didn't put him to work soon.

"Say hi for me. They're great guys."

"You want to come along? We could stay at Big Cedar Lodge," Rank said, giving her a wink. "We could stop by and check on Isabella on the way back."

It was tempting. She could use some rest and relaxation, and spending time with Rank at Table Rock Lake would be lovely, but could she afford to take time off? Dempsey sure wasn't on vacation.

"Come on, Stephens. You gotta live a little too."

She squeezed his hand. "I'll think about it and let you know."

And she was thinking about it. She was extremely attracted to Rank. Who wasn't? She'd always found it hard to resist his tall, dark handsomeness.

What are you doing, Stephens? This is the wrong time to start a new relationship.

THIRTY-SIX

Will

Hopeville Community Compound
Williams Junction, Arkansas
August 5th
Event + Eleven Months

Will wrapped his arm around Isabella's waist and helped her inside their two bedroom cabin tucked back in the woods. After all they'd been through, escaping to the forest sounded like heaven to him. He'd been pleasantly surprised when Isabella had agreed to leave the comforts of civilization in Texarkana and move away from the refugee center. They'd left behind electricity, as limited as it was, a stable food supply, and the safety of the military there. Normally, he'd say they were crazy for even considering such a thing, but starting a new community in the interior of Arkansas where they could live a somewhat normal life had become more important to them. Besides, they weren't that far from the military base in Little Rock where help and security would always be available if they could get to it in an emergency.

Due to her injuries, Isabella wouldn't be returning to active duty any time soon. Will's leave would be up in a week, and he was anxious to get their community up and running before he was called back to base. Colonel Sharp should be back from the Port of Houston after escorting the gold shipment to the Brazilian government's ship soon. Word was out that the US Army would be reinstituting a regular permanent change of station policy for soldiers soon. If this really happened, Will and Isabella could be sent somewhere far from home—married couples could even be sent to different places if the Army deemed it necessary. He wanted to be as sure as possible that his family and friends were in the best position possible to not only survive, but thrive in Williams Junction.

"Dad! Come see!" Cayden yelled from the doorway.

Will glanced down at Isabella.

"Go on. I'm not going anywhere," Isabella said as she plucked a paperback novel from the bedside table.

"He probably saw a deer or a raccoon," Will said, pulling on his trousers.

"Dad!" Cayden called again.

"He's so happy to have you back."

"Have us back," Will said, pecking her on the cheek. "On my way, Cayden."

Will looked back at Isabella as he exited the bedroom. He studied her for a moment. He'd almost lost her out there. They'd barely made it back to Cayden. They had so much to be thankful for, and none of it was lost on Will. Two things he had learned were to never take anything for granted, and to notice and appreciate the little things. Watching his beautiful wife reading a book in the past would be such a small thing, but in this new world, it was a luxury, and a sign that—for the moment— everything was okay.

~

Will stepped outside and stopped next to the horse and wagon Jason and the others had taken into town in their search for supplies. His mouth dropped open. "Where in the world did you find that?"

"In the meadow down by a creek just out of Perryville. He was just lying there sleeping. I waited to see if his momma would return before I put the rope on him," Cayden said, pulling on the rope tied around the small brown calf's neck.

Will stroked the mane of the horse pulling the wagon. He'd never expected to find farm animals. They were going to need a livestock trailer.

"Where's Jason? We need to do a search for that calf's mother. If we can get a milk cow, that's a game changer for our community."

"Can we keep him, then?" Cayden asked, as he slung his rifle over his shoulder and trotted toward Savanah's cabin.

"Of course!"

Will wasn't sure how they'd feed him if they couldn't find his mother, however. One of the two goats Jason had found a couple of days back looked pregnant, but who knew how long it would be before she delivered and could provide milk. Would she even produce enough for a calf and her kid or kids? He doubted it. A few minutes later, half the community had gathered around the young calf.

"This is no coincidence, Will. First the two goats and now a calf. There's a farmer somewhere missing his livestock," Savanah said.

"Maybe. We should search the area again and see if we can find out where they're coming from," Will said.

"We've already cleared everything within a two mile radius of town. We didn't find anything alive on any of the farms," Jason said.

"Maybe they're not on a farm. Maybe they're in town," Kendra said. "We rode through the city, but we didn't look in any of the backyards in the residential areas."

"It seemed pointless. Perryville looked deserted," Jason said.

"Let's send a team back and have them search again for signs of life," Will said.

"Can we spare people for a house-to-house search? We'll need to clear each house. That will take experience—and time," Jason said, looking to Tank.

"Not really," Tank said.

Will and Savanah's cousin, Tank, had been put in charge of security. He and Troy were training people as fast as they could.

"If there is more livestock alive out there, we need to find them," Savanah said.

Tank nodded. "I'll round up a team and head into town first thing in the morning. Will that work?"

Everyone knew how stubborn Savanah could be. They would be searching for that momma cow until they found it.

"I'll lead a team southwest of town and do a search farther out. I'm not sure how far these animals could have traveled from home," Jason said.

"What the hell is that?" a familiar voice called from behind Will.

He turned to find Rank and Aims heading across the field toward them.

"Hey there!" Will called back. "That there is a calf. Cayden found it near Perryville."

"Where's his mom?" Aims asked as they drew closer.

"We were just talking about going to go out to look for her," Cayden said, a broad grin spreading across his face.

"Well that would be some score if you find her. Might even be a bull somewhere out there," Aims said.

Wouldn't that be something?" Savanah said, running her hand down the calf's side. "He looks to be in great shape. He wasn't alone out there long."

"Good, I don't want to have to chase his mom halfway across the county," Jason said. He and Tank set off across the field toward the cabin to plan their mission while the others returned to their duties chopping wood and tilling the soil for a fall garden.

"What are you two doing all the way out here?" Will asked.

"We're heading to Branson to meet up with Lugnut and some folks. We're going to spend some time being lazy by the lake before Stephens ships us off on our next mission."

"I guess Sharp got that gold delivered to the Brazilians?" Will asked.

Rank smiled. "They did. Stephens said she nearly cried when Sharp described the ship leaving port after they had loaded all the gold onto it."

"How long before they return with the weapons?"

"At least a month."

"Does that mean we'll have some downtime before we get deployed again?" Will asked.

Savanah's head shot up, her gaze turning to Rank.

"Maybe," Rank said.

His gaze dropped to his feet. He was holding something back. Will liked the big man. He walked with an air of confidence that was rare these days. The world had beaten most people down a lot in the eleven months since the lights went out. Rank, however, still looked like he was ready to take on the world. The black T-shirt with the white skull printed on it he always wore looked like it had seen better days. Will imagined that it and the non-army-regulation, long-black beard would have to go when Colonel Sharp returned.

"Any word on Brad Smith?" Will asked.

"He's still in a coma from what I hear. The doctors down in Austin don't hold out much hope that he'll come out of it. If he does, they say he'll likely not be able to tell them anything useful about his interrogation anyway."

Will guessed that, in the end, Brad Smith had received what he'd deserved. He'd gotten a lot of good soldiers killed because of his "pillow talk" with Dempsey's spy, Simone Perez. There was no telling the far reaching damage he'd done with the information he divulged to her.

"Isabella's inside. You two want to keep her company while Cayden and I go find a place for this calf? We have a stew cooking over the fire. It should be ready by the time we get done. You're staying, right?" Will asked.

"Stew? Does a bear sh…" Rank turned toward the children playing a few feet away. "…poop in the woods? Of course we're staying."

"Thank you," Aims said.

Will was glad the two men where staying. He had questions. He wanted to hear all about the community they'd come from up in Missouri. For the time being, Williams Junction seemed to be a good place to settle, but it was good to know there were options— even way up in Missouri—if that changed.

While eating supper around the campfire, Will, Jason, Walker, and the others filled Rank and Aims in on what they knew of the new government and the recovery efforts down in Texas that Stephens and the general might not have shared with them. There were a few eyebrows raised at some of the freedoms that had been taken in the name of restoring law and order, but the progress being made to the infrastructure and manufacturing seemed to please the two men.

"I heard that they even have ice cream parlors in Houston," Jack said, smiling as he rubbed his knees. Will wondered how well equipped the hospitals were down there. Maybe there was something they could do to repair Jack's injured legs.

"I wonder if our house is still there," Cayden said.

The image of his deceased wife, Melanie, bent over her flower garden pricked his heart. Will tried hard not to think too much about their old life back in Houston. It was just too painful. "I don't know, son. That storm was mighty strong."

"Maybe we could go by and check if we ever visit there."

"Sure. We could do that," Will said.

Will doubted he'd be taking any vacations anytime soon. With trouble still on the west coast and rumors of General Dempsey's plan to push his control farther south, that could only mean more fighting in their future.

"You know, with our own milk cow, we might can make ice cream too," Savanah said.

"Really?" Kylie and Keegan said in unison.

Savanah turned to face them. "You two are supposed to be in bed."

"But I have to pee," Keegan said.

"And I need a drink of water," Kylie replied.

Jason stood slowly. "I've got them."

They were all still banged up and sore from their battle with Dempsey's army. In addition to the physical scars, Will was finding it hard to cope with the mental ones. Fighting fellow Americans was beyond disturbing, and it was unfathomable to think that before this was all over and the country was restored, they would probably have to kill more of them to bring Dempsey's reign to an end.

"I know an Amish family that has an ice house," Rank said. "Aims, remember John David harvesting the ice blocks when the lake froze over last winter?"

"Remember? Jacob and I helped him haul them. It was back-breaking work," Aims said.

"Life sounds good up there in Missouri," Savanah said. "Why'd you two want to leave?"

Rank glanced over at Aims. "I'm a Marine. My country needs me."

Will understood. He knew the drive to make the world a better place for the ones you love. He admired the man for it.

"Don't you miss your family?" Cayden asked.

"They're why I'm here. I made an oath to defend this nation against enemies, both foreign and domestic. I'm here to make sure that Maddie, Zach, and their mother, Beth, are protected from those enemies," Rank said.

"I came for the air conditioning," Aims chuckled, fanning himself with his hand. "Stephens and Colonel Sharp said there would be warm showers and cold beverages too."

"Speaking of showers," Savanah said, pinching her nose with her thumb and index finger. "Some of you need to take a swim in the pond with a bar of soap."

Will chuckled. He had no doubt his sister would have this compound turned into a sustainable homestead in no time, and regular bathing with her homemade and herb infused goat's milk soap and lotions would be mandatory. It was good to finally see her feeling free to be herself and back in her element. He prayed that trouble didn't find them there, and his family and friends could finally feel at home.

"Do you know where you're going from here?" Jason asked Aims, returning from putting the kids back to bed.

"I'll be heading down to Austin next week. Harding and I have a meeting with the president and his cabinet to discuss the situation up north."

With Aims and Harding being former FEMA officials, Will was sure they'd have great insight on the resources at Dempsey's disposal, and the challenges the military would face going up against them.

"Wow—we know someone who rubs elbows with the President of the United States!" Cayden said smiling.

"What about you, Rank," Savanah asked.

"I'll likely be heading out west to fight those commie bastards," he said.

Will hadn't thought much about the battle for the west coast much. It seemed so far away—almost like another country. He knew the Russians had bombed so much of it that it would be barely recognizable. With their east coast laid waste by the nukes dropped on it in the early days of the war, Will was glad they lived in the heartland.

"I'm heading in to check on Isabella. I'll see everyone in the morning. We'll head out tomorrow and see if we can locate where these livestock are coming from," Will said, standing and stretching.

His back hurt, his legs hurt—everything hurt—but he had to push on. He needed his family to be in the best position possible for when he and the others were called back to military duty. Although he hated to see Isabella in pain, he was glad she wouldn't be going back to active duty any time soon. Worrying about her in the midst of a battle was too much for him. He was grateful to know that she'd be there for Cayden for a while longer. Maybe, soon, all this fighting would be over and they'd all be together again as one big, happy family. That's what would keep him going, and what he'd be fighting for in the foreseeable future.

As the cabin's front door closed behind him, Rank, Aims, and Walker's satphones all chirped almost simultaneously.

"Isn't it great to be tied to these things again?" Aims said, reaching for his phone.

Inside the cabin, Will slowly made his way through the living room and the kitchen to the bedroom door.

"Are you finally coming to bed?" Isabella said, patting the pillow next to her

Will drew in a breath, let it out slowly, and climbed into bed next to his wife. This was living. This was all worth fighting for. He rolled onto his side and was about to take Isabella into his arms when his satphone chirped on the dresser.

~

Thank you for purchasing No Man's Land, book five in the Fall of Houston series. **Don't forget to check out the companion series, Days of Want as the story continues and our survivors head back to Missouri.**

Also I'd like to hear from you and hope that you could take a moment and post an honest review on Amazon. Your support and feedback will help this author improve for future projects. Without the support of readers like yourself, self-publishing would not be possible. **Don't forget to sign up for my spam-free newsletter at www.tlpayne.com to be the first to know of new releases, give-aways and special offers.**

No Man's Land has gone through several layers of editing. If you found a typographical, grammatical, or other error which impacted your enjoyment of the book, I offer my apologies and ask that you let me know so I can fix it for future readers. To do so, email me at contact@tlpayne.com In appreciation, I would like to offer you a free ebook copy of my next book.

Have you read my Days of Want series? If not, please check out the sample chapters for Turbulent, book one in the series or order your copy on Amazon today.

Sample Chapters

Chapter 1

Chicago O'Hare International Airport
Chicago, Illinois
Day of Event

Terminal Three of Chicago's O'Hare International Airport was filled with pissed-off passengers. After a four-hour delay, Maddison Langston was feeling cranky herself. Her flight from San Diego had arrived at eleven that morning. By three that afternoon, her connecting flight was still not boarding, even though the plane was at the gate.

When the lights in the terminal cut out and the flight departure screen went blank, Maddie sighed.

Looks like my flight will be delayed. Again.

Sitting in the dim light, Maddie pulled her cell phone from the Silent Pocket Faraday backpack Uncle Ryan had given her. Although she had promised him that she would keep her phone in the bag while she was in the airport, she was having social media withdrawal. She was not as concerned about a thief scanning her RFID chips as he was.

She pulled the charging cord from the pack and started to plug it into an outlet before realizing that it wouldn't charge with the power off. Maddie tapped a social media app on her phone, but it wouldn't load. Her phone did not have a signal. After shutting it down and restarting it half a dozen times, it still wouldn't connect to her wireless service provider.

To pass the time, she listened to songs from her music library. She usually listened to her favorite music using streaming services. Luckily, she had a few games on her phone.

Maddie looked up to see an angry man in a sport coat and trousers with one knee on the American Airlines service counter. The terrified woman behind the desk had her back pressed against the wall as far from the out-of-control passenger as possible.

Maddie pulled the earbuds from her ears.

Two men had gripped the arms of the angry man, who was yelling obscenities at the woman, as the woman yelled for security.

"Why can't you tell us what the hell is going on? My flight was supposed to leave three hours ago. Now the lights are out, and it is freaking hot as hell in here," another passenger yelled at the petite woman.

"I do not have anything to tell you. I am in the dark too," she said.

"Oh, is that your attempt to lighten the mood? De-stress the situation? Did they teach you that in customer service school?" the man mocked.

"My cell phone isn't working. I need to use a phone. I have to call my husband. He'll be expecting us to arrive in Nashville any minute," a woman called out.

A tall man in a sports jersey and jeans stepped forward. He towered over the other passengers. Holding an arm up, the man said, "Listen up, folks. All this yelling and getting aggressive with customer service isn't going to get us answers that the woman clearly doesn't have."

"Well, someone sure as hell better start explaining pretty damn fast," the man in the sport coat barked, shaking his arms loose from his captors.

"Look around you. It is a chaotic mess in here. It's not just American Airlines' flights that are delayed. No planes have taken off or landed here in over an hour. The power is out to the airport, and something has disrupted the phones, including cell phones."

Just then, an explosion rattled the windows. The ear-piercing sound of metal on concrete was followed by the cockpit of a jet skidding down the runway. It hadn't occurred to Maddie that planes might collide mid-air without access to tower control for guidance. People rushed from the shopping area of the terminal, dragging their wheeled bags behind them, and huddled near the window to stare at the burning wreckage of the plane on the tarmac.

Maddie slowly rose to her feet. Grabbing her backpack from its position beside her, she flipped it over her shoulder and reached for the extended handle on her suitcase. The terminal was in darkness, lit only by the windows where a surreal show of flames and black smoke was casting long shadows toward the center of the concourse.

As Maddie stared out the window with her mouth open wide at the flaming, smoking, twisted mass, a second Boeing 737 dropped from the sky in pieces, scattering onto the runway and bursting into flames. The lights were out, there was no cell service, and planes were colliding in the sky above them.

Maddie came to a startling realization. It had happened. The EMP—the electromagnetic pulse—her dad and Uncle Ryan talked about had really happened. Her hand shot up to cover her mouth. Maddie's feet would not move, even though her brain said run.

She couldn't catch her breath. While her fellow travelers stood with eyes peeled to the horrid sight and their mouths wide in shock and terror, Maddie ran.

Her bag's wheels skipped off the floor of the concourse as Maddie bolted toward a family restroom. Her backpack smacked the wall as she spun around to turn the lock. Maddie dropped her pack and suitcase by the door and slid to the cold tile floor. Hugging her knees to her chest, she sobbed, rocking side to side. Mixed with the crushing fear was a pang of guilt. She had mocked her dad for his paranoia. A wave of grief threatened to crash over her without mercy. As she cried, the years of repressed grief burst to the surface as she recalled the training and warnings her father had tried to communicate to her over the years.

Maddie hadn't cried this much since the accident. The day her dad died. The day her world changed forever.

As the tears flowed in torrents, Maddie rested her head on her arms. She was startled by loud banging behind her. She jumped to her feet and spun to face the door, her heart pounding against her chest. In the blackness, she couldn't see her hand in front of her face. Maddie pulled her phone from her back pocket and activated its flashlight feature. Holding it over her head, she turned and looked around the small room.

I can't stay in here forever.

How long before a plane came crashing through the terminal? How many were up there circling the airport? How many had diverted from their flight paths to land after they lost their navigation system and contact with the control tower? Pilots would only have line-of-sight to avoid a mid-air collision. How soon would it be before they ran out of fuel? Maddie's thoughts raced.

She had to get some place safe right now. That was what her dad always told her. The longer she hesitated, the more dangerous it would be.

Maddie stood and blew her nose. She bent over to reach for her pack.

She froze.

Maddie's heart dropped. She was stranded in one of the country's busiest airports in the middle of one of the most populated cities. And she had never felt more alone.

Maddie turned and put her back to the door. She slid once more to the floor, curling her arms over her head.

Dad was right.

Her friends had called her father, Greg Langston, a doomsday prepper—a title that brought Maddie embarrassment. Before he died, her father had taught her and her brother, Zach, survival skills and how to prepare for disasters. She never took it as seriously as she should have.

"What do I do, Daddy? What do I do?" she cried.

Her mind raced, searching for answers. Images of her rolling her eyes as her dad lectured her and Zach on what to do in a world-ending scenario brought a new round of guilt and shame.

"You were right, Daddy. I am so sorry I mocked you. I didn't listen to you, and now the shit has hit the fan, and I don't know what to do."

She curled into a fetal position. Time seemed to stand still in the tiny, cold room. She stared at the shadow cast by her cell phone. Her mind went blank. She slid into a familiar numbness. Sleep had been her comfort, her only solace in the days and weeks after her dad died. She wanted to go there. She let her breathing slow.

She was shaken back to reality by the sound of the growing chaos outside the bathroom.

Maddie heard her dad's voice in her head.

"Maddison Grace Langston, pay attention. Someday, you might find yourself alone when the shit hits the fan and you will need to know how to survive and get home."

She sat up, brushing loose strands of hair from her face.

The get-home bag her dad had given her containing all the essentials to survive on the road was in her dorm room in Ohio. It would do her no good now. But she had the everyday-carry items

243

with her. Uncle Ryan had picked up where her dad left off in making sure carrying her EDC was a habit. Maddie looked down at the plain, waterproof backpack on the floor next to her. There were times in the last few years when she had resented Ryan for trying to take her dad's place. At that moment, she was grateful he had.

Maddie got to her feet and walked over to the sink. She looked in the mirror. Mascara streaked her face, and her hazel eyes were bloodshot. She ran her hand through her long, blonde hair, pulling it into a messy bun on top of her head and securing it with the hair tie from her wrist. She stared at herself in the mirror.

"You've got this, Maddie. You can do it."

She pointed to the mirror with her index finger.

You have to.

Unzipping her carry-on bag, Maddie was relieved that she had brought her hydration pack on the trip. Knowing she would need to run every day to maintain her current level of endurance, she had thrown it in her bag. Pulling the vest pack from her suitcase and emptying all the pockets and pouches, she quickly inventoried its contents. With the Jelly Belly Sport Beans, sports gels, and energy bars, she had about ten thousand calories with her. Her hydration bladder and water flasks held at least two liters of water. She added the weight up in her head. She would be carrying around ten pounds.

When running a marathon or endurance race, she didn't take the hydration bladder or as many energy gels. There was an aid station along the route, and her crew would take position between stations in case she needed a quick pick-me-up. But Maddie had carried that much weight when she did backcountry and trail runs, so she knew she could.

In a Ziploc bag were two headlamps, extra batteries, a compass, and a multifunction mini tool—all requirements from her last race. From her every-day carry pack, she removed the emergency bivvy bag, her Sawyer MINI water filter, and a LifeStraw personal water filter. Maddie shoved them into the kangaroo pouch of her vest pack, along with a Ziploc bag of socks and thermals. The last thing in was a weatherproof jacket.

Maddie undressed and pulled on her running tights. After putting on a tank top, she put on a fresh pair of socks and slid on her running shoes. She wished she hadn't chosen to bring the red ones. They would stand out too much, but there was nothing she could do about that now.

Gathering up the water flasks and bladder, Maddie filled them in the sink. She pushed the bladder into the pouch and placed it in the hydration vest pack.

Placing her arms through the arm holes of the vest, she adjusted the straps across her chest. Her runner's pack was a vest-style. It wrapped around her, fitting snugly against her body. She tugged on the cords. It felt secure. After placing the soft flasks in the front pockets, she strapped one squeeze flask to her wrist. Lastly, she pulled on her dad's Marine Corps Marathon head-band and adjusted it to cover her ears.

She looked down at the half-empty suitcase and her clothes strewn about the floor. She picked them up and threw them into the bag. Maddie did not consider herself overly materialistic, but her suitcase contained some of her favorite clothes. It pained her to just leave them there.

This is crazy. How am I going to run all the way to St. Louis?

From her Silent Pocket Faraday backpack, Maddie retrieved her earbuds, car keys, and a pack of gum. As she placed them in the right-side pocket, her hands shook so badly that she dropped her car keys on the floor. She was alone in Chicago and the end of civilization as she knew it had occurred—just as her dad had predicted. She was scared shitless and was not afraid to admit it. Maddie shook her head, attempting to fight back the tears that threatened to spill down her face.

Harden up, Maddie.

No one was coming to save her. If she was going to make it,

she would have to protect herself. She couldn't afford to let self-doubt and indecision keep her prisoner in the airport.

St. Louis was about three hundred miles away. The previous week, she had run the New Hampshire 100-mile endurance race in twenty-six hours. So, with needing recovery time between runs, it would take at least a week or more to get home.

How long will it take if I have to avoid dangerous people?

She wanted nothing more than to sit back down on the cold tile floor, curl into a ball, and stay there until her mom came to her rescue.

Mom is not coming, Maddie. Mom is stranded in California.

She had gone with her mother to San Diego. They had brought her grandmother home from the hospital. Her mother wanted Grand to enjoy her last days at home in her own bed surrounded by the things she loved, including her one-eyed dog, Jack. The sudden realization that her mom might not be able to make it back home to Missouri shook her to her core. She had been so focused on herself that she had not even thought about where her mom and brother were. When she had last received a text message from Zach, he had been coming back from his school field trip to Washington, D.C.

Maddie placed her hands over her face and rubbed her forehead.

Where did he say they had stopped?

Maddie retrieved her cell phone from the floor beside her suitcase, opened her messages app, and clicked on the last message from Zach. He had been in Marshall, Illinois, right before the lights went out.

Maybe the lights aren't out there?

Although she was unsure where Marshall, Illinois, was, she doubted it was anywhere near Chicago. His bus had been heading southwest back to St. Louis.

He will be all right. There were six teachers on the trip. They'll get him home.

She checked for cell service one last time before putting her phone in the front pouch of her vest. The light from the phone shined through the mesh fabric. She patted her pockets, adjusted her straps, and pulled the cords tight.

Time to get going.

Maddie slowly unlocked and cracked opened the door. The scene out in the corridor was even more chaotic than before. She could hear raised voices and crying.

How long was I in there?

She checked her watch. It was four o'clock. She had at least two hours before it would be dark. Walking down the terminal toward the main hall, she could see that most of the activity centered on the restaurant area of the concourse. People were fighting over what was left of the food.

She needed a map. She had seen a place that sold books and newspapers when she'd gotten coffee earlier.

They should have maps. There are tourists here, right?

Maddie raced around a corner and saw a floor to ceiling mural of the city of Chicago. It wouldn't replace a paper map that she could take with her, but it would give her a direction to head out in at least. Not knowing the scale of the map, she made a fist and stuck up her thumb, using it as a ruler to calculate distance.

"Which way are you heading?" a man asked.

The voice startled her, causing her to jump. She twirled around to find a man in his mid-thirties. Beside the man stood a woman, maybe a little younger than him, and a girl of about ten years old.

"Um— I— South," Maddie stammered.

She chastised herself. She had just given out critical information to a stranger. She could hear her father scold her.

OPSEC, Maddie, her dad would say.

Operational security meant keeping your big trap shut about what you have and where you plan to go. She was sucking at this already. She looked at her feet.

"Your dad serve?" the man asked, pointing to Maddie's Marine Corps buff.

"He did. Did you?" she asked, pointing to the U.S. Army National Guard Minute Man logo on his hat.

"I did."

"Two tours in Iraq and four in Afghanistan," the woman added.

"Yeah, my dad spent a lot of time in those places too."

"Is he with you?" the man asked.

Maddie looked away and swallowed hard, resolved to fight back the tears. She would give anything to have her dad with her right now.

"I'm Rob Andrews, by the way, and this is my wife April and our daughter Emma."

Emma gave a timid wave as April stepped forward and extended her hand. Maddie shook it and said, "I'm Maddie Langston."

"Look, it is getting bad in here. It's going to get worse in the city very soon. We're not going to wait around for the lights to come back on. We're getting out of here, and it looks like you have the same idea," Rob said.

"Um... Yeah. I mean, I was thinking about it. With the airplanes crashing, I was trying to decide how to leave to avoid the runways. I need to head toward Interstate 55, but that is southwest, and it looks like most of the runways are in that direction."

"You could go due south and then cut over, say, around here." Rob pointed to 143rd Street on the map mural.

"I wish I had a map to take with me, in case I have to adjust course quickly."

"I have a map. We're heading south too. We live about fifty miles from here. You're welcome to join us until you need to head west."

"I don't know if I should."

"You shouldn't be out on the streets alone. It's not safe on a regular day, but now with the power being out..."

Maddie was leery of leaving the airport with strangers, but he was right. It wasn't safe to go alone. Safety in numbers, as her dad would say.

She looked the man over. He had been in the military like her dad. He had his wife and daughter with him.

It should be all right, right?

"Okay. When do you want to leave?"

~

Chapter 2

San Diego, California
Day of Event

Beth's drive back to her mother's house after dropping off her eighteen-year-old daughter at the San Diego airport was difficult. The doctor had put her mother on hospice care just days before. She hadn't had time to adjust to the news that her mother would not recover from cancer this time.

Beth's mother, Florence, had beaten breast cancer twice. The third time, it was in her bones. Her mother was sixty-eight and had led a full, vibrant, active life before this most recent diagnosis.

The traffic was heavy—heavier than Beth remembered from when she had lived there before marrying her first husband, Greg Langston. But that was ages ago. She had lived all over since then, settling in Missouri. When Greg left the Marines and took the job in St. Louis, Beth had been thrilled.

For the first time in their marriage, they had been able to settle in the place of their choosing. To be honest, though, St. Louis hadn't been her first choice. She could think of much nicer places to live, but Greg had received a great job offer from a military defense contractor. The job allowed him to be home with Beth and their children, Maddie and Zach.

Beth pulled the car into the third bay of her parents' three-car garage. She unloaded the groceries and placed them on the marble countertop.

"Beth, is that you?"

"Yes, Mom, it's me. Can I bring you some juice? I stopped at Panera Bread and bought you some of the chicken and wild rice soup you like."

"Maybe later, dear. I…"

She was getting weaker and sleeping longer. Beth wasn't sure if it was because of the cancer or the pain meds. She was incoherent a lot when she was awake. Beth had moved the dining table and china cabinet out of the dining room to set her mother's hospital bed up there. Her stepfather, Frank, was set up in the den, where he spent most of his time. He had suffered a stroke the year before, leaving his left arm paralyzed.

Beth finished putting the groceries away and went into the den to check on Frank.

"Frank, can I get you some soup or a sandwich?"

He didn't answer, so she said it louder. The television was blaring, so she had to yell to be heard over the commentator's gloomy newscast.

"Frank," she yelled.

"What? Why are you yelling at me?" Frank asked, glowering over his shoulder.

He turned back to stare at the television before she could finish her sentence. She rolled her eyes and went back to the kitchen.

"I'll just make him a tray, and if he's hungry, he'll eat it," she said out loud, exasperated.

"What did you say?" Frank called from the den.

Beth shook her head and pulled a bowl from the cabinet next to the sink. She made Frank a tray and set it on the coffee table in front of him.

"You're blocking the television," Frank barked, craning his neck around her.

China's president, Xi Jinping, is said to have facilitated the talks between North Korean leader Kim Jong Un and the United States. U.S. State Department spokesman, Robin Payton, said Monday that the president had rejected calls from China, Russia, and North Korea to lift sanctions imposed on the isolated state. The U.S. remains committed to only doing so when Pyongyang makes further progress toward denuclearization on the Korean Peninsula. Further talks between Chairman Kim and President Rhynard have yet to be scheduled.

"You can't trust those damn commie North Koreans. Are they nuts or something? What the hell are we talking to them for anyway," Frank yelled at the television.

Beth had never been so tired of listening to the news in her life.

Why in the world did they invent twenty-four-hour news stations, anyway? All they do is repeat the same bad news over and over.

～

Sandy, the hospice nurse, arrived shortly after one o'clock that afternoon. She took Florence's vitals and adjusted her morphine pump.

"She is sleeping most of the time now. Is it from the meds?" Beth asked as she walked Sandy to her car.

"Her urine output has decreased again. I increased her fluids, but I think her kidneys are shutting down."

The nurse put a hand on Beth's shoulder. Her eyes were full of sympathy.

"It is just a matter of days now—maybe three or four. If you have family to call in, I'd say now would be the time. She will likely slip into a coma in a day or two."

Beth inhaled and held it. She had known those words were

coming. She had felt it in her heart, and she'd thought she was prepared for it. Beth thanked Sandy and walked back into the house. All she wanted to do was go upstairs to her room, crawl into bed, and pull up the covers. That was what she had done after her husband, Greg had died. She had shut down. Sleep was her only comfort. She didn't have the luxury of retreat today, however. She had ill parents and a lazy, one-eyed dog to care for.

Jack slept in the bed with Beth's mother. He rarely left her side. She stroked the dog's head as she stared down at her mom. He lifted his head, shifted position, then put his head on Florence's leg. Feeling sorry for her mother's furry child, she decided she would reheat the chicken and rice she had made him the day before.

"Jack, you want some lunch?"

Jack's paws hit the wood floor, and a flash of white fur streaked by her feet. Jack loved food.

"What are we going to do with you, little guy?"

She hated the thought of taking him to an animal rescue, but her husband, Jason, would never allow her to bring him home with her. They already had a dog he didn't like.

As Beth followed Jack into the kitchen, an ear-piercing emergency alert tone came from Frank's television. Beth's first thought was the alert was for a wildfire. They hadn't had rain in a while. Beth placed the kitchen towel she held in her hand onto the counter and walked into the den just as the emergency alert message began to scroll across the screen.

~

We interrupt our programming. This is a national emergency. The Department of Homeland Security has issued a national emergency alert. Residents are asked to shelter in place until further notice. Stay tuned to this channel for updates. This is not a test.

Beth heard the alert tone on her cell phone and ran to the kitchen to retrieve it.

Presidential Alert
THIS IS NOT A TEST. This is a national emergency. Shelter in place until further notice.

"What the hell?" Frank said.

Beth clicked the news app on her phone to check for news about the emergency alert but found none. She opened the Facebook app and scrolled through the messages. She stared down at her phone as her news feed refreshed. A story from a San Diego station informed the city that the nation had been attacked. Beth dropped to her knees, her cell phone skidding across the floor. Crawling over to pick it back up, she leaned against the kitchen cabinets and read the article.

San Diego Daily News has been informed that at approximately twenty-three minutes past three this afternoon, a nuclear device exploded in the atmosphere above the United States. Information is still coming in regarding the extent of the damage this detonation has caused and the areas affected. But right now, we know that communications with most of the nation have been interrupted. An official with the governor's office has told Daily News that they have no information regarding further attacks. A state of emergency has been declared, and residents have been ordered to shelter in place until further notice. We expect a formal statement from the governor later today. Stay tuned for further details.

Beth kept scrolling through her news feed, hoping for more news. She tapped on contacts, selected Maddie's cell number, and pressed the call button. The call failed, so she couldn't even leave a voicemail. She opened her message app and typed a message to Maddie and Zach, then tapped the send button. She waited. A moment later, a message appeared telling her that delivery had failed.

Beth buried her head in her hands. Being cut off from her children during a national emergency was beyond any heartache she had ever experienced. Rocking back and forth, she tried to control her panic. She repeatedly tapped the message's send button, hoping desperately that it would go through.

Placing her hands on the counter, Beth pulled herself to her feet. She ran her hands through her hair. Her mind wanted to go numb, but she couldn't give in to that. Walking over to the sink, she washed her face and dried off with a kitchen towel. She heard a news anchor discussing the shelter in place order and headed back to the den.

Frank was unusually quiet as he and Beth sat staring at the television screen. All anyone could say was that no one knew what the damage was throughout the rest of the country. All planes had been grounded, and a state-wide curfew had been ordered. No one was allowed out of their homes except essential personnel.

It was hours before news reports came in about the blackout caused by the EMP. A so-called expert explained the effects of an EMP detonated at a three-hundred-mile altitude. As far as they had determined, the unaffected areas include parts of California, Oregon, Washington, and Alaska. Beth didn't need to listen to the rest. She understood the effects of an EMP. Her deceased husband, Greg had studied it as one of the possible scenarios he foresaw happening.

She was cut off from her children and her current husband, Jason. She was two thousand miles away, and there was nothing she could do to protect them. Worse yet, they were both away from home and separated from each other. Zach would have his teachers for help and support, but Maddie was stranded in an airport in a large, densely-populated city.

Beth paced the room. No matter how hard she tried, she couldn't think of a single thing she could do to help her children or even try to get to them. The roads were shut down. The authorities were not allowing anyone to travel. Walking two thousand miles without any gear was impossible.

"Beth? Where are you, Beth?"

"I'm right here, Mom. I'm coming."

No matter how desperately she wanted to get home to her children, she knew she could not leave her dying mother, and it would be foolish to go alone anyway. She wouldn't make it out of California, let alone across four states of chaos and devastation.

Even though every cell in her body wanted to get to her children, she would have to stay there and care for her parents.

Turbulent is book one of six in the Days of Want series. If you've enjoyed this sample of Turbulent, CLICK HERE to order your copy today!

Also, don't forget to check out my Gateway to Chaos series.

Also by T. L. Payne

Fall of Houston Series

No Way Out

No Other Choice

No Turning Back

No Surrender

No Man's Land

The Days of Want Series

Turbulent

Hunted

Turmoil

Uprising

Upheaval

Mayhem

Defiance (Pre-Order Now!)

The Gateway to Chaos Series

Seeking Safety

Seeking Refuge

Seeking Justice

Seeking Hope

Seeking Sanctuary (Coming Soon!)

About the Author

T. L. Payne is the author of the bestselling Days of Want, Gateway to Chaos, and Fall of Houston series. T. L. lives and writes in the Osage Hills region of Oklahoma and enjoys many outdoor activities including kayaking, rockhounding, metal detecting, and fishing the many lakes and rivers of the area.

Don't forget to sign up for T. L.'s spam-free newsletter at www.tlpayne.com to be the first to know of new releases, giveaways and special offers.

T. L. loves to hear from readers. You may email T. L. at contact@tlpayne.com or join the Facebook reader group at https://www.facebook.com/groups/tlpaynereadergroup

Made in the USA
Coppell, TX
03 September 2021

61765285R00156